See How Much I Love You

LUIS LEANTE

Published in Great Britain in 2009 and the United States in 2009 by

MARION BOYARS PUBLISHERS LTD
24 Lacy Road London SW15 1NL

www.marionboyars.co.uk

Distributed in Australia by Tower Books Pty Ltd,
Unit 2, 17 Rodborough Road, Frenchs Forest, NSW 2086, Australia

Printed in 2009
10 9 8 7 6 5 4 3 2 1

Mira Si Yo Te Querré by Luis Leante
First published in Spain in 2007 by Santillana Ediciones Generales S.L.

GOBIERNO
DE ESPAÑA

MINISTERIO
DE CULTURA

*Esta obra ha sido publicada con una
subvención de la Dirección General del
Libro, Archivos y Biblitecas.*

This book has been translated with a subsidy from the Spanish Government's
Department of Books, Archives and Libraries.

Recommended by pen

This book has been selected to receive financial
assistance from English PEN's Writers in
Translation programme supported by Bloomberg.

A CIP catalogue record for this book is available from the British Library.
A CIP catalog record for this book is available from the Library of Congress.

ISBN 978-0-7145-3181-6
Set in Bembo 11/14pt

Printed in England by J.F. Print Ltd., Sparkford

To Nieves

When I'm on foreign land,
And recognise your colours,
And think of your exploits,
See how much I love you…

Little flag you're red,
Little flag you're golden
Full of blood and full of riches
At the bottom of your soul.

Las Corsarias
Music and lyrics by Franciso Alonso

See How Much I Love You

LUIS LEANTE

Translated by Martin Schifino

MARION BOYARS
LONDON • NEW YORK

Chapter One

SHE SLEEPS THROUGH THE MORNING, INTO THE EVENING, she sleeps through most of the day. Then she stays awake for the best part of the night: it is an intermittent wakefulness, with moments of brief lucidity and others of delirium or abandon; she often faints. She is like this, day in, day out, for weeks. She is completely oblivious to the passing of time. Whenever she is able to stay conscious, she tries to open her eyes, but soon falls back into the depths of sleep, a heavy sleep from which she finds it hard to come round.

For days now she's been hearing voices in her moments of lucidity. They sound distant, as though they were coming from another room or the deepest end of her sleep. Only occasionally does she hear them near her, by her side. She cannot say for sure, but it sounds as if the unknown voices are speaking in Arabic. They talk in whispers. She doesn't understand a thing they're saying, but the sound of those voices, far from being disquieting, is comforting to her.

She finds it hard, very hard to think straight. When she makes an effort to understand where she is, she feels a great tiredness, and very soon falls back into her dreaded sleep. She struggles to stay awake, because hallucinations torment her. Over and over she is seized by the same image: the nightmare of the scorpion. Even when she's awake she fears opening her eyes in case the arachnid has survived the dream. But however hard she tries, her eyelids remain sealed.

The first time she manages to open her eyes she cannot see a thing. The dazzling light of the room blinds her, as if she'd been in a dungeon all along. Her eyelids grow heavy and give in. But now, for the first time, she is able to tell reality from reverie.

'*Skifak? Esmak?*' says somebody, very softly.

It is a soft, woman's voice. Although she doesn't understand the words, the tone is clearly friendly. She recognises the voice as the one she's been hearing over the past few days or weeks, sometimes very close to her ear and at others, in the distance, as if coming from another room. Yet she has no strength to reply.

Still conscious, she cannot rid her mind of the image of the scorpion, which is more troubling than an ordinary nightmare. She can even feel its carapace and legs creeping up her calf. She tries to convince herself that it is not really happening. She tries to move, but has no strength. In reality the sting was short and quick, like the prick of a needle. If it had not been for that woman's shouts of warning; '*Señorita, señorita*, careful, *señorita!*,' she wouldn't have seen it at all. But she turned to look as she was slipping her arm into the *burnous,*[1] saw the scorpion hanging from the lining and knew that it had stung her. She had to cover her mouth so as not to shout, and was distressed by the voices of the women who, sitting or crouching down, stared at her in horror.

She's never sure what posture she fell asleep in. Sometimes she wakes lying face up and sometimes face down. And so she realises that someone must be moving her, no doubt so that she won't get bed sores. The first thing she sees are the shadows in the ceiling where the plaster is coming off. Dim light comes in through a small window situated high up on the wall. She doesn't know whether it's dawn or dusk. No noises can be heard that might indicate life outside the room. Against the opposite wall, she discovers an old rusty bed. Her heart jumps when

---

[1.] *Burnous*: A long cloak of coarse woollen fabric.

she realises it is a hospital bed. There's no mattress on it. The bedsprings openly display signs of neglect. Between the two beds is a metal night table, which must once have been white but is now tainted by decay. For the first time she feels cold. She strains to hear a familiar sound. No use; there's nothing. She tries to speak, to ask for help, but cannot utter a word. She spends what little strength she has trying to attract someone, anyone's attention. Suddenly the door opens and a woman she has never seen before comes in. She realises that the newcomer is either a doctor or a nurse. A brightly coloured *melfa*[2] covers her from head to toe, and over it the woman wears a green gown with all the buttons done up. On seeing that she is awake, the nurse flails her arms in surprise, but takes a moment to react.

'*Skifak? Skifak?*' the nurse blurts out.

Although she doesn't understand the words, she assumes she's being asked how she's feeling. But she cannot move a single throat muscle to reply. She follows the nurse with her eyes, trying to recognise her features underneath the *melfa* covering her hair. The nurse leaves the room calling out for help, and presently returns with a man and another woman. They talk between themselves hurriedly, though without raising their voices. All three are wearing medical gowns, the women over the top of their *melfas*. The man takes the patient's wrist and feels her pulse. He asks the women to keep quiet. He lifts her eyelids and meticulously examines her pupils. He listens to her chest with a stethoscope. The metal feels flaming hot against her chest. The doctor's face shows he is perplexed. The nurse, who had left the room a moment ago, returns with a glass of water. The two women help her to sit up and drink. Her lips barely open. Water runs over the corners of her mouth and down her

---

[2.] *Melfa*: Traditional Saharawi woman's dress made of a single cloth wrapped around the entire body, including the head. Similar to the Indian sari. Can be of many different colours.

neck. When they lay her back down, they see her eyes turn white and she falls fast asleep, just as she has been for nearly four weeks now, since the day she was brought in and everyone thought she was going to die.

'*Señorita, señorita,* careful, *señorita!*' She's heard the voice in her dreams so many times that by now it is utterly familiar. 'Careful, *señorita!*' But at first she didn't know what all the shouting was about – until she saw the scorpion hanging from the lining of the burnous. At once she knew she'd been stung. The shouting spread amongst the women, and they covered their faces and uttered laments as if a terrible tragedy had taken place. '*Allez, allez,*' she shouted for her part, trying to make herself heard above the screams. 'Come with me, don't just sit there. *Allez.*' But the women either couldn't, or were refusing to understand her. They covered their faces with neck scarves and would not stop moaning. In the end she lost patience and started insulting them. 'You're a bunch of ignorant idiots. If we don't get out of here they'll rape us. It's outrageous that you let them treat you like this. This is worse than slavery, this is… this…'

Discouraged, she fell silent, because she saw that they did not understand her. At least they weren't shouting any more. She stood still and quiet in front of the twenty women who, frozen with fear, avoided her gaze. She waited for a reaction, but no-one took a step forward. On the contrary, they huddled together like pigeons at the back of the cell, seeking comfort in each other, praying and covering their faces. For the first time she thought about the scorpion. She knew that of the one thousand five hundred living species only twenty-five are poisonous. She quickly swept the thought aside.

There was no time to lose. Now it seemed certain that if no one had responded to the shouts it was because they'd been left alone, unguarded. She finished wrapping the *burnous* over her shoulders and covered her head with the hood. 'You can do what you like, but I'm leaving.' She pulled on the door and, just as she'd thought, found it padlocked. But she'd had it all planned since dawn. With a kick, she broke the lower planks; the wood was so dry that it splintered into smithereens. She waited a while and, seeing that no one was coming, gave it another kick. The hole became considerably larger. She gathered up her *burnous* and crawled out. The midday sun was intense. 'No, *señorita*, no,' was the last thing she heard before walking away. Her legs trembled; they felt weak. It had been more than ten days since she had walked such a long way without being watched – ten days that she and the other women had spent locked in that windowless hut built with bricks and cement blocks, with an asbestos ceiling that made the air unbreathable. Although she'd only seen the small oasis on the morning they'd brought them over as prisoners, she knew every inch of it through its sounds. The well was at the centre with a pulley to extract water; a few metres away was an enormous canvas which served as a tent. It was there that the men drank tea at all hours, chatting and arguing. There was rubbish everywhere. Under the palm trees, a more solid tent, with a rug at the entrance, provided shelter for Le Monsieur. Over the past nine nights, amid the silence of the desert, she'd heard his spine-chilling snores go on for hours. Near the tent she now saw the metallic glimmer of the Toyota. There was no one around. There was no sign of the truck except the tracks leading out into the inhospitable *hammada*.[3] She tried to stay calm and curb the euphoria she felt at being free.

She barely noticed the intensity of the sun in its zenith. She didn't think twice: walking faster, she headed for the four by four. She did not run but walked decisively, without giving in to the terror that was beginning to seize her. Not once did she look back, or even sideways. And so, when she heard someone

---

[3.] *Hammada*: A type of desert landscape consisting of largely barren, hard, rocky plateaus, with very little sand. Hammada areas form seventy per cent of the Sahara desert.

call out to her from behind, her heart jumped. Nevertheless she didn't stop; she walked on and only turned her head when she recognised the voice following her. It was Aza, the only Saharawi of the group. She was running behind her, clutching her *melfa*, which was slipping down her shoulders, with both hands.

'I'm coming with you, wait, I'm coming,' she said in good Spanish. She waited for Aza and took her hand. They ran the rest of the way to the Toyota together. The woman opened the driver's door and motioned to Aza to climb in from the other side. The Saharawi quickly did so. They sat for a while in silence, looking around, as if in fear that someone had seen them run towards the vehicle.

'Let's go, Aza; the nightmare is over.' She fumbled around the ignition, looking for the key, and immediately went pale.

'What's wrong?' asked the Saharawi. 'Are you afraid?' She showed Aza her empty hands.

'The key's not there.' Aza took a moment to understand. But she didn't seem worried; she gestured with both hands and placed them on her heart. Then she bent forward and slipped her hand under her seat. A black key, covered in dust, appeared.

'Is this what you needed?' The woman took the key and inserted it into the ignition. The four by four started with a roar. She was about to ask the Saharawi something, but Aza spoke first: 'That's where we keep them in the camps. Keys should be kept out of children's reach. Children are naughty; they're children.' The vehicle jerked forwards. If there had been a guard, he would have already reacted to the noise of the engine. They were definitely alone. She took a moment to get used to the controls and pedals. She followed the tracks left by other vehicles and gathered speed towards the distant horizon. Sweat dripped down her forehead, but instead of feeling hot she felt increasingly cold: she put it down to her anxiety and nerves. 'Not that way,' shouted Aza.

'Why not? Do you know any other road?'

'There are no roads in the desert, but there's no water that way, and we're not carrying any.' Aza lifted her hand and pointed to the southwest. 'That way.' The woman obeyed without saying a word. She took a sharp turn in a direction where there were no tyre tracks. By chance she glanced at the petrol indicator: they had a quarter of a tank left. Aza kept her eyes fixed on the the horizon. The vehicle lurched along, making the two women bounce. They did not talk. Inexplicably, her sweat stayed cold and she started to shiver. She started to feel a burning sensation on her neck where the scorpion had stung her. She had difficulty breathing, but thought it was nerves. Aza soon noticed that something wasn't right. The woman, who was clutching the wheel, noticed her legs were trembling, and her heart was beating arhythmically. In profile, her face looked worn. The Saharawi knew what was happening, so when the Toyota stopped she didn't ask her anything.

'I can't go on, Aza, I have no strength,' the woman said after being silent for a while. 'You'll have to drive.'

'I've never done it, I couldn't move it a metre. You'd better have some rest and try later.'

'I don't feel well, Aza.'

'I know: you were stung by a scorpion. It was bad luck.' Suddenly, they heard a much louder noise over the idling engine of the four by four. A truck appeared in the distance, and it was coming towards them, lurching up and down over the dunes. 'They found us,' said Aza. Making a tremendous effort, the woman pressed the accelerator and held onto the wheel as firmly as she could. The four by four was faster, but it stumbled against the dunes, zigzagging, and was soon losing ground to the other vehicle. The truck, on the other hand, pressed forwards in a straight line at a steady speed, getting closer to the two women. It was only a matter of time before they were intercepted. When they were close enough, the men on the truck started shouting at the women in Arabic and French. Le Monsieur, in his old-fashioned Spanish legionnaire's uniform, was wearing a frown that turned into the hint of a smile. He was sitting by the driver, pointing out the way over the sand or around the boulders. On his knees, he held a fully loaded Kalashnikov with both hands. As the woman drove on, her vision became clouded with more and more black spots. She had barely any strength left to press the accelerator. Eventually the vehicle crashed into a sand bank and came to a halt. Aza's head smashed into the dashboard, opening up a cut on her forehead. The Saharawi tasted the blood on her lips. Before the woman could react she saw Le Monsieur's men surrounding the car. Their eyes shone with a rage barely concealed by their fake smiles. They opened the two doors of the vehicle, and Le Monsieur shouted at them to get out. The Saharawi obeyed at once, but the other woman could barely move.

'Get out!' shouted the Spaniard.

'You have to take her to a doctor,' Aza shouted back, mustering her courage, 'she's been stung by a scorpion.' The legionnaire roared with grotesque laughter. The woman was barely able to hear him; she only felt his large hands grabbing her by the arm and pulling her out. She slumped to the floor and could not get up.

'A scorpion, eh?' He spat on her and made as if to give her a kick, but stopped a few inches short of her head. 'Where the fuck did you think you were going? Bloody whores. You should know,' he said, addressing Aza, 'that there's no escape from here. Or are you as stupid as she is?' From the floor, the woman was trying to ask for help, but only faltering words came out of her mouth. Nevertheless, she had enough presence of mind to recognise Aza's screams. And, although the woman couldn't see her, she knew they were beating her. She felt inexplicably responsible for it. Her throat was burning and she couldn't utter a word. In the narrow field of vision left to her by the legionnaire's boots, she saw the Saharawi run off towards the horizon. Aza knew she should not run in a straight line, and stumbled on her *melfa*. She ran clumsily but gave it all she had. The legionnaire put down his Kalashnikov on the bonnet of the Toyota and asked one of his men for a rifle. Looking up from the ground, the woman saw the whole scene play out as though in slow motion. Le Monsieur rested the rifle on his shoulder, moved aside his long grey beard so that it wouldn't catch, and took his time to bring the Saharawi into his sights. Aza was slowing down, as though she were certain that sooner or later she would be caught. The agonising run turned into a fast walk, she struggled not to look back or stop. Suddenly a short report was heard, and Aza's figure slumped onto the stony ground of the *hammada*. As if in mourning, an unexpected wind started blowing and gathered strength little by little. The last thing the foreign woman saw, before her eyelids fell shut, was an enormous sand curtain that was beginning to cloak the depths of the Sahara.

The patient screams and then opens her eyes. The nurse takes her hand at once, without saying a word, just looking her in the eyes as one would look at a newcomer. She tries to guess the woman's age: forty, forty-five. She knows that people elsewhere age better than in the Sahara.

'Aza, Aza!'

She's delirious, no doubt. The nurse touches her forehead, trying to calm her down. Now she's certain that the woman can see and hear her. She whispers a few words in hasania, vaguely hoping that she will be understood. She gives the woman some water, speaks to her in French, and tries to make herself understood in English. She tries all the languages she knows.

'Aza, Aza!' screams the woman again, now with her eyes wide open. 'They've killed Aza!'

When she hears this, the nurse shivers. She struggles to keep smiling.

'*Hola*. How are you feeling? Are you Spanish?'

The woman looks at her and grows calmer. She grasps the nurse's hand firmly.

'Where am I?'

'In hospital. You're alive, out of danger. You've been asleep for several days.'

'They've killed Aza.'

The nurse thinks the woman is still delirious. She hasn't left the side of her bed for many days. That lifeless face caught her attention from the moment a military vehicle left her at the hospital. The nurse had been the only one who seemed certain that the woman would live. Now she is sure that God has answered her prayers.

'You've got *baraka*[4],' the nurse says. 'You've been blessed by God.'

The nurse removes her *melfa*, revealing her shiny black hair. She cannot stop smiling. She doesn't want to let go of the unknown woman's hand, not even to go and spread the news that she's finally conscious after all these weeks. She puts a hand on her heart and then places her open palm on the woman's forehead.

'My name's Layla,' she says. 'What's yours?'

Layla's smile fills the woman with peace. She makes an effort to speak:

'Montse. My name is Montse.'

[4.] *Baraka*: An Arabic term for blessing or luck

Chapter Two

CORPORAL SANTIAGO SAN ROMÁN HAD BEEN WATCHING the unusual troop movements all day, from the barrack hut that served as a guardroom. It was four by six metres, and had a mattress on a metal bed base, a desk, a chair, a filthy latrine and a tap.

Dear Montse: soon it will be a year since I last heard from you.

It had taken him nearly an hour to write down the first sentence, but now it sounded affected, unnatural. The noise of the planes landing at El Aaiún aerodrome brought him back to reality. He looked at the sheet of paper and didn't even recognise his own handwriting. He could not make out much from the window of the hut except the security zone near the runway and part of the hangar. However, he could clearly see the depot and the Land Rovers that were constantly going in and out, the trucks loaded with new legionnaires and the official cars mysteriously coming and going. For the first time in seven days no one had brought him any food, and neither did they open the door in the middle of the afternoon for his walk to one end of the runway and back. In the last week he had barely exchanged a word with anyone, only eaten stale bread and tasteless soup, and seldom taken his eyes off either the door or the window whilst he waited to be collected at any moment, and put on a plane that would take him away from Africa for ever. They had told him, in a threatening tone, that it was only a matter of a day or two, and that later he'd have the rest of his life to miss the Sahara.

Time had stood still for Corporal San Román for the last seven days, ever since he'd been transferred from the guardroom at the barracks of the 4th Regiment of the Legion to the aerodrome, thence to be taken to a military court in Gran Canaria, far from the uprisings that were taking place in the African province. But these orders seemed to have been mislaid en route, and the procedure had ground to a halt without explanation. There was no difference between night and day now: his nerves and the anxiety of the wait gave him insomnia. And the fleas in the room did not help his discomfort and unease. His only break from the monotony was the few moments he stood at the end of the runway, guarded by an old legionnaire who always threatened him in the same way before climbing up to his watchtower. 'If you take more than ten steps at any one time or start running, I'll blow your brains out.' The man would then lazily get out his Cetme rifle , to make sure that the Corporal knew that he meant it. This was the only moment of the day when he was allowed outside the prison; he would scan the horizon, trying to make out the city's white rooftops, and fill his lungs with the dry air as if he were breathing it in for the last time. But on this November day no one had brought round his breakfast or lunch, and no guard had replied to his shouts pleading for food. There was no sign of life at all near the barracks. All the activity was concentrated around the runway and the hangars. No one came to open the door when it was the time for his walk. By mid afternoon he was sure that something out of the ordinary was going on.

It was only when the sun was about to touch the horizon that he heard the engine of an approaching Land Rover, and when he looked out of the window he saw the headlights of the vehicle as it went round the barracks. He sat on his mattress, trying to stay calm, until he heard the door being unbolted. Then Guillermo appeared in full regimental dress, carrying his white gloves in his hand, as if ready to go on parade. Behind him was a guard whom he'd never seen before, with his Cetme rifle slung over his shoulder.

'You've got a visitor,' the guard said, and closed the door behind Guillermo.

Corporal San Román didn't even have time to ask for his food. Suddenly he felt dirty. He was ill at ease in front of his friend; or rather, embarrassed. He stood by the window, leaning against the wall. They had not seen each other for over twenty days, ever since that fateful afternoon when he set out for a walk carrying a bag that wasn't his .

Guillermo was dressed impeccably, but didn't know what to say. He held his legionnaire's hat with both hands, crumpling it against his gloves. He appeared tense and was incapable of concealing it. Eventually he said:

'Have you heard the news?'

Santiago didn't reply, but he braced himself for the worst. Not that there was anything that could make things any worse.

'El Caudillo is dead,' Guillermo said, trying to get a reaction out of his friend. 'He died in the early hours of the morning.'

Corporal San Román turned away to look out of the window. The news didn't seem to affect him. Despite the late hour, the planes' activity had not stopped.

'So that's what it was.'

'What?'

'That's why they've been coming and going all day. Troops are being transported all the time. But I don't know if they're coming in or going away. It's been chaos for a week, and no one explains a thing to me. There's something else, isn't there?'

Guillermo sat on the dirty, sweaty mattress. He didn't dare to look his friend in the eye.

'Morocco is invading us.'

On the desk lay a letter that would never be written, let alone posted. They both looked at the yellowing piece of paper and their eyes met briefly.

'Guillermo,' said the corporal, choking on his words, 'they're going to execute me, aren't they? From what you say, the reason I'm still here is that they need the planes for other things, and not to fly out a...'

'Traitor?' said Guillermo with spontaneous malice.

'Is that what you think too?'

'It's what everyone is saying. And you haven't shown me any proof to the contrary.'

'What for? Would you believe me?'

'Try.'

Santiago approached the desk, crumpled the sheet of paper into a ball and threw it into the latrine. Guillermo watched his every move. Then he added:

'They're sending us away. No one wants a war with Morocco. Some people say they've secretly sold the province to Hasan and Mauritania.'

'I don't care about any of that. You'll be discharged in a month, and go back home, whereas I...'

'You'll go back too. As soon as you explain everything, they'll let you go.'

Corporal San Román went quiet, trying not to show the doubts that afflicted him. The din of a plane landing on the runway obliterated the silence of the barracks. Outside, a red sky blended with the line of the horizon, ablaze with mirages.

'Look, Santi, I know you don't want to talk about it, but I need to ask you anyway, for my peace of mind.'

Corporal San Román tensed up once more. He glared at his friend; he wasn't giving in. Guillermo looked away, but didn't back down either.

'At the barracks they say you're with the traitors; that you're a terrorist. I'm not saying I think that, but I'd like to hear it from you.'

Santiago felt he had no strength left to have an argument. He slid down, his back against the wall, until he was sitting on the floor. He covered his face with both hands. What he felt wasn't awkwardness so much as shame.

'I swear to you, Guillermo, that I didn't know a thing. I swear it on my mother's grave.'

'And I believe you, Santi, I do. But from the moment they arrested you they haven't let me speak to you. I'm fed up with working myself into the ground for you.'

'Then don't; it's not worth it. They're going to execute me anyway.'

'Enough of that nonsense: no one's going to execute you. As soon as you explain, they'll discharge you; if the worst comes to the worst, they'll open a file on you, but that'll be all.'

'They'll want to know everything, names and so on...'

'But you're telling me you didn't know a thing, so there's nothing to be afraid of.'

'I swear, I didn't know. I thought that the bag only had dirty clothes in it.'

Guillermo stared at his friend accusingly. Even in the dim light, Corporal San Román could guess, just by looking at him, what was going through Guillermo's mind.

'Santi, those 'dirty clothes', as you call them, weighed more than fifteen kilos.'

'So what? Do you think I don't know? I thought there might be an old carburettor, or a connecting rod in there. I knew that kind of thing isn't really allowed, but people do it. You do it, everyone does it. Carburettors, boots, all kinds of junk.'

'Yes, Santi, but that junk was grenades, detonators and who knows what else. At the barracks they say someone could have blown up the *Parador Nacional*[5] with all that.'

'But I wasn't planning to blow anything up. I was only

[5.] *Parador Nacional:* A large state run hotel common in many Spanish towns and cities.

doing someone a favour, the same as all the other times; only a favour.'

'Who, that girl? Were you doing that girl a favour?'

Corporal San Román sprang to his feet. He clenched his fists and stood still in front of Guillermo. His jaw was clamped shut and his teeth could almost be heard grinding together.

'That's none of your business. Don't interfere in my affairs, okay? I've told you before. I'm old enough to do as I damn well please and to see whoever I choose.'

Guillermo stood up, visibly hurt, and walked to the window. The whole thing made him miserable. He turned his back on Santiago to look at the first stars in the sky. Outside the air was fresh and pure. The beauty of the landscape contrasted sharply with his distress. He breathed deeply and felt relieved, though only for a moment.

'Look, Santi, I've made a huge effort to come and see you. You can't imagine how difficult it is. We're confined to the barracks while we're waiting for news. It was just lucky that I found out you wouldn't be transferred for another two weeks; that's why I've come over.'

Again they fell silent. It seemed as though Guillermo lacked the strength to go on talking. If he hadn't known his friend so well, he would have said Santiago was crying. But Santiago San Román had never, ever cried, least of all in front of someone else. Guillermo felt thoroughly confused when he saw Santiago pick himself up in the shadows, walk over and hug him like a helpless child. He froze, not knowing what to say, until he felt Santiago's tears against his face and could do nothing but reciprocate the gesture, holding his friend in his arms to console him as though he were a small child. He was even more startled to hear his friend's revelation, in a voice choked with emotion:

'I'm scared, Guillermo, I swear. I never thought I would say anything like this, but it's the truth.'

Guillermo tried to remain emotionally detached. In the

encroaching darkness he even considered the idea that it wasn't really Corporal San Román who'd blurted out that confession. They sat on the mattress while Santiago tried to calm down.

'I need you to do me a big favour, Guillermo. No one else can help me.'

The legionnaire braced himself, apprehensive of what might come next. He didn't dare to reply.

'I need you to help me get out of here. You've got to help me, Guillermo. It may be a long time until they take me to Canarias. If the Generalísimo is dead, things are going to get sticky.'

'Things have been sticky for a while.'

'Exactly. No one will give a damn if some shitty corporal breaks out from a shitty barrack. It's very simple, Guillermo. You won't get more than a month in jail. And that way you won't have to fight against those Moroccans.'

'You have no right to ask me that.'

'I know, but if you asked me I wouldn't hesitate for a second. It's very easy, my friend, and I'm the only one in danger – if they catch me.'

'You're crazy, San Román,' addressing him by his surname in an attempt to keep his distance and not get drawn into the situation. 'If they catch you they will execute you.'

'I'm at the end of my tether here. What I'm asking is that you sweet-talk the quartermaster into sending you on guard duty here. In the afternoon they take me for a walk to the end of the runway, where the planes turn around. I only need you to give me a two hundred yard start before you start shooting. With two hundred yards I can make it to the depot over there and get a Land Rover. After that it's up to me.'

'You're crazy: they'll catch you before you can jump-start it.'

'They won't. I'll take one of Territorial Police's vehicles. The Saharawis always leave the keys under the passenger's seat. It's a habit of theirs, I know it for a fact. You needn't worry; just give me two hundred metres before you start shooting. I'd do it on my own, but it's too risky. I might get one of those expert hunters from La Marcha, and they'd take me out clean.'

Guillermo didn't reply. His palms were sweating just from thinking about it. The lights from the hangar slanted in through the window. He stood up and started pacing up and down the six metres of the guardroom. Now, there were no planes taking off.

'Forget it,' Corporal San Román said eventually. 'It's stupid. If they're going to take me to a military court, the less they have against me the better. Besides, I don't want to deprive you of the pleasure of shooting Moroccans. I haven't eaten all day, you know? A man talks all kinds of nonsense on an empty stomach.'

Suddenly Santiago started shouting to attract the guards' attention.

'I'm starving here! You arseholes, I hope they cut your throats out there. Fucking cowards! Chickens! That's what you are. When the Moroccans catch you, you're going to pay for what you're doing to me now.'

He was shouting as if possessed. Even his voice sounded like it belonged to someone else. Guillermo took a step back, looking for the door. He didn't know what to say or do. The door opened and the same soldier as before appeared holding his Cetme rifle with a finger on the trigger. As soon as Guillermo saw him, he slipped out, trying to conceal his unease. The door closed and it was quiet again. The Land Rover drove away and was soon out of sight.

Alone again, Corporal San Román held the window bars and pressed his mouth and nose against them to catch the fresh air. A dry pleasant wind made it difficult to believe that autumn was at an end. The smell of the earth, after the recent rains, was more intense than ever. A flaky moon cast its light over the distant dunes, revealing the cunning foxes. The lights of the runway slanted towards the barracks. For a moment Santiago saw Andía's image, as clearly as if she were in front of him.

He thought he could hear her voice and smell her dark skin. The echo of a far-off bugle broke the silence and dispelled the image of the girl. Inexplicably, the legionnaire felt a pleasant sensation that made him appreciate the air blowing on his face. The smell gave him strength and transported him far away from the aerodrome, above El Aaiún and the Sahara. With his eyes half-closed, he recognised the sensation as the same one that had coursed through his whole body, like a shiver, on a certain September morning in 1974, when the hatch of the Hercules had opened noisily and the ramp came down, leading out into the most beautiful and dazzling of deserts. In Zaragoza, he'd had to put up with the north wind for as long as he was stationed there; he would never have imagined that what awaited him on the runway at El Aaiún would change him for ever. In a few hours he went from living under a pale winter light to the deep blue of the Saharan sky. All ninety-three soldiers who had voluntarily transferred from the army to the Legion remained seated on the benches of the Hercules, motionless, until the voice of a sergeant with a Seville accent shook them out of their daydreams.

'Everyone stand up,' bellowed the legionnaire. And all ninety-three novices stood up at once, before he'd even finished the sentence. But Santiago San Román's mind was already outside the C-130. He almost floated down the ramp, carrying his bag and unbuttoning the top of his shirt like the legionnaires that waited below with their chests stuck out, chins cocked and eyes staring straight ahead. He placed himself in the first row, was the first to fall in line and so was the first to feel the warm December air – the warmest of Decembers, so different from the one in his native Barcelona. His whole body tingled as he took everything in out of the corner of his eye. Among the various flags and insignia, the uniforms of the Territorial Police attracted his attention: those pale army jackets which brought out the Saharawi's dark skins. Opposite him was the office

building. An enormous balcony crossed it from one end to the
other, almost as high up as the roof, and the men on the balcony
were dressed in black and blue turbans and long *djellabas*[6], as if
to enliven the monotonous reddish tinge of the landscape. The
purring of the Land Rover, the noisy propellers of the Hercules,
the instructions coming through the loudspeakers all seemed
like a play staged for the new arrivals, rehearsed for years for
the benefit of the young soldiers who came from the Iberian
peninsula. He felt as though it had all been there for centuries,
awaiting the moment that Santiago San Román got off the
plane to see it. The desert and the Saharawis' faces struck him as
the oldest things on the planet. Everything fitted together: the
landscape, the light, the faces of the native people. However,
he came back to reality when he saw Guillermo's pale face, his
faithful friend Guillermo, whom he had only known for forty
days, but from whom he had become inseparable. Guillermo
was very pale and found it hard to remain standing. Santiago
realised that his friend had had a rough flight. He hissed to
attract his attention, but Guillermo barely raised his eyes and
kept his gaze fixed to the floor. Santiago San Román felt
somewhat responsible, because had it not been for him, his friend
would now be posted somewhere quiet in Zaragoza, sitting out
the months until he was discharged and collected his pay. But
he, Santiago, had interfered, as had that legionnaire, a second
lieutenant who had appeared in Zaragoza and spoken to them
about the Legion, showing them his tattoos, a few photographs
and a Super-8 film in which the legionnaires marched with a
martial step, their chests puffed out; at that moment Santiago
had decided that Zaragoza was not far enough from Barcelona.
He did a mental calculation of the distance between the Saharan
province and his neighbourhood and concluded that he could

[6.] *Djellaba:* A long, loosely fitting hooded outer robe with full sleeves. Worn
by both men and women.

not possibly get any further away. That evening he rang Montse's house once again, to let her know that he was leaving to go to the end of the world. But once again he was told that she was away. They were lying, and he knew it all too well. He slammed the phone down as hard as he could. He tried to tear Montse's image into a thousand little pieces. Unable to sleep, he tossed and turned in his bed all night, right next to Guillermo. After reveille was sounded and he had a moment, he went straight to the recruitment office and said the second lieutenant: 'Sir, I want to become a legionnaire.' And the lieutenant, without asking him to repeat it, warmed up his ballpoint pen with his breath and wrote down Santiago San Román's name. Then he asked: 'Can you sign, lad?'

'Yes, sir.' The legionnaire turned the page and pointed to where it said 'signature and printed name', and Santiago San Román put his name down, for he wanted to go to the end of the world, get a tattoo like the second lieutenant's, which read 'A mother's love', and forget Montse, never to return.

But now, seeing Guillermo's gaunt and anxious face, he wasn't sure that he'd done the right thing dragging his friend along with him, the first true friend he'd had in a long time. Still, it had been Guillermo, not him, who had insisted on volunteering to the Legion on seeing Santiago's recently signed piece of paper. Santiago was touched just thinking about it. No one had ever done anything like that for him.

The music coming through the loudspeakers of the aerodrome caught his attention. The first few bars of that *paso doble* turned his stomach and also disconcerted him. Like the wines from Jerez and from Rioja, went the song. The energy of the music was in sharp contrast to the soldiers' exhausted bodies. Are the colours of the Spanish flag. On command they started loading their bags onto the two trucks at the end of the runway. When I'm on foreign land and see your colours... Santiago San Román could not think straight. And think of your exploits... It was as though Montse's face were right in front of him. See how much I love you.

'What did you say?' she had asked, her eyes fixed on his own.

'See how much I love you,' he had replied. And she had touched her lips to his in a way that he'd never felt before. And he had repeated, 'See how much I love you.' But now this devil of a sergeant was shouting at them by the truck, flailing his arms like a crazy windmill, spitting insults at the new legionnaires to hurry them up. Santiago San Román's pride was hurt. He climbed up the truck and jumped in, then grabbed his bag and went to sit at the back, on top of the spare wheel. He pushed Montse's image out of his mind by taking a look around. The Saharawis' faces were the colour of the earth they trod on. For a second he thought they were one and the same thing. It looked as though the older ones, idling away the hours in the shade outside the military building, had been there all their lives. They shaded their eyes with their hands and looked at the new soldiers with a mixture of compassion and indifference. The truck pulled out, and the music died away behind it. The passage of the vehicles whipped up a mountain of dust. At the side of the road, the few surviving bushes were completely white. It was a short journey: soon the first houses of El Aaiún came into view. Santiago San Román saw a woman wearing a brightly coloured *melfa* and caught his breath. She walked with her head held up, in a straight line, holding a cloak in her hand, as if she were on a catwalk in Paris. She didn't even turn when the truck passed by. Her image receded into the distance as they pressed on along the city streets. Santiago San Román didn't know where to look.

Everything caught his attention. A little while before reaching the barracks, as they went by the market, Montse's image had vanished from his mind. By the time they got off the truck, he was sure that this was where his wounds would heal.

Chapter Three

When Doctor Cambra started her twenty-four-hour shift on the 31st of December, she couldn't have guessed that the new century would usher in a radical change in her life. Nor did she suspect that the events of that night would help her make decisions she didn't think she was ready for.

She wasn't actually supposed to be on duty that day, but she swapped her shift with a colleague because she would have found it very hard to spend New Year's eve at home on her own for the first time in her life. In the last few months she'd taken extra shifts on numerous occasions. Still, this one was something special, given what the arrival of new century meant for so many people. The Casualty Ward of the Hospital de la Santa Creu i de Sant Pau was prepared for a very busy night. Few staff were hoping to get more than two or three hours' sleep. But, in fact, before midnight they admitted fewer, less serious cases than on a regular day. Although she didn't have much to do, Doctor Cambra walked up and down trying to keep herself busy. She would go to the pharmacy, restock the cupboard with gauze, and make sure they had received as many bottles of saline solution as had been ordered. Every time she walked into the staff room where the TV was on, she would hang her head and sing to herself in a mumble to stave off her despair. She was afraid she might break down in front of her colleagues at any moment, like that time she had burst into tears in the middle of an examination, while the nurse looked on in distress, not sure whether he should tend to the doctor or to the elderly woman who couldn't breathe because a rib was pressing on her lungs. Now, every time Doctor Cambra heard her name through the loudspeakers of the casualty ward, she went wherever she was needed without thinking about anything except her work. At times an intern with a badly receding hairline and an aquiline nose would remind her of Alberto, who was still her husband. But, unlike a few months before, she was able to smile. She could even picture him cooking dinner with that radiologist who was obsessed with the gym and the hairdresser's; he who had never done the dishes and had never opened a kitchen drawer except to take out a corkscrew. The last time she'd seen him it looked as though he had dyed the grey hairs on his temples and sideburns. She also imagined him belly dancing for the radiologist, and chasing her around a coffee table, in one of the wild cat-and-mouse games that he hadn't played with her for years. Her feelings for Alberto had changed from sadness to irony, and from irony to sarcasm. She would never have imagined that someone who had been such an important part of her life since her youth would become, in barely ten months, a sort of rag doll, an empty, fake being – a veritable bastard. She found it hard to remember what he looked like when they'd met, at the time when he drove around Barcelona in that white, impeccable, polished, perfect Mercedes of his, it was just like him. A doctor from a family of doctors, a young cardiologist with a brilliant career, he'd been seductive, intelligent, handsome. Now, Doctor Cambra could not rid her mind of the image of her husband of twenty years chasing the young radiologist. When she bumped into Doctor Carnero, the anaesthetist on duty, she was still wearing a sarcastic smile on her face. They looked at each other in complicity.

'This is the first time I've seen anyone smile on a New Year's Eve shift,' said the anaesthetist as she walked by.

'I guess there's a first time for everything.'

A voice called Doctor Cambra through the loudspeakers. Before the message was over, she was at her station.

'In number four there's a young woman with fractured limbs. A motorcycle accident.'

Doctor Cambra's blood boiled. Her face flushed and her heartbeat accelerated. She walked over to the room they'd indicated, to find a very pale young woman being tended to by a nurse and an assistant. The girl looked scared and helpless, and the doctor immediately felt her legs grow weak. She tried to regain her composure, and said, in an annoyed tone:

'Who took her helmet off?'

'They brought her in without one. She probably wasn't wearing it.'

The doctor lifted the girl's eyelids and shone a little torch in them. She couldn't help taking her hand and squeezing it. The girl's other hand looked dead and was scratched all over. The doctor pressed gently on her thorax, spleen, kidneys, and stomach, saying: 'Does this hurt? And here?' The girl moaned, but shook her head.

'Let's see. Tell me how it happened.'

The girl mumbled something, but she couldn't string her sentences together.

'Do you feel a bit sleepy?' asked the doctor. 'Don't fall asleep now. Go on, tell me what you can remember.'

As the girl tried to make herself understood, the nurse took her blood pleasure.

'We're going to need a CAT scan.'

The assistant wrote it down. The girl went on talking, now more coherently.

'Blood pressure's eleven-eighteen.'

'How old are you?' asked the doctor.

'Nineteen. I have to be home for dinner.'

Doctor Cambra held her breath and looked away. That may have been the same thing her daughter had said six months before, when a doctor at the casualty ward had asked her what she had just asked the unknown girl. Nineteen. Her daughter had turned nineteen in March. As they took the girl away for her scan, Doctor Cambra left the room. Her daughter's death would not come between her and her work, but she could not forget it either. Just like this girl, she'd been nineteen, and was riding her moped with her helmet hanging from her arm, heading home for dinner with her mother. However, it had been her father who got the call. At the hospital, Alberto's name was well-known. They didn't even have to look up his number in the dead girl's diary. It was on file, at reception, along with the frequently used numbers. Montse didn't know what hurt her the most, how long they'd taken to let her know, or the fact that it had been her husband, in a deep voice filled with self-possession, who had told her that their daughter had died. Besides, he had shown up with the radiologist, as if he wanted his lover to witness his fortitude.

An hour later, when Montse bumped into doctor Carnero in the staff room, her sarcastic smile had been replaced by a vacant gaze. On seeing her, the anaesthetist knew her friend was about to slip back into that deep hole she was trying to climb out of.

'Coffee?'

Doctor Cambra nodded. It felt good to be surrounded by people and talk about mundane things.

'How's your son?'

The anaesthetist squinted at her and tried to smile.

'Oh, he's fine. But how are you? A moment ago you were smiling to yourself and now I come here and find you…'

'I'm fine. My head's not always where it should be, that's all.'

'We all get that, Montse. It doesn't really make you special, you know.'

'Nothing does, Belén. I'm the least special person on the planet.'

Belén tried not to take her friend's observation too seriously. She knew better than anyone that Montse didn't need words or advice but time for her wounds to heal.

'Listen, Montse,' said the anaesthetist. 'What are you doing tomorrow?' ·

'Nothing much, I guess: I'll watch the ski jumping and the waltz competition on TV, and get fat with no regrets.'

'I was thinking you could come round for dinner. Matías has brought some of that cod you like so much from his hometown.'

'Cod on New Year's Day? What about turkey and rice? The tradition that made our cuisine so great?'

'You couldn't be more old-fashioned!'

The door opened and an intern walked in, wearing gloves and surgical mask at a crooked angle.

'Montse, we need you.'

Doctor Cambra stood up and left her coffee on the table without having even sipped from it.

'All right,' she said before leaving, 'tomorrow at yours. If you like I'll tape the ski jumps.'

'No thanks. I'll watch them live. My son loves them.'

Between eleven and twelve-thirty, the Casualty Ward was particularly quiet. A few staff members went over to the cafeteria for a bite to eat; others preferred to share home dishes in the staff room. It was the worst period of the night for Doctor Cambra.

The girl's parents appeared a little before the clock struck twelve, harrowed by their daughter's accident. Doctor Montserrat Cambra took special care of them. Against hospital regulations, she even allowed them to go in and see their daughter for a few minutes.

'She's been very lucky,' she told the parents, who wept in front of the badly injured girl. 'Don't be scared by the intubation and all the bandages. It's only saline solution and pain killers. Her head is absolutely fine. She's broken a collarbone and a tibia. The worst thing, though, are the injuries to her hand, but with surgery and proper physical therapy there'll be no serious consequences.'

The mother burst into tears as soon as she finished the report.

'But she's fine, trust me. In a month she'll be nearly back to normal.'

Doctor Cambra was doing her best to lift the parents' spirits, but she herself was sinking deeper into the terrifying hole. As soon as she could, she excused herself and walked away. Back in the staff room, the doctors and nurses on duty were toasting the new year in with plastic cups and making confetti out of old spreadsheets. The new century had crept in. A doctor from traumatology kissed her and wished her a happy new year. He was nervous and particularly clumsy, and nearly spilled coffee all over her.

'You haven't called me all week,' he said, trying not to sound reproachful.

'I didn't get a chance, Pere, honestly. I had a million things to do here.'

'Well, if that's the only reason...'

'Of course it is. You're a great guy, honestly.'

The doctor walked off, wary of prying eyes. Belén approached her friend from behind and whispered in her ear:

'You haven't called me all week, Montse.'

She blushed so much she thought everyone would see .

'You're a great guy, honestly,' continued the anaesthetist, imitating Montse's affected tone.

'Will you shut up ! Don't you realise he's listening?'

'Who, Pere? He's deaf in one ear, as I'm sure you know. I myself anaesthetised him for the operation.'

'You're a witch.'

'And you're a bit jumpy today. Didn't you know Pere is the hospital's most eligible bachelor?'

'And did you know that the most eligible bachelor falls short where it matters?'

Belén covered her mouth in a exaggerated gesture of surprise.

'Really!'

'You heard me.'

'Well, nobody's perfect, darling.'

The rest of the shift went as everyone expected: people coming and going up and down corridors, opening and closing doors, pushing gurneys in and out of rooms. It would have ended like any other shift Doctor Cambra had worked in her long career, had it not been for a series of coincidences that took place in the first hours of the new century.

At three-fifteen in the morning, an ambulance from the Casualty Ward of the Hospital de Barcelona picked up a twenty-five-year-old Arabic pregnant woman, who had been run over at the airport. First coincidence: the ambulance, which was speeding at over ninety kilometres an hour along Gran Via de Les Cort Catalanes, encountered a traffic jam when it reached Carrer de Badal; three cars had crashed and were on fire. That was the shortest way to the Hospital de Barcelona, but it was now impossible to pass through the fire engines and police cars gathering in the area, and so the driver carried on along the main road looking for the nearest hospital. Second coincidence: when the driver radioed the Hospital Clinic i Provincial, who told him they were expecting four people with severe burns, and advised him to proceed to his initial destination. Third coincidence: when the ambulance was about to take a turn at Plaça de les Glóries Catalanes in order to go back up Diagonal towards the Hospital, the driver made a mistake while turning a sharp corner and ended up on the wrong road. Fourth coincidence: as the driver was trying to orientate himself, he chanced on the main façade of the Hospital de la Santa Creu i de Sant Pau, and before he knew where he was, he saw the red lights of the Casualty Ward. The moment the stretcher crossed the threshold, the woman lost all her vitals, and presently a nurse realised she was dead. Fifth coincidence: just when doctor Cambra was seeing an old man who'd been admitted with an asthma attack, an orderly and an intern left the gurney with the body of the pregnant woman next to her. A certain something made Doctor Cambra take notice of that woman: perhaps the beauty of her features, the colourful piece of cloth wrapped around her, or her advanced pregnancy. Though no one asked her to, Doctor Cambra took her pulse at the throat; then she lifted her eyelids and found the pupils dilated and non-reactive, which confirmed that the woman was dead. Her features were placid, as if she'd died with a smile on her face. At reception, meanwhile, there was a bit of a commotion, and a discussion started between the administrative and ambulance staff. Doctor Cambra, without really meaning to, learned all the details. The victim's husband, who had not been allowed on the ambulance, had taken a taxi to the Hospital de Barcelona, where he was no doubt asking about his wife at that very moment. Also, all the woman's papers, passport and documents were in Arabic, so no one knew who to contact about the death. Doctor Cambra stepped in and tried to make some sense of it all.

'Call the other casualty department, explain what's happened, and tell them to send the husband over as soon as he gets there.'

They looked at each other, with all the tiredness one feels at half three in the morning.

'And don't mention she's dead.'

Doctor Cambra looked again at the woman's disquietingly peaceful face. In other circumstances, it would have looked contented. As two assistants put what the woman carried in her pockets and purse on a little table, Montse picked up a form and examined her injuries, trying to figure out how the accident had happened. In the form she entered the estimated age of the victim: twenty-five. It made her shiver. For a moment she saw herself at that age, walking arm in arm with Alberto, or dancing with him at Caldaqués, pregnant and envied by the resentful girls from Barcelona also on holiday at the seaside. Then, another coincidence, she leaned on the small table to write more comfortably, and the woman's personal effects fell off. This wouldn't have mattered much in itself if, on bending down to pick them up, Montserat Cambra hadn't seen three or four photographs, one of which strongly attracted her attention.

It was in black and white. Two men appeared in the centre, shown from the knees up. They were the same height. Both smiled at the camera, as though they were the happiest people in the world. Behind them was the front of a Land Rover with a spare wheel on the bonnet. Further back there were countless Bedouin tents, lined up all the way to the horizon. Among the tents there were groups of goats lying on the ground. The two men had their arms around each other's shoulders, in a gesture of comradeship. They were very close to one another, their faces nearly touching. One of them had Arab features: he was wearing military clothes and making the V sign with his hand. The other was clearly a Westerner, in spite of his attire. He was dressed like Laurence of Arabia, with a long white tunic and a dark turban, undone and hanging loose over his shoulders. He had very short hair and an old-fashioned moustache. In his right hand he was holding a gun in a very cinematographic gesture. What most attracted the viewer's attention were the men's smiles.

The picture confused Doctor Cambra. A moment later, when she held it up in her shaking hands, she realised why: the moustachioed man in desert clothes was Santiago San Román. She traced the image with her finger, not sure whether it was an illusion. But her doubts were soon dispelled. She flipped the picture and discovered what seemed to be a dedication in Arabic, in blue smudged letters. Underneath it read clearly: "Tifariti, 18-1-1976". The date was so conclusive that it left no room for uncertainty. If Santiago San Román had died in 1975, as she had always thought, that young man could not be the guy who, on a hot July afternoon twenty-six years to this date, had approached her and her inseparable friend Nuria while they were waiting for a bus on Avenida del Generalísimo Franco.

It happened in the early summer of '74. Montse would never forget the date, no matter how many years went by. It was the first time her parents had gone on holiday to Cadaqués and left her at home. She'd never been on her own in her life, and that summer she wasn't either. A maid called Mari Cruz, who cooked, made the beds and looked after her, had stayed at the house on Vía Cayetana. Montse had turned eighteen barely a month before, and had graduated from secondary school with excellent marks. Still, her father thought that in order to study medicine one needed more than an outstanding student record, so Montse was denied a summer holiday for the first time in eighteen years. And, while the days blended into each other by the sea, she attended a private academy in the morning and afternoon, where she brushed up on maths and chemistry and took up German.

The Academia Santa Teresa was situated on the mezzanine of a building on Avenida del Generalísimo Franco. There was a dance academy on the floor above it, which in the summer gave full-immersion courses from eight o'clock in the morning till nine in the evening. While Montse and her inseparable friend Nuria tried to focus on their logarithms, the desks of the classroom would vibrate to the stamping heels of the flamenco dancers or the broken rhythms of a tango. In those conditions it was easy for one's eyes to stray to the window, and one's attention would follow the same way, focusing on a handsome guy or the shops across the road. But the monotony was soon to be broken, on a day when Montse and Nuria were waiting for the bus, having lost all hope that something would save them from the boredom of the summer and the heat.

Perhaps it was boredom that made the two friends glance at the white convertible with very big plates that stopped on the other side of the road. It was a foreign car, possibly American. Apart from the unusual model, they noticed that inside it were two young, handsome, very well dressed guys who would not stop staring at them. Neither Montse nor Nuria dared to say something, but they both knew that sooner or later something out of the ordinary would happen. And indeed, in a dangerous, spectacular move, the car drove across the road and screeched to a halt by the bus stop. That was the first time Montse saw Santiago San Román. Although the boy was only nineteen, his brilliantined hair, his clothes and the car made him look more mature. He and his friend got out of the car at the same time and approached the girls. 'The service on this line has been suspended,' he said in an accent that instantly gave away that he was not from Barcelona, 'me and Pascualín have just found out.' The other people waiting at the bus stop exchanged incredulous glances. Only Montse and Nuria smiled, their curiosity piqued. 'It'll take a day or two at most,' added Pascualín. 'But if you don't want to wait that long, myself and my friend here can give you a ride to wherever you're going.' As Pascualín spoke, Santiago pointed to the splendid car. Pascualín opened the door on the passenger's side, and Montse, acting on an impulse she'd never felt before, said to her friend. 'Come on, Nuria, they're driving us.' Nuria sat in the back with Pascualín, and Montse in the spectacular front seat, which was ample and luxurious, covered in very pale tan leather. Santiago San Román hesitated for a second, his eyes wide open, as if he couldn't believe the two girls had taken him up on the invitation. He got nervous at the steering wheel when Montse asked: 'And what's your name?' 'Santiago San Román, at your service,' he replied, in a ridiculous-sounding stab at humbleness.

It was the craziest thing Montse had ever done. Sitting next to Santiago San Román, she felt the heat and the boredom float away. They drove in silence, all four enjoying the sensation, lost in their own thoughts. And so, when they went round Plaza de la Victoria and past Vía Layetana, Montse didn't say a thing. They drove into Plaza de las Glorias Catalanas as though they were part of a triumphant parade. Every now and again Santiago would glance at her, or turn to look at her head-on as she lifted her hair for the breeze to run through it. After a while they stopped at the Estación del Pueblo Nuevo. The sea air smelled of stagnant water. Once the car was parked, Montse opened her eyes as though she were waking up from a slumber. 'Why are you stopping?' she asked, with forced self-confidence. 'This place is horrible.'

'Okay, but you haven't told me where you live.'

'On Vía Layetana,' replied Nuria quickly, less at ease than her friend. Santiago did a U-turn and drove back the way they'd come. Suddenly Montse became talkative and started asking all kinds of questions.

'It's my father's car, I don't make enough to own a Cadillac.' 'In a bank, I work in a bank. Well, actually, my father's the manager, and I'll be the same one day.' 'Yes, Pascualín too; we both work at the same bank.'

Meanwhile, Pascualín and Nuria were oblivious to the conversation. As Santiago answered the questions, he dug himself deeper and deeper into a hole. 'Pull up here, please. This is where Nuria lives,' said Montse all of a sudden. In fact the girls were neighbours, but Nuria realised what her friend's intentions were, and reluctantly got out of the Cadillac.

'Will you not walk her?' said Santiago to Pascualín, reproachfully. The convertible proceeded down the road and stopped where Montse indicated. For the first time she looked him in the eyes; he struck her as the handsomest guy she'd ever met. She let him tell more lies. Santiago, however, didn't ask any questions. It was hard enough to have to reply to the ones Montse was continually asking him. Eventually, he said: 'This feels like an interrogation.'

'Do you mind my questions?'

'No, no, I don't mind them at all.'

It's just that when I jump into someone's car I like to know who the guy is,' said Montse, coyly. 'Don't go thinking, though, that I do this every day.'

'No, no, I don't think that at all. But the thing is, I've told you everything, and you...'

'What would you like to know?' she cut in.

Santiago hesitated before asking: 'Do you have a boyfriend?' For the first time Montse's confidence faltered. Now it was she who hesitated before replying: 'No, not a boyfriend as such – but I've got admirers,' she said, trying to keep her cool. 'What about you, do you have a girlfriend?'

'No, no; I don't like commitment.' Even before finishing the phrase he wished he hadn't said it. Confused and without exactly knowing why, he placed a hand on her back and stroked the nape of her neck. Montse, also without thinking clearly, drew near and kissed him on the lips. But when Santiago tried to hold her in his arms and kiss her more deeply she slipped away, pretending she was offended.

'I have to go now,' she said, 'it's getting late.' She opened the door, got out of the car, and only stopped when Santiago San Román shouted to her worriedly:

'Do you want to meet up some other time?' Like a capricious child, she walked back to the car, left the books on the bonnet, scribbled something in her notebook, tore out the page, put it under the windshield wiper, picked up her books again and, after a few steps, turned and said:

'Give me a call first. There's the number. I've also written down the address and the number of the flat, so you don't go around asking the neighbours.' That was all. She walked to the doorway and, with some difficulty, pushed open the enormous iron door. Santiago San Román didn't even get a chance to reply. After Montse had disappeared, he was still looking at the empty space where she had been. The girl did not have enough patience to wait for the lift. She ran up the stairs two steps at a time, hastily opened the front door, dropped the books on the floor and ran to her room, ignoring Mari Cruz's hello. From the balcony of her room she just caught sight of the car driving into the traffic and disappearing towards the harbour. Still, she could see that the page was no longer under the windshield wiper. She pictured it folded in four, hidden in Santiago's shirt pocket: an immaculate, nicely cut white shirt, without a crease, its sleeves rolled up to the elbow, and with a distinction that contrasted with the social class he so tried to hide.

Doctor Montserrat Cambra was walking down the corridor of the casualty ward in a considerable state of confusion. She held the pocket of her coat as though she were afraid that someone might snatch the picture she had just stolen from a dead woman out of it. For a moment she didn't even know where she was. Then she thought everyone was watching her. However, none of the staff she passed looked at her. She walked into the doctors' room and closed the door behind her. She had difficulty breathing. She sat down and swallowed a pill. It was the last in the box. The coffee that Belén had poured her hours before was still on the table. She downed it in one, without even noticing it was cold. She picked up the receiver of the phone on the table, dialled reception and said in a trembling voice:

'Doctor Cambra speaking. Please listen carefully. When the husband of the woman from the airport comes in, I need you to let me know. Don't forget. It doesn't matter if I'm busy. Let me know. It's important. Thanks.'

After hanging up, she put her hand in her pocket and touched the photograph. She sat down without taking her hand out. She experienced the absurd sensation that the picture might disappear at any time. Then it would all vanish as in a dream: another dream turned into a nightmare.

Chapter Four

THERE'S SOMETHING GHOSTLY ABOUT THE SMARA HOSPITAL
at four o'clock in the afternoon. Outside, the scorching sun and
the dry, biting wind make it impossible for life to go about
its business normally. Inside, the dark empty corridors seem
entangled like a spider's web that reaches far into the building.
From a distance, the Smara Hospital looks like a mirage
emanating from the redoubtable *hammada* of the Sahara.

Dressed in an olive-green uniform, Colonel Mulud Lahsen
walks into the lavatories, dusting off his clothes and removing
the turban from his mouth. His chauffeur waits for him in the
car, under the sun. Mulud Lahsen does not take his glasses off
even though the corridors are dark. Suddenly, after walking
over the threshold, it seems as though he'd left the desert far
behind. It smells of disinfectant. The colonel wrinkles his nose;
after so many years he has never got used to the intense smell.
He knows the hospital like the palm of his hand. He's seen it
grow from the foundations up, when there was nothing but
sand and stones in the site. He strides confidently through the
maze of corridors. He stops at the director's office without
having crossed a soul. He doesn't knock before going in. The
director is a small, restless man. Sitting behind his desk, he has
his eyes fixed on a mountain of papers. He wears tortoiseshell
glasses. What little hair he has left is grey. His skin is tanned
and hardened by the sun. On seeing the colonel by the door, he
smiles broadly. They go through a lengthy greeting of Arabic

formulae, looking each other in the eye and shaking hands.

Colonel Mulud Lahsen is tall and heavily built. In comparison, the director of the Smara Hospital looks like a child.

'Mulud, Mulud, Mulud,' says the director when the greeting is finally over and they let go of each other's hands.

'With that coat and those glasses you look like a doctor.'

The director smiles. They've known each other since they were children, long before they had to leave their country.

'You're the last person I was expecting today,' says the director.

'I would have visited earlier, but I've been away.'

'So I've heard. How's the minister?'

'He's got a fever,' says the colonel with a broad smile.

'The health minister with a fever? Doesn't he know we have plenty of beds in our hospital?'

They both laugh. The colonel takes off his sunglasses and leaves them on the desk. His eyes are bloodshot.

'He's that pigheaded, you know him.'

'Yes, yes, I know him all too well.'

As he speaks, he takes two glasses out of a drawer and places them on the desk. Then he walks across the room and lights a cigarette on the gas stove. He fills up a kettle and puts it on the hob.

'How's everything here?' asks the colonel.

'Fine, fine, as usual. We're finishing installing the new machines. Everyone's trying to get them to work.'

'Is that why the hospital is so quiet?'

'Yes. Well, in fact, we haven't admitted anyone today. The nurses are finishing tidying the library, and trying to work out how to operate the dialysis machine. All the reagents and instructions are in German.'

'No one's been admitted...'

'Today we discharged a boy who had a toothache.'

'No one else?'

'In fact, yes. I had almost forgotten. We've had a foreign

woman for three weeks. As I see her every day I forget she's not really a member of staff. She almost died.'

'A woman? A foreign woman?'

The director leaves the preparation of the tea for a moment and approaches the colonel. Very carefully he lifts his eyelids.

'Let me see those eyes.'

Colonel Mulud patiently submits to the examination. His eyelids are opened wide, and the conjunctiva examined.

'I sent you a message the day she arrived. In the report I explained all the details of her admission. I was surprised you didn't reply, but then so many papers get lost en route.'

The director goes on speaking as he carefully studies Mulud's eyes.

'You have very serious conjunctivitis,' he tells the colonel.

'It's the wind.'

'And the sun. Yesterday I would have given you some drops, but we've run out. If you come back in a fortnight, perhaps I'll be able to do something for you. I don't like the look of this eye.'

At that point the colonel searches his jacket and takes out a letter. He unfolds it on the desk. The director stares at the piece of paper and instantly recognises his own handwriting.

'So you got the report in Rabuni.'

'I found it the day before yesterday among the papers I had to forward to the Ministry. As I say, I had to go away for a while. But what you say here attracted my attention.'

'It's an unusual case for me too. That's why I wanted to know what procedure to follow.'

'You say the woman will live.'

'Yes, though a week ago I wouldn't have been so sure.'

The two men go quiet for a moment. The director wipes his glasses with a flannel until they sparkle.

'It's difficult to say what happened, but now you're here I'm glad to be able to discuss it with someone.'

'Tell me. I'm intrigued.'

'Well, you see, about a month ago an army patrol turned up

with this half-dead woman.'

'A patrol, you say?'

'Two men in a four-by-four. They said they'd left from Smara that morning with a group towards the Wall.'

'Do you remember any names?'

'No. I'd never seen them before, and they didn't identify themselves.'

'It's all very strange. No patrol has informed me that they found a woman or brought her to this hospital.'

'From what they said, they were part of a convoy travelling to the free territories. They didn't explain much, but I understood they'd left at dawn and, thirty kilometres later, found a woman in the middle of the desert. She was one of us, a Saharawi, and signalled to them from a distance to attract their attention. When they went over, she said another woman had been left for dead about a day's walk to the north. From what she explained, the woman had been stung by a scorpion.'

'One of us, alone in the desert?'

'That's what they said.'

'Did you speak to her?'

'She was not in the vehicle. She stayed where they found her, about thirty kilometres away from Smara. And on her own, as they said, because the convoy continued towards the Wall.'

'It's all very strange.'

'I thought so too. That's why I sent the letter to the ministry. I thought you'd reply a lot sooner.'

Colonel Mulud ignores the last remark. He'd rather have an explanation. Eventually he asks:

'Didn't any of the soldiers give any more details about the women?'

'They were in a hurry. For them it was just a hassle. I suggested they write a full report, and they gave me a withering look.'

'But it was their duty.'

The director pours the tea into the glasses. The sound of the falling liquid fills the room. For a moment words are swept aside, and both men are engrossed in the contemplation of the shiny tray.

Aza was convinced she was going to die. As she fled, she was trying to avoid running in a straight line. The sun was in front of her, so she had a slight advantage, but her legs moved more slowly than her mind dictated. She ran in a tortuous zigzag, looking for an elevation on the ground, a little mound, a slope where she could dive for cover. In a daze of anxiety, she ended up going in the worst direction. She was so nervous she couldn't decide what to do. Before she even realised, she was running on soft sand. Her stride became shorter and clumsier. With each step she sank up to her calf. She knew she only had a very small lead, and didn't even want to turn round to check on it. She ended up walking with her eyes fixed to the ground, in a straight line. Her shoulders felt weighed down, and her legs were burning; besides, her *melfa* was getting in the way, although she didn't want to cast it aside and leave it behind. Then she heard a clear metallic sound that she knew well. Someone was loading a rifle – and was taking his time. She summoned all her strength and ran a bit further. At that moment a gust of wind blew around her, but even in those conditions she heard, as if right next to her, the report of the rifle. The *melfa* got tangled in her legs and she fell forward onto the sand. It all happened so fast that at first she didn't know whether it was her own clumsiness or the bullet that brought her down.

All she could hear now was the whistling of the wind as it whipped up huge clouds of dust. Her whole body ached, but her mind was regaining awareness. Lying on the ground she couldn't see her pursuers, which meant they couldn't see her either. She moved a bit and touched her back without rising. She was unhurt: the bullet had missed her. Almost instinctively she clung to the ground and started digging into it. The sand was very soft, and the wind helped . Her mind reacted surprisingly quickly. In a frenzy, she started digging with her feet, her legs, her whole body. After a few minutes she had hollowed out a considerable space in the sand. She rolled into it and started to cover herself. She placed the *melfa* over her face and covered it with some difficulty. The wind took care of the rest. After a while she was completely buried, with her face barely a few centimetres from the surface. She could hear the sound of the wind and even, depending on which way it blew, the voices of Le Monsieur and his men.

Many times Aza had heard her elders tell stories about the war. She had heard them so much that she'd stopped paying attention, but she'd never entirely forgotten them. The Saharawi shepherds who, in the seventies, had become warriors and fought the same way and using the same tactics as their ancestors. When laying ambushes for the Moroccans, the Saharawis had often buried themselves. Aza's uncle had told her many times how, buried in the sand, he'd felt an armoured vehicle pass over him. You needed a lot of sangfroid, as her uncle had often said as well. Aza tried to remember those stories as she was in the sand, and regretted not having been more attentive, she had not anticipated how useful those guerrilla tactics might be.

Her heart felt like a bomb about to go off. Aza knew her worst enemy would be anxiety. She tried to think of pleasant things. She thought of her son and her mother. She remembered the seafront in Havana, with those old cars miraculously winding up and down the street. The desert wind started to resemble the wind of the Caribbean, whose fearsome waves broke against the rocks of the jetty. She recalled the day of her wedding. Though breathing with difficulty, she calmed herself little by little, until her thoughts blended in with the voices of the despicable men who thought they had killed her. Then she recognised Le Monsieur's voice, speaking in French with the mercenaries who followed him everywhere. Now and again he uttered curses in

Spanish. She knew they were desperately looking for her, no doubt thinking she'd been gunned down. When her body did not appear they began to blame one another. They came so close she could hear their laboured breathing. And above their voices, she heard Le Monsieur, insulting them all and threatening to cut their throats. Aza feared her heart would give her away. She was trying to breathe deeply but very slowly. A few grains of sand slipped through the cloth of the *melfa* covering her face. She knew she wouldn't be able stand the horrible situation for long. However, she would rather suffocate, buried, than fall into the hands of those criminals.

Every time Le Monsieur's voice drew near, her body tensed up and her jaw locked. He got so close that for a moment she thought he would tread on her. The voices would alternately move away and return. The men were obviously walking in circles around the area where they'd seen her go down. It was an extremely tense atmosphere, and the mercenaries soon started arguing with each other. Aza knew men like that, and they were perfectly capable of killing one another because of an offence or a few insults. But the voice she heard most often was Le Monsieur's. He was shouting himself hoarse. In the meantime, the wind was working in Aza's favour. Not only had her footsteps been erased, but also the sand kept accumulating on the imperceptible mound that her body made on the surface of the desert, so that she became better and better hidden.

As the voices grew distant, Aza weighed up her chances of survival. It had been ten hours since she'd last drunk any water, which of course didn't help. Also, after running away from the mercenaries, she had started sweating, and moisture was seeping out of her pores. In spite of the wind, the sand was burning hot in the sun. Any Saharawi knew full well what it meant to be stranded in the desert without water. She'd seen cases of death by dehydration, and it was a terrible end. For a moment she wondered whether it would be worse to be shot or die of thirst. But she was so scared that she was incapable of deciding. If the men went away in both vehicles, her chances would be slim. She anxiously thought of the washing-up bowl filled with filthy water near the hellish oasis. And, listening to the maddened voices of her pursuers, she reached the conclusion that it was preferable to withstand the terrible effects of thirst to being captured by them. Her mouth felt dry and full of sand. She strove not to lose control of her body and mind. She closed her eyes and pictured herself in her *jaima,*[7] with her son next to her. She tried hard to distract herself. For a while her heartbeat almost went back to normal.

When she heard the engines of the truck and the four by four, her body tensed up once again. She wasn't sure how much time had passed – perhaps several hours. The wind had dropped. However, she could still hear the roaring engines, as though the mercenaries were driving in widening circles and then closing in on themselves until they were very near her. Aza thought of the Spanish woman who had stayed in the Toyota. Although she hadn't heard any more shots, she was sure that the woman would soon die. Aza herself had seen the scorpion that had stung her, but she hadn't had enough time to warn her. If those men had not already killed her, the poison would spread through her veins and cause cardiac arrest. She pitied the woman. The noise of the vehicles was unnerving. The more upset she felt, the drier her throat became. Now and again she noticed the sweat on her skin. She didn't remember ever having been so thirsty. She tried not to think about what would become of her if those bandits didn't find her and she stayed at the mercy of the desert. She knew that the feeling of thirst started after the body lost half a litre of water. After two litres, the stomach shrank and it was no longer capable of holding the amount of water the body needed. She'd seen cases like that, especially in old people.

[7.] *Jaima*: A large tent used in the Sahara.

People suffering from this condition stopped drinking long before the body had met its needs. Doctors called it 'voluntary dehydration'. Still, that wasn't the worst case scenario. If the body lost five litres, symptoms of fatigue and fever would appear, one's pulse would quicken and one's skin would turn very red. After that came dizziness, intense headache, absence of saliva and circulatory problems. In a less hostile environment, you reached that phase in three days, but in the Sahara you could get there in twelve hours of intense heat. Buried in the sun, with her mouth all doughy, she knew she was sweating, but found it impossible to estimate how much water she'd lost. She had a momentary panic attack. It felt as though her skin had stuck to her bones and was beginning to harden and crack. She even felt that her eyes had sunk into their sockets as the hours had gone by. However, she drew some comfort from the fact that she could still hear very clearly what was going on, even in the distance. What she feared most was delirium, and so she tried to calm down once again so as not to be overwhelmed by the heat. Aza couldn't get the idea out of her head that death was not caused by thirst, but by excess heat: the blood thickened in one's veins and couldn't carry the internal body heat to the surface of the skin. Indeed, what ended up killing you was the heat, as your body temperature rose unexpectedly and irrevocably.

She was about to fall asleep when her eyes opened with a start. Suddenly she couldn't hear the wind, or the mercenaries' voices, or the roaring of the vehicles. The absolute silence was spine chilling. She had the horrible feeling of having been buried for several days. The light that reached her through the sand felt less aggressive. She tilted her head forwards and, with great difficulty, pushed it out into the open air. Grains of sand slipped over her body. Her arms and shoulder ached. She struggled again and unearthed half her body. She removed the *melfa* and surveyed the deserted, silent *hammada*. In two hours the sun would set, so the heat was no longer so intense. With a great effort, Aza managed to sit up. She was so frightened she didn't dare to remove her clothes to shake the sand off her body. It was a long time before she was totally sure that the mercenaries had gone. Nevertheless, she knew that even in the immensity of the desert the men might be able to find her. The tyre tracks left by the two vehicles were all around her: from the looks of it they must have circled around for hours, probably until the petrol tanks began to run out. Although she was dying to get away, she kept her wits about her and decided to wait for the sun to set. Under the canopy of the stars it would be easier for her to orient herself, and of course her body would lose less water while walking. While she was sitting down, on the alert, she thought she saw a moving shadow in the distance. Her first reaction was to crouch down and stay still, but she soon realised what it was. She walked in the direction of the figure, glancing everywhere around her in case it was a trap. But it wasn't. From a distance of a hundred metres she could see that it was the Spanish woman. Aza couldn't even remember her name. She approached and knelt down beside her. The woman must have been lying there for over five hours. With a string of insults that she'd learned as a child, she cursed the men who'd abandoned her there. She turned the woman over and raised her head, but there was no reaction. She put her ear to the woman's chest; the situation looked desperate. It took a while before she could hear the heartbeat. It was faint and irregular, arrhythmical, as if the heart was announcing that it would stop imminently . Aza looked frantically for the spot where the woman had been stung. It was too late to try to extract the poison. She knew that the woman would die, and there was nothing she could do about it. The thought of death distressed her horribly. She tried to remain calm. Soon it would be dark and her chances of escape would improve.

Without looking back, Aza started walking the minute that the blinding sphere of the sun dipped below the horizon. A few

Denise Vondra
New Horizons
Cell
970 - 420 - 5842

970 - 223 - 7400
Conf # 005033261. 4

moments later the surface of the desert started cooling down. Each time the wind blew, she got goose-pimples. She didn't waste any time. After checking one last time that the foreign woman's heart was still beating, she set forth towards the south-east. She weighed up her chances again. She didn't have a clear idea of how far the nearest camp would be. Besides, although most Saharawis were capable of finding their way perfectly in the desert at night, she had had little opportunity to learn to do so. She had spent half her life in Cuba as a student. The desert, at times, was as hostile to her as to a foreigner, even though she had not left it for the last three years. In any case, she knew that if one wanted to reach a certain place it was vital to be precise and always walk in a straight line; a small deviation might mean straying several kilometres from the intended destination. She walked slowly so as not to tire herself out. She tried to ignore her thirst. If she didn't sweat too much and lay down as soon as the sun was up, she might be able to walk for one more night. But that was just a guess. Meanwhile, her steps became clumsier and clumsier. She frequently stumbled and fell forwards. Her eyes clouded with fatigue. Although there was a full moon, she could barely make out the terrain five or six metres ahead. She hadn't eaten anything for over a day. Eventually, a few hours before dawn, she fell to the ground and could not find the strength to pick herself up again.

A noise, almost a vibration, awoke her. Her eyelids were stuck together, and she didn't remember where she was. She had covered herself with the *melfa* to keep insects from biting her. It was very cold. As the noise became clearer, she feared she was experiencing the onset of hallucinations. Her head ached horribly. She sat up and took a good look around, but saw nothing. The sun had been up for at least two hours. She lay back down on the ground, and this time the noise made her jump to her feet. There was no room for doubt: it was a truck engine. She listened, but the wind changed direction.

However, a plume of dust rising on the horizon revealed the presence of several vehicles. It didn't even occur to her that it might be Le Monsieur and his mercenaries. Although she could not yet see the shining surface of the cars, she figured out that they were moving quite slowly, judging from the height of the cloud of dust. She traced a mental line in their direction and started walking over to intercept them. They were probably two kilometres away. It was difficult to calculate distances. As she pressed on she shook the dirt off her clothes, and wiped her eyes and the corners of her mouth with saliva; she cleaned her ears of sand and put on the *melfa* as if she had just got up on a normal day. About five hundred metres from them, she started waving her arms, but trying not to reveal her desperation. They saw her a moment later. Four trucks with canvas covering the back and two four-by-fours. Even from afar she could see the surprised faces of the young soldiers. In a fit of embarrassment, she prayed to Allah that none of those men would know who she was.

The convoy changed course directly after seeing the woman signal to them from the most inhospitable area of the *hammada*. As they approached, the drivers and passengers could hardly believe their eyes. They were all , staring fixedly at the same spot. One of the four-by-fours ran ahead and stopped a few metres from the woman. An officer got out. His stripes made it obvious that he was the one in charge. As he walked up to her, he took off his sunglasses and loosened his turban. He started a long formulaic greeting, all the time studying the woman. If his men had not been following his every move, he would have touched her arm to make sure she was not a mirage. The greeting finished, his neutral tone changed and his surprise showed through. 'What are you doing here? Where did you come from?' he asked in an obviously annoyed voice.

'I got lost.'

'You got lost?' he asked again, not believing her. 'How did you get lost?'

'It's a long story, and I haven't got much time,' she replied, respectfully. The officer seemed spooked, as though he were talking to a ghost . 'And how did you get here? How long have you been lost?'

'I need to drink some water, I'm about to collapse.' The rest of the convoy had stopped in a long line, and the soldiers got out of their vehicles. The officer opened the door of the four-by-four and took out a canteen covered in leather. Aza drank as much as she could. The water went into her mouth and flowed out of her pores, as if from a fountain. Then she sought the shade of one of the trucks. The soldiers looked at her without really grasping what was going on.

With a shout, the officer ordered them to go back to their vehicles. 'Now explain to me how it was you got lost.'

'It's a long story, and there are more important things to be done.'

'More important?'

'Yes, over in that direction there's a dying woman. She's foreign. She was stung by a scorpion nearly twenty-four hours ago. She may be dead already.' The officer grew agitated. He called over the driver of one of the four-by-fours and asked Aza to tell him where the exact place was. 'It's in that direction. I've walked in a straight line for eight hours. You could get there in twenty minutes.' The driver and two soldiers left immediately. Meanwhile, the soldiers were forming another line near the woman, trying to remain inconspicuous. The officer began to lose his patience when no more information was forthcoming. 'I need to go to my *wilaya*[8],' said Aza. 'My two-year-old son needs me.'

'What *wilaya* is that?'

'Dajla,' she lied.

---

[8]. *Wilaya*: An Algerian administrative area akin to a province.

'God help you, woman. You'll never get there from here.'

'Where are you coming from?'

'Smara'

'Is that very far?'

'Twenty kilometres.' Aza saw the hand of Allah in what was happening. She looked around and mentally calculated the direction in which the Ausserd camp was. 'I've got relatives in Ausserd,' she said, trying to conceal the truth.

'We'll take you to Smara. As soon as they find the sick woman, a vehicle will take you to the hospital, and someone will inform your family in Dajla.' Aza didn't know how to get out of the situation. She was so ashamed of the truth that she would have preferred to start running and die in the desert than let those men even suspect what had happened. 'I cannot go to Smara,' she explained as casually as she could. 'My sister is getting married in Ausserd in four days and she needs me.' The lie irritated the officer.

'You'll go to Smara and there you'll explain all there is to explain.'

'If you take me to Smara I'll accuse you of kidnapping me to the *wali*.'[9] The officer clenched his fists and put on his sunglasses to hide his rage. He looked around and then strode away towards the plain of the desert. Aza went on drinking water, but now in smaller sips. The young recruits looked at her without even blinking. No doubt, the apparition of such a beautiful woman in the most deserted area of the *hammada* seemed miraculous. 'Have you got any food?' she asked calmly. All at once, the soldiers rummaged in their bags and took out dry biscuits, goat's cheese and sugar. Aza sat down in the shade of the truck and began eating slowly, savouring every bite.

Less than an hour had gone by when the four-by-four returned with the foreign woman. The officer looked inside the

---

[9.] *Wali*: Administrative head of a *wilaya*.

vehicle and could not believe it. If the Saharawi woman had told the truth, perhaps she was not, as he had thought, crazy. 'Is she dead?' he asked the driver. 'I couldn't tell for sure.' The officer approached Aza and pointed to the vehicle firmly.

'Get in the car. My men will take you to Smara. Then you can go wherever you please.' Aza stood up, put away the leftover food, drank some more water and said: 'I need to know the way to Ausserd.' The officer was about to lose his self-control. He bit his lip so hard he drew blood. He suspected that, if he insisted, that woman would make a fool of him in front of the troops. 'Fine. If that's what you want, carry on in that direction and don't stray even this much. Walking steadily, you'll reach Ausserd in ten hours.' He emphasised the last sentence, in the vague hope that the woman would reconsider before walking away.

However, Aza put the water canteen on her head and approached the four-by-four where the foreign woman was. 'Hurry up,' she told the driver. 'She's been in a coma for hours.' Then she began to walk in a straight line, without losing sight of the point on the horizon that was her only chance of salvation. The soldiers didn't take their eyes off her until they heard their superior's fearsome shouting.

The foreign woman's hospital room is half in darkness, in spite of the furious sun outside. Layla is sitting on a rug on the floor, numb with heat, when the director of the hospital walks in, followed by his friend Mulud. On seeing them Layla stands up and buttons up her white coat. She exchanges an endless greeting full of formulae with the colonel. Then all three silently turn their eyes towards the patient. Layla adjusts her *melfa* and covers her head properly. The foreign woman is asleep, drawing deep breaths.

'She's had some food,' explains the nurse to the director. 'But she sleeps most of the time.'

'Layla spends whole days here,' the director says.

'Only when I'm not busy,' adds Layla.

The colonel smiles. He's curious to learn the foreigner's story.

'Is she getting better?' he asks.

'She no longer has a fever,' replies Layla. 'Sometimes she hallucinates, but no fever. All I know is that her name is Montse and she's from Spain. She's obsessed with something, but I haven't managed to find out what.'

'Obsessed?' asks the colonel.

'She talks in her sleep and says the name Aza all the time.'

'She's obsessed with that name,' echoes the director.

'When she's awake and I ask her about it, she says they've killed Aza. But she gets so upset that she can't explain herself any further.'

Colonel Mulud stares at the foreigner. He is intrigued, but also very busy; he hasn't got much time.

'We need to ascertain how she arrived here,' he says eventually. 'Surely she hasn't travelled alone. Someone must have reported her missing.'

'Soon it will be a month,' says the director. 'It's too long for a woman not to be missed.'

'That's true. The more I think about it the less sense it makes.'

'I could try to find out,' Layla says. 'She's better every day, but she's really scared. I don't know what happened to her, but she's frightened. If I can get her to trust me, she might tell me.'

'And in the meantime?' asks the director, matter-of-factly.

'In the meantime there's nothing we can do,' says the colonel. 'We'll ask the people who deal with Spain. If they don't know anything, we'll have to wait for her to get better to send her back home.'

By the time he finishes the phrase, Mulud is in the doorway. The director goes after him. Both say goodbye with a short formula, and the nurse remains alone with the patient. She sits on the edge of the bed. She has got used to the foreigner's presence, but she's very curious about her story. She touches her forehead and looks one more time at her tangled hair, her white skin and soft hands. Suddenly the woman gives a start and opens her eyes. She doesn't know where she is. Her eyes are full of fear.

'Aza,' she says, delirious. 'They shot Aza. You have to tell everybody.'

'Who's Aza?' asks Layla, tying to appease her.

'Aza? She escaped with me and they caught us. That murderer killed her. It was my fault. I should have escaped on my own.'

'Who killed her?' insists Layla.

The foreign woman closes her eyes and goes quiet. From her breathing, it is obvious she's suffering. Layla squeezes her hand, determined to stay by her side until she calms down.

Chapter Five

FOR SANTIAGO SAN ROMÁN, THE OASIS WAS THE CENTRE of the universe. Leaning on the bar, or sitting at one of the oilcloth-covered tables, he felt that the world revolved around him. Never before had he felt so comfortable. A glass of cognac in his hand, and the company of Guillermo, was all he needed to forget the thorn that had been lodged in his conscience since he had left Spain.

The officers gathered at the Casino Militar and the *Parador Nacional* in El Aaiún. The Oasis was reserved for the troops. On Saturday evenings no other place in the city, or for that matter the province, was as crowded. Its owner, a world-weary Andalusian, was called Pepe El Boli. The place was the only one where the authorities turned a blind eye to prostitution. At the Oasis one could find whores, bingo, poker, brawls, hash and the cheapest cognac in the Western Sahara. On Saturday nights it looked like a battlefield. The prostitutes, dressed as waitresses, could barely cope, and the shouts of the gamblers vied with the TV turned on at full blast. No other place in the city had such a faithful clientele as the Oasis. Sooner or later, everyone who had a permit for an evening's, or a week's, leave, dropped by.

When he spent time at the Oasis, Santiago San Román forgot about his obsessions for a while. And 'his obsessions', at the time, really meant Montse, the treacherous Montse. As his blood warmed up with a second glass of cognac, he would regain his self-confidence, and Montse would be relegated to the background. Then he could devote his time to his friend Guillermo and anyone else who wanted to share their time away from the barracks. Guillermo had not only become his confidant, but was also the most loyal person he'd ever known. He would write the letters Santiago sent to Montse, listen to him when he needed to vent to his anger, and keep him company in silence when he didn't feel like talking. Guillermo had been provisionally assigned to the 9th regiment of engineers as a sapper. He spent his days digging ditches and pits for the construction of the El Aaiún zoo. Like the rest of the legionnaires, he wasn't thrilled at mixing with regular soldiers. Santiago, for his part, was initially a mechanic in the 4th Regiment of the Alejandro Farnesio Legion. However, chance aligned his destiny with that of a group of Nomad Troops, under commander Javier Lobo.

The Nomad Troops, like the Territorial Police, were a corps made up mostly of Saharawis, even if the officers were Spaniards. From the first day Santiago San Román had been fascinated by the Saharawis. In the eyes of someone newly arrived from Spain, these dark-skinned young men, with their curly hair and peculiar habits, were a constant surprise. The first time he had direct contact with them was when a Nomad Troop Land Rover was pushed into the garage where he worked by four Saharawi soldiers. The soldiers, covered in grease up to their eyelids, parked it and lifted the bonnet. When Santiago went over to take a look at the engine, he whistled sharply, attracting the other mechanics' attention. The wires, connections and patches on that Land Rover were in such a tangle that they hid the cylinder block from view. 'Major Lobo sends us,' said one of the soldiers, and he spoke so formally that it was as though he were on parade. The other mechanics wanted nothing to do with the business. Only Santiago San Román took care of the four lads. 'We cannot make it start,' continued the young man. 'If we can't fix it, we'll be arrested.' Santiago could not take his eyes off the four Saharawis. Presently the other mechanics laid down their tools and went out to lunch. Their faces made it quite clear they had no intention of getting stuck with the job. Santiago was annoyed at their behaviour, but didn't want to get into an argument. The Saharawis looked like castaways in the middle of the ocean. Without further ado, he stuck his head into the jaws of the vehicle and started untangling the web of wires. When his colleagues came back from lunch, Santiago was still waist deep in the bowels of the Land Rover. The four Saharawis looked on in silence, not daring to break his concentration. As in a trance, Santiago spoke to the engine of the vehicle and, every now and again, said something to the soldiers. They looked at each other, wondering whether the legionnaire might be a bit crazy. After several hours changing parts, examining hoses and sweet-talking the engine, Santiago San Román got in the vehicle, turned the key, and the car started with a sickly cough. He revved it up a few times, releasing black smoke which soon turned lighter, and then the Land Rover started sounding more normal. 'Jump in,' he told the Saharawis, and all four obeyed as they would an officer's orders. Santiago San Román drove a few times round the barracks, tested the wheel and the brakes, and finally stopped in front of the Nomad Troops' block. He got out of the car without cutting the engine and said: 'It's all yours. You can tell Major Lobo he's got a Land Rover for another ten years.' As he went off, the Saharawis seemed lost for words, but when he was a few metres away they called him back. He stopped. 'Thanks, my friend, thanks.' Santiago brushed aside their thanks, but one of the men ran after him. The Saharawi took his hand and kept it in his.

'I'm Lazaar.' Santiago San Román introduced himself. 'We're always here, in this block. Come and pay us a visit; you are always welcome. You'll make many friends.' That day, when Santiago walked into the soldiers' mess, he had the impression that the words had been sincere.

The first time Santiago San Román set foot in the Nomad

Troops' block he thought he had ventured into another world. The soldiers, away from the officers' watchful eyes, behaved as if they were in a large *jaima*. Seated around a stove at the very entrance, a dozen of them were chatting in Hassaniya and drinking tea, and were so relaxed that the place didn't look like a barracks at all. When they saw Santiago, however, they grew serious, and conversation ceased. San Román was about to turn round and retrace his steps when he spotted the reassuring presence of Laazar. 'I didn't mean to disturb you,' he excused himself. 'I didn't know...' Laazar addressed his friends in Arabic, and the conversation resumed. The Saharawi took him by both his hands and asked him to sit down near the tea. It wasn't long before Santiago began to feel more comfortable.

'Do you play football?' asked one of the Saharawis.

'Of course, I taught Cruyff how to play.'

'I support Real Madrid,' replied Lazaar seriously.

'Well, I also taught Amancio, you know.' From that day on, Santiago San Román played every afternoon as a goalkeeper in the Nomad Troops' team; and, every time they beat the Spaniards, the guys from his own battalion accused him of being a traitor.

Now, leaning over the bar at El Oasis, Santiago could see the soldiers of the passing Nomad Troops look in through the window with a mixture of curiosity and disdain. He finished off his cognac and promised himself that he wouldn't drink whenever a Saharawi might see him. He'd never felt so ashamed before. Sergeant Baquedano, the only regiment NCO who frequented the Oasis, would strut around amongst the waitresses, pinching their backsides and brushing against their breasts. His breath, always reeking of alcohol, gave him away wherever he went. Terrible stories were told about him. He was around forty, and the only things that mattered in his life were the Legion, alcohol and whores. On one occasion,

they said, he had shot a recruit in the foot for marching out
of step. When one saw him drunk, rubbing his groin against
the prostitutes, it was easy to believe the stories. Most soldiers
avoided him, but a few loudmouths would laugh at his jokes and
follow him everywhere, celebrating his displays of bravado and
buying him drinks. Usually they ended up being humiliated
by him and were forced to endure his insults like animals. It
was the prostitutes who tried hardest to stay out of his way;
they knew him all too well. Sergeant Baquedano was the only
person in the bar who frightened them. They were perfectly
aware that if they faced up to him they might lose their job
or end up in a gutter of the Smara road with their throat slit
open. Sergeant Baquedano acted as a kind of gangster for Major
Panta. Prostitution at the Oasis had to be supervised by Major
Panta, but no high-ranking officer would have approved of his
visiting a dive like that. Officers never shared whores with the
troops. Not even corporals and sergeants. Nevertheless, they
could not allow the local mafias to run the show, trafficking
women from Spain, Morocco or Mauritania. Major Panta
looked after the Regiment's health and made sure that things
ran smoothly. But the major had never seen Baquedano dead
drunk, staggering between the tables, cupping his balls with
both hands, and slobbering over the breasts of the prostitutes
dressed as waitresses.

Santiago San Román looked away on the two or three
occasions when he crossed the sergeant's gaze. When he saw
Baquedano leave, he felt a lot more relaxed, in spite of the
racket the troops were making. The music merged with the
TV, the thumping of bottles on the marble bar, the shouting at
the poker tables, the bingo numbers being called out, and the
incredibly loud conversations. Suddenly all the noise dissolved
into a second of silence, and the military marches gave way to
Las Corsarias, Pepe's favourite paso doble. When San Román
heard the first few bars, he felt as though the ceiling had fallen

on his head. Instantly Montse's image reared up its ugly head. The noise had become inexplicably hostile.

'Another cognac?' asked Guillermo.

'No, I'd better not. I've got indigestion.'

'A beer then.'

'You have one, my stomach aches,' lied Santiago.

'Is that all you're drinking tonight? It's Saturday.'

Santiago San Román gave his friend a grave look, and Guillermo understood at once. He didn't reply. He was perfectly familiar with his friend's bouts of melancholy. They both left the Oasis and stumbled out into the February breeze. They sauntered in silence. The streets looked oddly empty, at least until they reached Plaza de España, where the whole city seemed to have congregated. The noise of the bars spilled out into the street. The Territorial Police patrolled the area on foot and in their vehicles, trying to look inconspicuous. Santiago and Guillermo stopped under the marquee of a cinema. Under the title of Serpico, a colour drawing of Al Pacino jumped out of a poster. Guillermo stood in front of it with his feet apart, imitating, not very well, the posture of a cop from the Bronx. He pushed his cap down to his eyebrows and fastened the strap on his chin. The girls in the queue looked at him and laughed ,covering their mouths.

'Stop playing the fool,' said Santiago reproachfully. 'Everyone's looking at you.'

Guillermo hooked his thumbs on the huge silver buckle of his belt and blew the girls a kiss as they laughed.

'I need you to do me a favour, Guillermo. I swear it's the last time.'

Guillermo lost his party mood. He was more than familiar with those words. Santiago started walking slowly, his body slumped.

'Let's get out of here. This place is crawling with sergeants.'

Every rank favoured a certain area of the city. Sergeants

and corporals avoided the surroundings of the *Parador* and the Casino Militar, in order not to have to salute their superiors all the time. The rank and file, in their turn, did not walk along main roads, which was where NCOs' favourite bars were.

The two friends headed for Avenida de Skaikma without saying a word. They knew they would be away from the legionnaires' eyes and walked in silence, as if they could read each other's mind. Stopping at a telephone booth, Santiago took out all the coins he was carrying in his pockets. For some bizarre reason, the air in that spot smelled of thyme. He passed the coins to Guillermo.

'I want you to call Montse. Well, first...'

'I know, I know,' Guillermo cut in, impatiently.

'Tell them you're a classmate from university and that you have to speak to her...'

'Santi!' shouted Guillermo, who felt like slapping him.

'What?'

'Do you know how many times I've phoned your girl?'

'She's not my girl, Guillermo, I've told you. And if you really don't want to do me this favour...'

Guillermo passed his arm over Santiago's shoulder, trying to appease him.

'I'll call her, okay? I'll call her. But don't explain to me what I have to say, because you told me a thousand times. It's me who calls, me who writes to her, in the end it'll be me who...'

Guillermo stopped, regretting his words. Yet his friend was so upset he didn't even pick up on where he had been going. Guillermo put the coins in his pocket and stepped into the booth. Santiago stood a few metres away, as if embarrassed.

The last phone call had been full of drama. On that occasion he had also rung her from a booth, a few metres from the archway at Vía Layetana. When Montse finally came on, it was nearly ten in the evening. Santiago had been standing in front of her house for four hours. It was the early days of a humid, cold December, and by then he was frozen through. When he heard her voice, he went quiet, not knowing what to say. Then he regrouped and tried to control his nerves.

'It's Santi,' he said in a trembling voice.

'I know, they've just told me so. What do you want?'

'Look, Montse, I've been calling you all evening.'

'I've been to the library; I've just come back.'

'Don't lie to me, Montse, don't do that.'

'Are you ringing to call me a liar? You've got some cheek, you know?'

'No, I didn't mean to call you a liar, but I've been at your door since six and I haven't seen you come in or go out.' After that there was a longer, more dramatic silence.

'But do you think I have to explain myself to you?'

'No, Montse, I don't want you to explain yourself; I've only rung to say I'm leaving.'

'Well, goodbye, then.'

'I'm leaving for Zaragoza.' Again, silence. 'I've received the summons from the recruitment office at home. I have to join up the day after tomorrow.' Montse was still quiet, and that gave Santiago confidence. 'Have you spoken to your parents?' he asked, mustering all the courage he had.

'My parents? What should I speak to my parents about?'

Santiago got furious. 'About the kid, for God's sake, about our child.' She wouldn't hear another word.

'Look, the kid is my affair, and mine only.'

'But, I mean, it's not like I've got nothing to do with it.'

'Well you should've thought of that before,' said Montse, who was now on the brink of tears.

'Before hooking up with that blonde hussy, before snogging that...'

'I haven't snogged anyone.'

'I won't have you lying to me.'

'I'm not lying, Montse, I swear on my mother, on all that's holy. She's only a friend.'

'And that's how you kiss your friends?'

'I've told you a thousand times that we were together some time ago. But we were children. For fuck's sake…'

'God, I've been such a fool.'

'Montse, the kid.'

'The child is mine, do you hear? I want you to forget you've ever met me, to forget the child, to forget everything.' The receiver went dead. A continuous beep announced there was no longer anyone at the other end. Furious, Santiago head-butted the glass of the booth. People passing by jumped when they heard the blow. He cut his forehead, and the blood started running down his face. He didn't know what to do with the receiver. Eventually he banged it as hard as he could against the telephone and cracked it in two. He stepped out of the cabin like a wild animal, looking about him in a rage. He'd never felt as humiliated, as impotent as in that moment . He couldn't hit anyone, couldn't tell anyone how things stood, couldn't give vent to all his rage.

Guillermo came back with a very serious face. In his hand he had the coins which hadn't been used.

'She's not home.'

'She's not home or she's not coming to the phone?'

'What's the difference?'

'None. But I'd like to know. Who picked up?'

'I don't know. Her sister, maybe.'

'What did you tell her?'

'That I was a friend from university.'

'And what did she say?'

'That Montse was not in Barcelona. She asked me for my name and number, in case she wanted to call me. I said that it wasn't urgent, that I would call back another time.'

As they left the main road behind, the noise of the traffic was replaced by that of the TVs in ground-floor flats. It was a warm night. Everything was still except for the February wind occasionally stirring things around. They stopped at a corner, far from the city centre. Barely any cars went by. In the distance, the moon was reflected on the shallow Saguía river. They smoked in silence. Guillermo didn't dare disturb his friend's thoughts.

'Never again, I swear, never again,' said Santiago San Román unexpectedly. 'I'm done with her.'

'Don't take it like that.'

But Santiago did not seem to be listening.

'No one's ever treated me like that. Fuck it. From now on Montse is dead. Forever. Do you hear?'

'I do.'

'If I ever mention her name, or ask you to call her, or write to her, I want you to punch me in the face. Very hard. You get me?'

'As you wish.'

'Swear it.'

'I swear.'

In an outburst of emotion Santiago hugged his friend and held him close to his body. Then he kissed him on the cheek.

'What are you doing? Let go, damn it. If anyone sees us they're going to think we're queer.'

Santiago let go and smiled for the first time that evening.

'Queer! Get out! We'll have a good one tonight. Even if we wind up in jail.'

Guillermo seconded his friend's sudden enthusiasm.

'Let's go back to the Oasis,' he said.

'Fuck the Oasis. We do that every Saturday. Let's get a couple of whores, but good ones.'

'And the money?'

'We're bridegrooms of death. Who cares about the money. Fuck the money!'

At the end of the street a Territorial Police vehicle appeared.

The two legionnaires instantly grew serious and straightened up, as if the Saharawis were able to read their minds. The patrol went past them very slowly, but didn't stop.

'Have you ever been up there?' asked Santiago, pointing to the 'Stone Houses'.

'Of course not. Do you think I'm crazy? Besides, there aren't any bars or whores up there.'

The Zemla quarter, in the high part of the city, was a Saharawi area. It was also called 'Stone Houses' or 'Hata-Rambla', which meant 'line of dunes'. Apart from the Saharawis, only a few people from the Canary Islands lived there.

'Tell me something. Aren't you curious about what's up there in those streets?'

'Not at all. Are you?'

'Let's take a walk. No one in the regiment has enough balls to go up.'

'And you do?'

'I've got what it takes.'

'You're wrong in the head, man.'

'I can't believe you're scared.'

'I'm not, Santi, don't be stupid. But you've heard as well as I have what they say about the area.'

'All lies, Guillermo. Do you know anyone who has actually gone up there?'

'No.'

'Well I do.'

'Saharawis don't count. They live there. But haven't you heard about the demonstrations? Those crazy guys from the Polisario are poisoning people. They've kidnapped two lorry drivers. Do you know what happened in Agyeyimat? Lots of legionnaires died.'

Santiago's enthusiasm cooled as his friend talked. Yet since his first stroll around El Aaiún he'd been intrigued by that part of town, however ugly it looked.

'That happened far away from here. We're in civilisation. There are no traitors here. But if you're not sure, if you're frightened...'

'Fuck off. I'm going back to the Oasis.'

Guillermo started walking, annoyed, and his friend followed him with a smile on his face. Santiago felt like he had always lived in that city, and knew it better than his own. He mentally summoned a picture of his old neighbourhood, his house, his mother's tobacconist's, but these images were hazy. Suddenly he thought of Montse, and he was incapable of remembering her face.

Chapter Six

AT EIGHT IN THE EVENING VIA LAITENA WAS TEEMING WITH cars and people. The new century seemed to have begun with a race against time. It was impossible to get a cab. The stores were overcrowded, its windows steamed up with customers' breath. Streams of people exited from Jaume I metro station, dispersing in all directions. The Gothic Town absorbed tourists as a dry sponge absorbs water. The Christmas music and the hot air of the shops spilled out onto the pavements. Montse had to wait for a crowd to come out of the metro before moving on. She'd been walking for over an hour, and her feet hurt. She knew where she was going, but she was putting off the moment when she would have to face up to the ghosts of her past.

The living room seemed like the set of a horror movie. After ten years everything looked old-fashioned and smaller. Even the light-bulbs struck her as weaker. Most of the furniture was covered with dust sheets, which gave the room a dismal appearance. It smelled musty. The rolled-up carpets gave off a stale, humid, odour. The curtains were faded and out of fashion. She tried to open the shutters to let some air in, but a couple had to stay closed, as the wood had swollen. The noise of the traffic, in any case, was as audible as if one were on the ground floor. When Montse looked around she felt desolate. Nothing was the way she remembered it. During the last few years, she had made it a point to think of the house as little as possible, so it now seemed unreal, as though the décor was made of washed out papier-mâché. How long had it been since the last time she'd been in the house? It was easy to calculate. She hadn't come back since her mother had died: exactly ten years before. She started removing the sheets covering the furniture and left them on an armchair. When she uncovered a sideboard, she was startled by her own image, reflected in the moon-shaped mirror. She felt out of place, as though she were an intruder who had broken into this sanctuary through a crack in time. How many times had she put on her hair-band in front of that mirror before going out? How many times had she straightened her shirt or flattened her hair? How many times had she looked at her adolescent self – beautiful, full of plans and fury – just for pleasure? She closed her eyes, and out of nerves accidentally knocked down a picture frame. The whole sideboard was bristling with them, as if it were an altar. She looked at each one. She appeared in none. Her father, mother, grandparents, sister, brother-in-law and nieces, all were there. Her daughter too. She picked up the frame with the picture of her daughter in her first-communion dress, but didn't feel anything. She smiled with disappointment when she realized that her mother didn't have a single picture of her, and tried to convince herself, while staring at her reflection in the mirror, that she didn't care at all. Then she turned her back on her reflection.

Her bedroom, on the other hand, was just the way she remembered it. When she sat down on the bed in which she'd slept as a girl, she felt a pang of nostalgia. But she couldn't cry. For the last two months her tear ducts had refused to shed any more tears. She lay down on the bed, rested her head on the pillow and put her feet on the blanket. She fleetingly remembered how much that used to annoy her mother and smiled at the thought of what she would say if she saw her now. She recognised the cracks in the ceiling as if she hadn't been away for twenty years. The shadows cast by the chandelier in the middle of the room made shapes: a top hat, near the window; a snail, in the centre; Franco's profile. She smiled, overcome with emotion. Irrepressible images and sensations surfaced. She closed her eyes, the smile always on her lips, trying to believe that time had not gone by, that she was still eighteen and her life had not taken a nosedive. The noise of cars crept in on her thoughts and acted as a powerful soporific.

She woke up with a start. She'd dreamt that the phone was ringing and no one had picked up. Holding her breath, she tried to separate dream from reality. It was hard to tell how long she'd been asleep. The echo of the phone still resonated in her head, but it wasn't real. For a moment she thought that Mari Cruz would open the door and say: 'The phone, *señorita*. It's for you.' But the door wouldn't open. The phone had been disconnected for ten years. She was over forty now, and the dead did not return from their graves just like that, as if nothing had happened. She sat up and looked for the cigar box in the drawer of the night-table. She put it on the bed and took out a hair clip, a box of matches, old stamps, a one-peseta coin, a museum ticket, lipstick. The letters were tied together with red ribbon.

She had found them in her mother's jewellery case. She remembered it well. Her sister had been sitting across the table, the case between them like a recently exhumed coffin. They both knew neither would wear their mother's jewels, but couldn't leave them there: they were worth too much money. It had been her sister who'd finally opened the case and sorted them into two piles. She looked like a professional valuer. She had seen them so many times that she was capable of listing them and their price without opening the case. After taking out the last pearl necklace, she went on looking at the bottom of the case. 'This is yours,' she said. Montse looked at her, turning pale, as if she expected to find a Saint's preserved finger. She put her hand in the case and took out a bunch of letters tied with red ribbon. 'No, I don't think it is,' Montse replied, without looking at them. Her sister leaned back on her chair and lit up a cigarette. 'It is now.' Montse felt a shiver down her spine. She untied the ribbon and instantly recognised her own name and the Vía Cayetana address. The envelopes were yellowing. She quickly calculated that there must have been between fifteen and twenty letters, each complete with their three-peseta stamp from when Franco was in power. She didn't get it. She placed them on the table in a fan. They were all unopened. She picked one up and read the sender's name. The letters slipped from her hand. Her sister remained impassive, unsurprised. Montse flipped all the envelopes. The sender was the same on every last one: Santiago San Román, Chacón, 4th Regiment of the Alejandro Farnesio Legion, El Aaiún, Western Sahara. She blushed and shook slightly. It seemed as though the dead were rising to torment her. She looked for an explanation in her sister's eyes, but Teresa didn't even blink. It wasn't Santiago's handwriting, that was for sure. 'What's this, Teresa? Don't tell me you knew about these letters.' Teresa didn't reply; she was stroking her mother's jewels as if they were a cat. Finally she said: 'Yes, Montse, I did know about them. The porter handed some of them to me. Others reached mum's hands first. What I didn't know was that mum had kept them all this time.' Montse remained silent. Sixteen years after the event she could no longer feel betrayed, but for a moment she did not know her sister. She checked the postmark. The letters were ordered chronologically: from December '74 to February '75. She didn't dare to open them in front of Teresa, who said: 'You were in Cadaqués; you know what I mean. Every letter that came in put this household through hell.' 'Yes, but you always…' Teresa banged on the table, and the two piles of jewels collapsed. 'No, Montse, I didn't always anything. You went through hell yourself, but I had my purgatory,' she said in an outburst of rage, 'and I didn't have anything to do with it. Now listen to me and don't get angry as though you're a tragic heroine. While you were in Cadaqués, hiding for the sake of mother's shame, I had to put up with her every day. Every last one, do you understand? Every time a letter came in or there was a call, it was me who had to suffer mother's anger. It was me who had to tiptoe around; me who went to bed at nine to avoid her moods; me who stopped going out with friends because I couldn't bring myself to ask her permission. I got fed up with her shouting and unfair reproaches. Fed up with being the perfect daughter who had to make up for her sister's sins.' Suddenly she went quiet, visibly shaken, trying to contain her anger. Now it was Montse who didn't blink. It was the first time she'd seen her sister beside herself with fury. That seemed more momentous than the discovery of the letters. Teresa, her little sister, had always acted like the older one. She'd always been a buffer between Montse and her mother. Teresa represented intelligence, coolness and serenity in moments of drama. Seeing her like this was earthshaking for Montse. They looked at each other for a further few seconds, trying to calm down. 'You choose,' said Teresa eventually.

'Sorry?'

'Choose a pile and take it.'

'Shouldn't we draw lots or something?' Teresa took out her diary, tore out a page and divided it into four. She scribbled figures, made two balls and let Montse choose. That decided it. Teresa put her part of the jewels in a handkerchief, tied a knot in it and pocketed them. She stood up. Montse felt awkward. She didn't dare to ask any more questions.

'Are you coming?' asked Teresa.

'I think I'll stay a bit.'

'Don't forget to turn the circuit breaker off. And lock twice.'

After she'd read them several times, the letters, always tied with their red ribbon, stayed for a further ten years in the night-table drawer in her mother's house. Now they were in front of her once again, like yellowing, stale, outdated ghosts. She untied the knot and spread them over the bed, opening one at random. In spite of all the time that had gone by, she remembered every sentence as though she had just read it. Montse knew it wasn't Santiago's handwriting, but the words did sound like him. No doubt a friend had written them down. Most letters were accompanied by a photograph, and all were very similar: Santiago dressed in uniform, in front of a combat vehicle; on top of a lorry; with a rifle slung over his shoulder; by the flag. She seemed to be looking at his face as if it had only been a month since they had last met. She had obsessively, maddeningly dreamt of that face every night for years.

Details, gestures, smells she thought she had completely forgotten now came back to her. For a moment she could almost hear the floorboards in the corridor creak under Mari Cruz's short steps. The clicking of the housekeeper's heels was part and parcel of her adolescence, as was the view from the balcony of her bedroom. She had listened to that clicking going up and down the corridor on a certain hot July afternoon, while she sat in bed pretending to read, overcome with anxiety, biting her nails. It was the first time she had missed a day of class without justification. True, she'd been to the Academia Santa Teresa in the morning, but after lunch she told Mari Cruz she didn't feel well: she had a terrible headache. Then she asked Mari Cruz to let her know if anyone rang. But time went by and no one did. Montse wasn't sure she'd hear the phone from her bedroom, and so she listened to the maid's heels, alert, gauging every noise, every move. Through the window she heard the belfries of the Gothic Quarter tolling the hours one after another. All she could think of was the boy who had driven her home. Perhaps she'd been a bit cold when she'd said goodbye in front of her house. Perhaps she should have said something else when she gave him her phone number. Perhaps she had misjudged him, had misread his mysterious dark eyes. Or perhaps Santiago San Román could have any girl he wanted just by offering her a ride in his white convertible, as he'd done with her. She was afflicted by doubts and anxiety. She looked up the surname San Román in the telephone directory. Even if she found his number, she wouldn't dare to call him, but she liked to think that she could. Every now and again she was startled by Mari Cruz's heels. Montse went out onto the balcony at least ten times. Maybe the boy was laughing at her. No doubt he had a girlfriend and all he'd done was show his friend Pascualín how easily he could pick up girls. Maybe she shouldn't have kissed him. Maybe she should have let him kiss her. As the afternoon wore on she grew more and more in thrall to her own nerves. It was infuriating to think that she had missed class for him, and yet she was unable to think of anything except this jumped-up nobody who had tried to dazzle her. But when she heard Mari Cruz's heels going faster than normal, and then stop at her door, knocking on it softly and saying, '*Señorita* Montse, there's a call for you,' her heart almost jumped out of her chest. She ran as if half-crazed to the living room, closed the door behind her and, almost out of breath, picked up the receiver.

'It's Santiago San Román,' she heard at the other end. 'From yesterday evening?'

'Santiago San Román?' asked Montse, trying to conceal the affectation in her voice. There was a tense, equivocal pause.

'I drove you home yesterday and you gave me your phone number. Well, actually, I asked you for it...'

'Oh, yes, the guy in the white convertible.'

'Yes, that's right. Well, that's me. Anyway, would you like to go for a spin?'

'A "spin"? A spin where?' Montse didn't like to be cruel, but didn't know how else to do this.

'Around, wherever you like. Out for a drink and all that.'

'Your friend, you and me?'

'No, no, just you and me. Pascualín is busy.' Montse counted to seven before replying.

'I've got to study. I'm quite behind with my German.' Santiago was not expecting that answer. He didn't know what else to say.

'Well, it's a pity. I'll call you some other time then.' Montse swallowed and did something that went against all her principles.

'Wait. Where are you now?'

'Across the road from you, in a phone booth.'

'Stay there. I'm coming right over.'

That was the last day Montse attended the Academia Santa Teresa. From then on, the summer turned into spring, the books into flowers, and the stifling heat into a light breeze that went on brushing against her skin for several months, even after the humid cold weather had come in from the coast along the Ramblas and settled on the streets of the city.

On that first afternoon the sky was an intense red that Montse had never seen before. Santiago San Román was wearing the same white shirt, rolled up to his elbows. He looked taller than the day before, darker, more handsome. She took an hour to get ready and come down, but the boy didn't say a thing; he just waited in front of the booth.

'Where are you taking me?' asked Montse flirtatiously, as soon as she was close to him.

'Do you want to go for a walk?'

'A walk?' Santiago had not been expecting that question either.

'Did you not drive here?' He blushed. For the first time he looked vulnerable. He took Montse by the hand, and they walked down the street as if they were a couple.

'I haven't got the convertible today,' he said, as he opened the door of a yellow Seat 850. 'It's at the mechanic's.' Montse got in without replying. Inside it smelled of grease and tobacco.

Yet once in it, with the windows down to let the air in, Montse felt as good as the previous evening in the convertible. She looked at Santiago out of the corner of her eye: he drove as if he'd been driving all his life. They went across the Gothic

Quarter and into the Ramblas. San Román got out of the car and ran around it to open her door. She failed to conceal how much the gesture pleased her. Without asking her anything, Santiago pointed to a bar and led the way. She knew the place but had never been inside. They sat at the bar, and Santiago asked for two beers without asking her what she was having. He acted perfectly naturally; he was clearly in his element. Montse, on the other hand, felt ill at ease. She felt that everyone was watching her: waiters, customers, the passers-by on the other side of the huge windows. She tried to imagine what her friends would say if they saw her at that moment. She could barely pay attention to what Santiago was saying; his words came out in a torrent and gave her no time to reply. As she drank the first beer of her life, Montse tried to guess what lay behind his words. She drank as though she loved the bitter beverage. She accepted a cigarette and smoked it without inhaling so as not to start coughing. Everything seemed magical this afternoon. She listened to Santiago talk and didn't ask him any questions. When they said goodbye at around ten, she let him kiss her. For the first time she trembled in the arms of a boy. She got out of the car with the combined taste of beer, tobacco and kisses in her mouth. She felt dizzy. As she opened the front door, the glass reflected San Román leaning on his car, looking at her chivalrously, perhaps smiling. She told herself she would never get in a car with him again, never again agree to see him. The experience of that afternoon was enough to gossip about with her friends for months. Nothing remotely like it had happened to any of them. She turned to say goodbye and had to squint when she saw him standing there – so handsome, so attentive to her movements, so dashing.

It wasn't quite eight in the morning, and Montse was already standing at the corner of Vía Layetana in front of the shoe shop, waiting for Santiago's yellow car to appear. He turned up in a red one. The night before, as soon as she'd opened the door,

Mari Cruz had told her there was someone on the phone for her. It was Santiago, calling from the booth across the road: 'Are you my girlfriend?' he had asked point-blank.

Montse had felt a tingle reach her neck. She'd been tipsy and happy. 'Yes,' she'd answered, trying to sound calm .

'Then I'll see you tomorrow at eight at the corner of the shoe shop.' And she hadn't said anything, just hung up. She knew it wouldn't be easy to get the boy out of her mind.

She held her books and folder to her chest, as she would a pillow. In her pencil case she'd put lipstick and mascara. She hadn't dared to apply the make-up at home. She was so nervous that she had to lean on the window of the shoe shop to stop her legs trembling. This wasn't the way she should be doing things – she knew she should have played hard to get – but she wasn't able to control her impulses. On hearing the horn of a red car and seeing Santiago lean out of its window, she ran across the street, barely looking at the traffic. She opened the back door, threw the books on the seat and climbed in the front.

'Is this your father's car, too?' She asked it without irony or malice, but Santiago turned red with embarrassment. Montse touched her lips to his. 'What did you put back there?' he asked.

'My books. At home I have to pretend I'm going to the Academy.' Santiago smiled.

'Clever girl.'

'Haven't you got work to do today?' she asked, and this time the question was dripping with sarcasm. But Santiago didn't notice.

'I'm on holiday.' They spent the muggy July morning driving around Barcelona. As the hours passed the sun started to bleach the colours of the streets and the buildings. Santiago wasn't in a hurry; he drove as calmly as if he were sitting at a bar. Today it was Montse who did the talking. She was euphoric. Everything attracted her attention: the siren of an ambulance, a beggar at a zebra crossing, a couple of lovers, a man who resembled her uncle. Santiago listened to all of it and smiled without interrupting her. They went across the city from north to south and then back, stopping for lunch at a bar for tourists with an outdoor terrace. When Santiago suggested going to the amusement park, Montse could barely hide her eagerness.

Before getting out of the car she put on the lipstick and applied mascara, looking at herself in the rear-view mirror. From the Montjuic viewpoint she surveyed the harbour as though she were an empress. Things were happening so fast she had no time to think. 'You look like a princess,' Santiago said, and Montse felt butterflies in her stomach. She let him hug her and, as her gaze flew from boat to boat, thought of the boys she had met in the past. None was like Santiago. They all seemed immature, childish. She let him hold her tight. Had it not been for the shiver she felt, she would have thought it was all a dream. But it wasn't. No one would understand what she was feeling just then. The little house in Cadaqués flashed into her mind. It now seemed she had wasted many summers there, thinking it the centre of the world. 'Can you swim?' she asked out of the blue.

'No, I've never had a chance to learn. You?'

'Me neither,' she lied.

They ate candyfloss at the amusement park. They shot at silhouettes in the shooting gallery. They climbed into the bumper cars. They strolled like a couple of lovers from ride to ride. Santiago made suggestions, and Montse went along with them. On the rollercoaster they held each other so tight that their arms ached. They lost themselves in the crowd, trying to go unnoticed among the few tourists. She kept on talking nervously. 'I'd like to smoke,' she said. And Santiago ran to a tobacconist's to buy a packet of Chesterfields. Every time he had to pay for something he took out a roll of one-hundred-peseta notes which he wielded as if he were a bank teller. 'Now tell me, are you really rich?'

'Of course, richest man in the world, with you here.'

At noon Montse called home to tell the maid she was having

lunch at Nuria's.

'Don't you have to call your parents?' she asked Santiago.

'Never. I don't owe them any explanations. I'm independent.' 'You're lucky!' They ate at an expensive restaurant. Santiago tried hard to make Montse feel at ease. Later, when she opened the door to her building, with the books pressed to her, it seemed as though the world was spinning. She turned to say goodbye and felt him push her gently against the door. 'What are you doing?'

'What do you think?' They kissed. Montse felt a pair of hands reaching where no one had ever reached before. Her books fell to the floor with a thud. She had to make an effort to tear herself away. In spite of her tiredness she found it difficult to fall asleep. She thought she wouldn't brush her teeth, so as to keep Santiago's kiss in her mouth, but the taste of cigarettes was too strong. Daydreaming, she scribbled in her diary. In the morning she only hoped her family wouldn't find out.

Montse phoned her father early the next morning. She spoke to her sister Teresa and her mother as well. She told them she found the classes at the Academy boring and, lying, said she wanted to come to Cadalqués. At half past nine she was standing by the shoe shop, nervously holding her books. Santiago appeared in a white car, though not the convertible. Montse got in as if this were part of a daily routine, smiling, wanting to be near him. 'I don't believe for a second that you work in a bank, or that your father is the general manager.' The boy tensed up, stepped on the accelerator, and drove into the traffic. 'Santi, you're a liar. And I haven't lied to you at all.'

'Nor me, Montse, honest. I'm not a liar, I swear.' She realised she was putting him on the spot. She leaned back on the headrest and gently placed her hand on his leg.

'Tell me something, Santi. Have you loved many women?' Santiago San Román smiled, trying to relax.

'No one as much as you, sweetheart.' Montse felt as though petals were raining down on her. Her ears tingled and her legs trembled.

'You're a liar,' she said, squeezing his leg, 'but I love it.'

'I swear I'm not lying to you. I swear on...' He trailed off. Judging from his face, a dark thought must have crossed his mind.

For a week Montse's books travelled in the back seat of a number of different cars. She had the feeling of seeing the world from above, of gliding over the city, only to put her feet back on the ground when she went back home. Every evening, before saying goodbye, Santiago would push her into the huge central shaft of the spiral staircase, and she would let him explore her body. They would kiss for hours, until their stomachs ached. Thousands of questions popped in her mind, but she didn't dare ask them for fear of breaking the spell. Santiago's background was obvious. He sounded like an outsider, behaved impulsively, contradicted himself. Although he tried to hide his hands, his broken, grease-stained nails looked more like a factory worker's than a banker's. But whenever Montse hinted at it he would squirm, and she didn't feel like giving him a hard time. Later, lying on her bed, she tried to take a step back and see things clearly. Every night she promised herself she would speak to Santiago the next time she saw him, but when it came to the crunch she was afraid of frightening him away.

Almost twenty-six years later, lying on that very bed, she was turning the same thoughts over in her mind. The pictures of Santiago in military uniform had sent her back in time. She seemed to have been looking into that gaze of his only a few hours ago as they had said goodbye huddled in the staircase shaft. She looked at her hands and felt old. Remembering these things was like digging up a dead person. She took out the picture she'd found in the hospital and placed it on the blanket, next to the other photographs. It was him, no doubt about it. She tried to recall her feelings when they told her that he had died. She could perfectly remember the faces of the tobacconist and her husband. Had it been Santiago's idea? Had he tried to take his revenge on her by faking his own death? Had it been some macabre joke or a rumour no one bothered to confirm? Montse's eyes stung from staring so hard at the pictures. She decided to go through with her plan, and took her mobile out of her bag. She looked up the number she'd quickly scribbled in her diary and dialled it. Her stomach was a bundle of nerves. It felt like lifting a tombstone to make sure the body was still there. She waited impatiently as the rings went on. Eventually someone picked up. It was a man's quiet voice.

'Mr Ayach Bachir?'

'Who is this?'

'My name is Dr Montserrat Cambra. May I speak to Mr Ayach Bachir?'

'It's me. I'm Ayach Bachir.'

'Oh, hello, I'm calling from Santa Creu hospital.'

'The hospital? What now?'

'Nothing, rest assured, nothing's happened. I just wanted to have a word about your wife.'

'My wife is dead. We buried her two days ago.'

'I know, Mr Bachir. I signed the death certificate.'

There was a silence at the other end of the line. Montse found it almost unbearably painful. She took a deep breath and continued.

'You see, I only wanted to tell you that, when they gave you back your wife's belongings, something was left behind in the hospital. It's a photograph. I'd like to give it back to you in person and have a word with you.'

'A photograph? What photograph?'

'One of the ones your wife was carrying in her bag.'

'They gave me those back.'

'I'm sorry to insist, but one of them was mislaid,' lied Montse, still firm. 'I know this is not a good moment, but if you don't mind I'd like to give it back to you. I can come to your house if you like.'

Again there was a pause.

'To my house? What did you say your name was?'

'Montserrat Cambra. I got your address from the hospital files. I've got your file right here,' she lied again. 'Carrer de Balboa. Is that correct?'

'Yes, that's where I live.'

'So if you don't mind...'

'I don't, that's very kind of you.'

Montse breathed out, relieved, as though she had just walked over quicksand.

'I'll come by tomorrow then, if that's convenient, of course.'

'It is convenient, yes. Any time. You'll be welcome.'

Montse hung up and put the phone in her bag. She tied the letters together with the red ribbon and returned them to their place. Her hand touched something inside the drawer. It was a blackened silver ring. She took it out and looked at it against the light, as though it were a prism. Her heart quickened once again, and she realised that a tear was rolling down her cheek and into the corner of her mouth.

Chapter Seven

It is the beginning of March, and in the middle of the day the heat in the camps is stifling. There is a considerable temperature difference between the hospital rooms and the patio. The foreign woman finds it pleasurable to look at objects in the sunshine. She enjoys the heat on her skin. As soon as the biting cold of the morning lifts, she starts washing herself calmly, as though she were observing a ritual. She has learned to wash herself from head to toe with barely a litre of water, and likes doing it very slowly, like someone preparing for an important ceremony. It takes her over an hour to complete the task. Her movements are slow. She tires quickly. It is not easy to lift her arms to comb her hair. When she is finally dressed, she sits on a chair and only then glances at herself in the mirror. She is almost unrecognisable. She looks awful, but is amused by the image reflected in the glass. Her hair is badly damaged, her skin burnt, her lips parched, her face blistered, her eyes reddened. She has lost a lot of weight. And yet she is happy. Everything around her is recognisable: the flaking ceiling, the small window, the bed without a mattress across from hers, the metal chair that once was white. This is the third day that, after marvelling at her huge empty room, she comes out into the patio. She knows the way, and today no one needs to walk with her. She is overwhelmed by the solitude of the empty corridors. Even so, its smell is thoroughly familiar, and the place feels like home.

As soon as she steps out into the courtyard, she sees a nurse.

Although she knows her, she cannot remember her name. She takes the chair she's offered – the same one as the last two days. The nurse only speaks Arabic, but is obviously saying good morning and asking the foreigner how she's feeling. Both women seem equally happy, and the Saharawi doesn't stop smiling. From across the courtyard a young man says hello to them, but Montse cannot remember his name either. She's not even sure that she's met him before, although his face looks vaguely familiar. She sits down. Getting dressed and walking has tired her a good deal. The sun comforts her. She half-closes her eyes. The early-morning wind has stopped blowing. She tries to remember what day it is. Yesterday she asked Layla, but she's forgotten. Suddenly she remembers the month – March. Today was the first time she woke up and didn't see Layla by her bed. It felt strange. She is so used to the nurse's face that she misses it. Relaxed in the sun, she closes her eyes and falls asleep.

Yet again somebody rescues her from the nightmare. She is about to feel the sting of the scorpion in her neck when a cold hand on her face awakens her. It's Layla, smiling as always. The nurse is not wearing a green coat, which disconcerts Montse.

'They tell me you got dressed on your own.'

'All on my own. And I've walked here.'

Layla looks excited at the news. She crouches down and takes Montse's hand.

'I wish I'd seen it.'

'You'll see it tomorrow, I promise. Where have you been?'

Layla stops smiling. She seems upset.

'But, Montse, I told you yesterday. Don't you remember?'

Montse is disconcerted by the nurse's sadness. Suddenly she feels useless, a nuisance. Her memory blanks are oppressive. It is upsetting not to be able to remember things, or to see only fragments of sentences or images flash in her mind. Layla strives to hide her disappointment. She tries to make light of the problem and speaks to her as if she wasn't aware of it:

'I've spoken to the Council. They've received a communication from Rabuni.'

'And what do they say in Rabuni?'

Montse gives Layla her full attention, pretending to understand everything.

'Good news. You're no longer a ghost. They've checked the records of the last few months and found you. You were on the passenger list of a flight that arrived on the 31st of January from Barcelona.'

'I told you.'

'Yes, you did. But it seemed very strange that no one had reported you as missing.'

Montse's face clouds over.

'It's not that strange. I didn't tell anyone I was coming. Only Ayach Bachir knows: he gave me all the information.'

Once again the foreign woman proves she's full of surprises.

'The *wali* said everything will be arranged. In ten days there's a flight to Spain from Tindouf. They'll get you documents and a passport. They've already contacted your embassy in Algiers. Somebody's coming tomorrow to take your picture and personal information.'

Montse makes neither a gesture nor a comment. Her face looks neutral. Layla can only guess at the many things she does not know about this woman whose path has accidentally crossed hers. As she always does, she places her hand on the woman's forehead to make sure she doesn't have a temperature.

'How old are you, Layla?' asks Montse, as if she were waking up.

It's the same question the nurse has been meaning to ask.

'Twenty-five.'

'God, you're so young.'

Layla smiles, revealing her glistening white teeth.

'And you?'

'Forty-four.'

'Forty-four! You must be joking.'

Montse smiles, amused.

'That's very sweet of you, but I swear it's true.'

'Where's your husband?'

She takes some time to reply.

'Could I not be single?'

'Yes, but I don't think so,' replies Layla.

'He left me for someone else. A pretty young blonde radiologist. We're separated. We'll be divorced in a few months. Blondes have always brought me bad luck.'

Layla looks at her with a grave expression, trying to read her eyes. But Montse does not appear to take her words too seriously.

'I'll get over it. Especially after this.' Layla smiles. 'What about you? Are you married?'

'Not yet. I'll get married at the end of the summer. I went to study in Cuba when I was eleven and only came back seven months ago.'

Now it is Montse trying to guess what lies behind those beautiful dark eyes.

'Aza was in Cuba too,' she says almost without thinking.

Layla has heard the name so many times that it is has become familiar. She sits on the floor and waits for Montse to add something about this enigmatic woman. But Montse remains lost in thought, as though she is too tired to talk.

'Does she really exist, that woman?' asks Layla, fearing her question might sound offensive.

Montse looks at her. Layla resembles Aza. Perhaps Aza was darker, but they both have the same peaceful eyes.

'I don't know. I'm not sure of anything. Sometimes I think that it was all a nightmare, that nothing happened in reality. I mean, Aza, the airport, all those people I always see in my dreams. If my body weren't so weak, I'd think I imagined it, that I'm crazy.'

'I don't think you're crazy. No one does. But the story of the woman is puzzling. You said you saw her die.'

Montse tries to find understanding in the nurse's eyes.

'Why don't you tell me everything you can remember?' suggests Layla. 'Maybe it's good for you.'

'Maybe, but there are so many things I can't remember.'

'Do you remember the day you arrived at Tindouf? Did you meet Aza on the plane? Do you remember the plane, the airport?'

How could she forget? She had never seen anything like it. She was the first to walk down the gangway. The air, tremendously dry, slapped her in the face. She had to make an effort to fill her lungs and breathe. The sky looked leaden, as if ready to fall on the planes at the end of the runway. For a moment she didn't know what time it was, dawn or dusk, midday or late afternoon. She lost her bearings when she set foot on the runway. A soldier was telling everyone where to go. For no particular reason, Montse felt hurried. The terminal was housed in an ochre, colonial-looking building. There were barely two hundred metres between the plane and the customs gate. The passengers crowded around a narrow entrance which didn't allow groups to pass through. Leaning against the façade, or crouching down on the pavement, the Algerians cast sullen looks at the new arrivals. The black-and-blue turbans, the tunics, the covered faces, the military uniforms, the military aspect of the bureaucrats, not to mention the guns, made it all look rather sinister. Montse was nervous, and the long, slow-moving queue irritated her. She didn't know anyone and was not in the mood to start up a conversation. Time seemed to stand still. The wait felt longer than the flight. By the time a beardless soldier took her passport, she was beginning to understand that this was no tourist destination. The soldier looked at the passport picture a thousand and one times, trying to confirm that it corresponded to the face on the other side of the glass. Then he made sure that the information in the form Montse had filled for the Algerian police matched the one in the passport. He dwelled on every accent, comma and dash. At times he double-checked figures to avoid any confusion. It was a tense fifteen minutes, without a word exchanged – only looks – and no idea of what was going through the soldier's mind.

When she finally dragged her suitcase out into the car park, Montse was exhausted. The Spanish travellers' voices, the mountains of backpacks, the general hustle and bustle confused her. She took out the piece of paper with the name of the person that was meant to come and collect her. It would be difficult for them to find her amid so many people. The Saharawis who'd flown in from Barcelona sorted themselves into groups and climbed onto two trucks and a bus. As the foreigners sat down in the vehicles, the crowd slowly thinned out.

'Are you not coming with us, señora?' called out a Saharawi man, who was about to get on a truck. Montse shook her head. The man stopped in his tracks and approached her.

'I'm waiting for someone,' said Montse, before he had even asked her anything.

'They're coming to pick you up?'

'Yes, someone should be here soon.'

'What camp are you going to?' Montse showed him the piece of paper. To her all the names and places sounded the same. The Saharawi deciphered her writing. 'It's quite far from ours. We're going to Dajla. If you want, we can take you there in a day or two.'

'But what if they come to pick me up?' The Saharawi cast a look at the truck. The driver was shouting at him and beeping the horn. They were ready to go.

'Listen, *señora*, maybe they've come to collect you and left already. The plane was twelve hours late. There was a last-minute change of plans and perhaps they never found out.' Montse was bewildered by all the shouting on the truck.

'Go, don't keep them waiting. I'll stay. If they are late, I'm sure

I'll manage.' The Saharawi walked off, not entirely convinced. He jumped on the truck, and they drove away.

Standing on the pavement with the suitcase between her legs, Montse had the feeling that all the idle men in the airport car park had their eyes fixed on her. For over two hours she stood there waiting. Eventually she sat on the suitcase, defeated. She was so tired she could hardly think what to do next. Night was falling, and fewer and fewer vehicles remained at the entrance to the terminal. There was no information available anywhere, and the gates had been closed after the passengers of the last flight had come out. In the distance the lights of a city were visible. Distressed, still hanging on to her suitcase, she approached one of the remaining vehicles. The driver was just sitting there with the door open, as if he was waiting for someone. Montse tried to ask him where she could find a hotel for the night. The man didn't understand. He replied in French and Arabic. Montse said a few words in English, but he still didn't understand. She tried explaining herself with gestures, and at that point the man opened his eyes wide and let out an exclamation. He seemed to be praying. Then he picked up Montse's suitcase and threw it onto the back seat. He motioned her to climb in the front. She wasn't entirely sure that he had understood her, but she got in without protest. The man shouted something, and a boy appeared and climbed in the back, next to the suitcase. They pulled out, driving with all windows down. The two Algerians conversed in shouts. Montse didn't understand a word. She felt increasingly confused and anxious, but made an effort to appear calm. They drove towards Tindouf along a road that looked as though it was painted onto the desert sand.

As it lurched along the road, the old vehicle left a cloud of smoke behind it. The dashboard was covered in sand. When they entered the city, Montse's heart sank. It was already dark, and the buildings, dimly lit by a few street lamps, looked terrifying. Barely any cars went by. Only a few people could be seen in the street. Now and again they passed a bicycle or a donkey pulling a cart. Montse had the impression they were driving through a recently bombed city. The two men still communicated in shouts, as if they were angry. Sometimes a building appeared in the distance which seemed in good condition, yet after they left the centre of Tindouf the city looked increasingly desolate. They entered an area where unlit lamps hung from wooden posts. The houses were made of brick. The doors and windows were simple holes in the walls. Yet there were people living in them. Later Montse saw constructions made of concrete blocks, without plastering or cement: two metres by two cubes, with only a curtain for a door. The car stopped in front of one of those countless cubes on an unlit street. A dog was barking like crazy. Montse saw the young man pick up her suitcase and walk into the makeshift dwelling. The other asked her to follow him. She obeyed without daring to ask anything. What she found behind the curtain sent a shiver down her spine. Six or seven children, sitting on the floor, looked at her as if she were an apparition. In the centre of the dingy room was a small gas lamp. Two women were making dinner, sitting on a faded carpet. At the back, oblivious to everything, was an old woman. The neighbour's children soon started peering in, but the man shooed them away as if they were chickens running into the house. The two women stood up and, with their eyes fixed on her, listened to the driver's tale. Without making a single gesture or comment, they sat back down in their places and finished making dinner. Montse tried to get the men to understand that she needed a hotel for the night. The Algerians replied at the same time, and she felt increasingly bewildered. The women, sitting on the floor, still paid no attention. With a feeling of impotence, Montse picked up her suitcase and tried to leave the house. The older man grabbed her arm and pulled her back in. She stumbled on one of the children and fell on the floor. The men went on talking to her, alternately pointing to the street and the meal, and shouting angrily. Montse bit her lip to stop herself from crying. She was trying not to lose control. She stayed on the floor, no longer trying to explain herself. An adolescent boy walked in and sat down by the women. He didn't seem surprised at finding a foreign woman there. He barely exchanged a word with the men. Before Montse realised what was going on, a woman offered her a plate of dates and a cupful of milk. The rest of the family started eating from a dish in the middle of the room. Montse didn't know what to do. She wasn't hungry, but she picked up a date and nibbled at the tip. The woman took another one and show her how to dip it in the milk. Montse imitated her. Her stomach was churning, but she guessed that a refusal of food might be construed as an offence. She was so tired that her jaws ached when chewing. No one spoke or looked at her again. Outside one could hear the barking of dogs and the crying of a child. Not quite understanding what was happening, Montse succumbed to drowsiness and eventually lost consciousness.

She opened her eyes, hoping it had all been a nightmare. Everything was real. The first, timid rays of sunlight came through the curtains. The old woman she'd seen the previous night was now in the centre of the room, making tea, her gaze lost on the floor. Beside her was the adolescent boy, who could not stop looking at Montse. He approached and offered her a piece of bread. It was hard as stone. There was nobody else around. The suitcase and the bag were where she had left them. She opened the latter to make sure her passport was still in it. She sat up. Her whole body ached. She peered out into the street and, once again, the view distressed her. All the houses looked the same: windowless blocks with curtains for doors. Half-naked children played among the junk of abandoned cars, engines and trailers without wheels. At the entrance of the house there was a goat tied to a piece of metal. Its coat was filthy, and it was coughing as though in agony. From across the road a dog started barking at Montse. She took a few steps away from the façade, until she saw a woman run towards her with her face covered, shouting and holding her head in her hands. The woman took Montse by the arm and dragged her back into the house. She was one of the women who'd cooked dinner the night before. Montse didn't understand a word. She tried to explain that she needed to find a telephone. The woman kept talking in Arabic and French. In despair, Montse ran to the door and out into the street. She was prepared to cry for help, but when she saw the serious looks on the neighbours' faces she couldn't do it. The woman went after her, still speaking angrily. Montse held on to her handbag and walked on, giving her suitcase up for lost. At least, she thought, she was carrying all her documents and money with her. She strode away as quickly as possible, leaving the woman's chastening voice behind. All the kids in the street tailed behind her, shouting and laughing, and aping her walk. It took her a while to escape from the ruins of the labyrinth, because all the streets looked the same.

She felt greatly relieved when, after many twists and turns, she found a main road. Most of the children had stayed behind, only three little girls had kept up with her. She turned to them and recognised some of the faces from the night before. 'Go home,' she shouted, 'home! À la maison, à la maison!' They girls looked serious. They stopped and, a little later, went on walking behind her. The eldest looked barely ten. Increasingly anxious, Montse sat on the kerbstone. The girls stood on the other side of the road. She beckoned them over. They approached after thinking about it for a long while. 'I want to make a phone call, do you understand? A phone call?' The girls just stared at her. Drivers slowed down to see the unusual sight. 'Telephone, telephone, where?' she said in French. The oldest girl pointed to the end of the street. Then the other two did the same. Montse stood up and headed in that direction. Suddenly she felt the youngest girl's hand taking hers. The other two remained walking behind her, but not very far. As they walked on, the streets became more crowded. People stared at Montse. Men stopped and turned. Women covered their mouths with their head scarves. There were no telephone booths in sight. A man riding on a donkey repeatedly shouted at Montse without her knowing why.

She stopped at the entrance to a bar with a thatched roof. By the door were a few dirty white plastic tables. Two old men, who were smoking, fixed their eyes on her. One of them was wearing a pair of glasses with one of the lenses missing. He closed one eye to bring her into focus. Montse plucked up the courage to walk into the bar. There were a dozen men sitting around tables, chatting and smoking. As soon as they saw her they went quiet. Montse tried not to look them in the eye. The old man who'd been sitting by the door went in behind her, driven by his curiosity. There was an ancient telephone fixed to a post. Montse tried to find out who the owner was, but it proved impossible. 'Telephone,' she said in a broken voice as she pointed to the receiver. 'I need to telephone.' One of the men approached her, took her by the arm and pushed her towards the door. Montse resisted. Suddenly there was a commotion that she couldn't understand . The men started arguing between themselves. The racket was phenomenal. They gesticulated, shouted and even made as if to hit one another. The two old men jumped into the argument and started shouting at her too. Montse was so scared that she couldn't even see the exit. Two men took her by the arms, and both started pulling her towards them. She dropped her bag. Terrified, unable to control her nerves, she started to scream. Someone held her by the waist and pulled her away. Before she realised what was going on she was back in the street. The adolescent she had seen in the house was still dragging her by the arm to make her run. Montse did so as if the boy were her guardian angel. Behind her she heard the men's voices, still shouting and insulting each other at the entrance to the bar. She only stopped after she'd turned the corner, and sat down on the kerb once again. The boy had her bag slung over his shoulder. He gave it back as if it burned his hands. The three girls were sitting across the road, their eyes wide open, taking in every detail. The boy was talking to her, but Montse didn't have the strength to look him in the eye.

Back in the house, the woman was sitting in the middle of the room, along with the grandmother. She gave Montse a serious look but didn't say anything. The suitcase was still there. Montse slumped on the floor, letting go of her bag. The boy apparently began telling the women what had happened. A few female neighbours came in, while children peered in through the curtains without daring to enter. Montse burst into tears. She'd been trying not to cry from the moment she found herself alone at the terminal of Tindouf airport.

Layla squeezes Montse's hand. The sun is getting very strong. After hearing the story, the nurse has a smile on her face. This is surprising. She and Montse look at each other.

'You're not at home, but there's nothing to be scared of,' says Layla with a touch of sadness.

'What do you mean?'

'That it can be difficult to understand Islamic culture from the outside. Those people must have thought you were asking them for a place to sleep, and though they were poor they offered you what they had. To some it's not easy to understand our customs. But hospitality is sacred among Muslims.'

'I can understand that much.'

'If you accept someone's hospitality, you must follow their rules.'

'Meaning?'

'Algerian women are not like us. They are old-fashioned. They don't understand that a woman might walk alone in the street, let alone if she's a guest or a foreigner. As for walking into a men's bar... Well, some would think it as serious a sin as walking bare-armed down the street.'

Montse ponders Layla's words, which sadden her. The nurse realises that something is wrong and puts her hand on Montse's forehead, although the patient doesn't have a temperature.

'Don't be sad. You'll get back home soon and will be able to tell the whole story as if it were a film.'

Montse's face hardens into a grimace. Layla is disconcerted. She cannot get used to her patient's mood swings.

'Are you all right, Montse?'

'No, I'm not really. It's hard to explain it, even to myself.'

'Try explaining it to me. Maybe I'll get it.'

Montse swallows with difficulty. She combs her hair with her hands.

'I don't feel like going back. Just thinking about it makes me feel like I'm falling into a deep hole I won't be able to come out of.'

'Don't you have any children?'

'Only a daughter, but she doesn't need me,' replies Montse without hesitation.

'Have you got a job?'

'I do, but I've taken time off. There's no one waiting for me. If I never return, no one will miss me.'

They fall silent. A few nurses walk across the courtyard and say hello, exchanging a few words in Arabic with Layla. Then they're alone again.

'Would you like to come to my house?' asks Layla. 'I can extend a formal invitation. Next week it's the Feast of the Sacrifice. It's a time to spend with the people you love. You could meet my family.'

Montse smiles. She likes the sound of the nurse's words.

'Do you mean that? I mean, is it possible?'

'Of course it's possible. I only have to ask. You can go back home on the next flight, or the one after that. Whenever you like. My family would be pleased to have you.'

Montse hugs her with some difficulty. She's still exhausted.

'And will you cut my hair?' she asks with a schoolgirl's enthusiasm.

'Your hair?'

'Yes. It's a mess, look. Will you cut it for me?'

'If that's what you want, I'll cut it. And I'll dye it red. I've got lots of henna at home. Is that a "yes" then?'

'Yes, Layla. It's the best invitation I've ever had.'

And as she says this a cloud of sadness descends on her.

Chapter Eight

SANTIAGO SAN ROMÁN LOOKED AT HIS WATCH OVER AND
over again, as if impatience would make time go faster. The last
half an hour had been the longest in his life. What the hell was
he doing there on a Saturday night, past two in the morning,
behind the steering wheel of a Seat 124, waiting for a signal to
drive off at full speed? The more he thought of it, the less he
understood how he'd become involved in all this. They had
tricked him into it like a novice. He was angry and upset. The
weapon he was carrying under his jacket burnt his skin. He felt
like flinging it into the bushes of a garden and running away.
Then he thought of Sergeant Baquedano, and was paralysed
with fear.

Against his orders, he got out of the car and paced up and
down the pavement, trying to remain calm. He felt awkward
in civilian clothes. This too was against the rules, but at the
moment it was the least of his worries. He walked back and forth,
always within fifty metres of the Seat. The car had a Western
Sahara plate number, and nothing indicated that it was a military
vehicle. In the glove compartment he found the driver's license
and the identity card of an unknown Saharawi shopkeeper. All
very suspect. Could it be a joke devised by veteran legionnaires
to ruin his weekend? Whenever he touched the gun under his
clothes the theory vanished. Why would they give him a gun
if they were only mocking him? Just thinking of Baquedano he
felt a shiver rippling through his whole body.

He sat behind the steering wheel once again. He lowered the window, lit his last cigarette, and threw the empty packet onto the back seat. He resisted the impulse to look at his watch. Instead, he fixed his eyes on the corner around which he had seen Baquedano and his two accomplices disappear half an hour ago. He was certain that the three men were up to no good. He imagined the consequences he'd have to face if he washed his hands of the whole affair and left. For a moment he saw himself lying in a ditch by a desolate road, with his stomach cut open. Only Guillermo would miss him, and by the time they found him he would have rotted under the desert sun. He definitely didn't have the courage to run away. He felt like shit. On Friday, during break time, when Sergeant Baquedano approached him and started getting him into all this, he had not had the courage to say no. He had seen no way to extricate himself.

Friday and Saturday afternoons in the barracks were different from other days. The soldiers became especially animated as they waited to be handed their passes for the evening or the weekend. That Friday Santiago San Román was the last remaining person in his pavilion. After all, however fast he ran, he would have to queue up at the gates to show his pass like everyone else. He sprinkled himself with all the Varon Dandy left in the bottle and fastened the cap strap under his chin. When he heard a voice calling him, he thought it was a colleague hurrying him up. He turned, saw Sergeant Baquedano, and his face froze. More than the NCO's presence, what really made him nervous was the fact that Baquedano had called him by his surname. Santiago had never exchanged a word with him, not even a gesture. He even avoided the man's eyes. 'Attention, San Román!' Santiago stood to attention, stuck his chest out, pulled his stomach in, clicked the heels of his boots and saluted, saying that he was at Baquedano's command. The sergeant stood still a few metres away, with his legs slightly apart and his fingers hooked on the buckle of his belt. 'At ease, soldier. What I've come to tell you is strictly confidential.' He outranked Santiago. Baquedano looked him up and down and cleared his throat before proceeding. It was the first time Santiago had not seen him drunk. 'They say you're the best driver in the regiment. Is that true?'

'I'm a mechanic, sir.'

'Same thing, don't interrupt me. They tell me you can do a complete spin on the runway without touching the yellow lines.' He paused without taking his eyes off the soldier. 'Major Panta has heard about you and requires your services.' A drop of sweat rolled down Santiago's forehead, from the cap to his eyebrow. It struck him as awkward and dangerous that Baquedano had heard about him.

'People exaggerate, sir. Besides, it's easier to drive a car when one's not the owner.'

'Don't be modest, soldier, no need for that with me.' The sergeant came closer and casually put a hand on his shoulder. 'You see, San Román, if I've come to look for you at your pavilion instead of calling you to the Major's office, it's because no one must know about this. You understand?' Santiago had no time to reply. 'I'm glad you do. The Legion needs you, lad, and that should make you proud as a bridegroom of death. But if anything of what we're about to discuss leaves this room I'll cut your balls off and sent them to your dad by special delivery. You understand?' Santiago didn't, but couldn't utter a word. 'Tomorrow the soldier San Román won't get a leave permit. We need a driver with enough experience and sangfroid. Needless to say, the mission is top secret and very important. The less you know, the better for everyone. All you need to know is that tomorrow I'll be waiting for you at the hangar at ten pm; come in uniform. Don't carry any papers or documents that might help identify you. You'll have a bag with civilian clothes, in case we need to blend in. Tomorrow I'll tell you the rest, the same time as I brief the other courageous legionnaires who are coming with us. Don't ask questions and don't mention this to anyone, absolutely anyone, not even Major Panta. Understood?' Santiago couldn't talk. 'Understood?'

'Yes, sir. At your command, sergeant sir!' Baquedano patted him on the shoulder, as though he were giving him his blessing.

'You'll feel proud of your uniform. And then... Well, Major Panta will sign a permit for seven days' leave to those who volunteered for the mission. Seven days, San Román, seven days to do whatever the hell you want. And all you have to do is carry out your duty.'

'At your command, sergeant, sir!' Baquedano was about to turn but stopped.

'And another thing, San Román: unless there's another officer around, don't ever call me sergeant again. You'll call me Señor. Here I'm El Señor. Understood?'

'Sí, Señor. At your command, Señor!'

Guillermo crossed Baquedano at the door. He caught his breath and stood to attention. When he finally found Santiago, his friend looked very pale. He was leaning on a filing cabinet, his breathing was laboured, and his eyes seemed about to pop out of his head.

'Are you all right, Santi?'

'Yeah, yeah, it's my stomach again, giving me trouble.' Guillermo believed him.

'We're the only ones left, Santi. If we stay here any longer we won't find anything to drink at the Oasis.'

'Let's go then.'

Guillermo didn't connect the encounter with Baquedano with Santiago's strange behaviour. He resigned himself to taking a walk when Santiago said he didn't feel like going to the Oasis. They went near the zoo under construction. Guillermo was proud of the building, as though the design had been his. Although in Barcelona he'd already worked as a builder, this was the most important development he'd ever taken part in. Now, seated on cement blocks, the two friends smoked and imagined what the zoo would look like when it was finished. Santiago had difficulty talking. He couldn't get Baquedano out of his mind. He suspected that the affair would cause him nothing but trouble. If it was the Major's idea, it was no doubt about prostitutes. But if it was Baquedano's, it could be anything: dope, smuggled tobacco, LSD.

'I'm not allowed out tomorrow. I'm on duty.' His friend didn't look surprised.

'Well, you're screwed.'

'No, not at all. Afterwards they'll give me a seven-day permit.' This did surprise Guillermo.

'You were born lucky, mate, I've always said so. There's no one I know with as much luck as you.' San Román couldn't bring himself to tell Guillermo the story about Baquedano. Deep down he expected his friend to sound him out, to feel intrigued, to detect something strange about all of it. It was not to be.

'Let's go get a drink before it's too late.' Santiago suddenly started walking – he felt nervous, reckless. 'Let's go up to see the Stone Houses.' He meant the Zemla quarter, where the Saharawis lived.

'Not again. You must be wrong in the head, Santi. Don't break my balls with the Saharawis.' Santiago pressed on. He stopped after a while and turned.

'You're such a shit, Guillermo! I can never count on you for anything out of the ordinary.' To Guillermo, that felt like a punch in his stomach. He reddened, locked his jaw and gritted his teeth. He was about to shout something, but held back. Santiago walked away without turning. He had to get rid of his obsession with that part of the city.

He gave a start on hearing Guillermo's voice behind him. 'That's not fair, Santi. How can you forget everything I've done for you so quickly?' Santiago turned around. Guillermo had followed him for a quarter of an hour like a faithful lapdog. Santiago knew that his friend didn't deserve that kind of treatment. He was suddenly sorry. He threw his arm round Guillermo's shoulder and held him.

'Don't go all queer on me, Santi, you know I don't like it.' Santiago made as if to kiss him, and then ran off, with Guillermo giving chase in an attempt to kick him.

The Saharawis called the Zemla area Hata-Rambla; it was a sort of peninsula that tore itself away from the modern part and its four-storey buildings. From afar the stone houses looked like they were made of papier-mâché. Most dwellings only had a ground floor. As the two legionnaires proceeded up the hill, they left behind what were known as the 'half-egg' houses, which had white roofs like upturned egg shells, especially built to channel the heat upwards. It was a holiday for Muslims, and on that evening the streets were unusually quiet. There were children playing football where the terrain was flat, but on seeing the two soldiers they ran away as if they'd never seen anything like them. The women, for their part, would go straight into their houses, only to peep through the hand-woven curtains covering the doors and windows. The men came out to take a look at the legionnaires, and would blatantly stare at them, with impertinent, clearly hostile gazes. Neither of them felt comfortable, but Santiago concealed his feelings better. He talked to Guillermo without meeting the Saharawis' eyes. He was familiar with some of their habits and knew that it was best to act naturally. A man in a turban approached them. 'Have you got a light, lads?' he asked calmly, as though he were used to coming across legionnaires in those back streets. Santiago San Román offered him a box of matches. As soon as he'd heard his voice, he knew he was one of the men from Canary Islands who now lived there. Most were road hauliers or ex-legionnaires who hadn't returned home after being discharged. The man touched the light to his pipe, a copper cylinder that got wider at the tip and was adorned with engraved lines. 'The legion has improved since my days, my friends. They didn't provide us with uniforms like that, and we had no money to spend on cologne.' Santiago knew he meant his Varon Dandy. 'Things change, gentlemen, even in the army.'

Guillermo felt ill-at-ease under the scrutiny of the man in Saharawi clothes. His rotten teeth and world-weary reflections didn't inspire confidence. The man knew this; he gave the matches back to Santiago. 'You bet things change. A few years ago none of us would have dared to come to up here, on a holiday, dressed like that.' Guillermo pulled his friend by the arm. The man from Canary Islands noticed his suspicion. 'You'll allow a piece of advice from someone who wore your uniform too: if you're not going to come and live up here, don't strut around the streets of Hata-Rambla. People are very sensitive here, you know, and they might regard it as a provocation. Tempers have been running a bit high. And Muslims are not like you, *compañeros*.' Then the man went back the way he'd come. With his clothes and morose walk, he looked just like a Saharawi.

Santiago dragged his friend away by the arm. Although he tried not to act like a tourist, everything he saw attracted his attention. The jambs and lintels of many doors were skirted with a band of indigo which stood out against the whitewashed stone walls. 'Let's get some tobacco.' San Román wanted to visit one of the tobacconist's he'd heard so much about among the Nomad Troops. He knew one could buy anything in those shops, however exotic it might seem, and that they were open every day of the year, day and night. He saw one a moment later and motioned Guillermo to follow him. They stepped into a room stacked up to the ceiling with all kinds of objects, and perceived a strong smell of leather and hemp. Neither knew where to look. On seeing them a Saharawi rose from the floor. '*Salama aleikum*,' Santiago said immediately. '*Aleikum salama*,' replied the shopkeeper, surprised. '*Asmahlin*,' went on the legionnaire, apologetic in front of his friend's incredulous eyes. The Saharawi welcomed him to his store: '*Barjaban.*' San Román, for his part, thanked him: '*Shu-cran.*'

'For a foreigner, you speak my language very well,' said the man. Guillermo was beginning to wonder whether it wasn't all a joke to see what he would do.

'I've got Saharawi friends,' explained Santiago. 'And I'm a fast learner.'

'What can I do for you?'

'I'd like a packet of tobacco, please.' In fact, the tobacco was only an excuse to enter the shop, as Santiago didn't want his curiosity to seem impertinent. 'Try this one: it's very good. American. Fresh off the boat.' The shopkeeper was still smiling. Santiago gave him a one-hundred-peseta note and waited for the change, smiling back. Then he tried to say goodbye, but the shopkeeper came out from behind the counter and stood in front of the door. 'You cannot leave Sid-Ahmed's house just like that.' Santiago understood what he meant, but Guillermo was growing nervous.

'You'll smoke some of my tobacco and drink some tea.' Sid-Ahmed left the shop through a door concealed by a curtain.

'Let's get out of here, Santi. Are you mad?' said Guillermo agitatedly. 'This guy wants to sell us dope.'

'Shut up, you fool. Who do you think you're with? Do you think I'm an idiot?' Guillermo swallowed his words. He didn't know how to react. Then Sid-Ahmed appeared carrying a teapot and a few small crystal glasses. He moved away some dirty glasses on a silver tray, and invited the legionnaires to sit next to him on a carpet while the water boiled. Guillermo didn't open his mouth. Only Santiago and Sid-Ahmed took part in the conversation. They smoked long thin cigarettes. As they waited for the water to boil, the Saharawi talked about his business, football, and how expensive life was. He showed the legionnaires a photo of his football team, which was hanging among his goods. 'Signed by Santillana,' said Ahmed. 'Real Madrid is my favourite team. That Miljanic is very clever. If we had a coach like him, we'd have a first division team, *fahem*? You know what I mean. Here we have players as good as Amancio or Gento, but we're missing a good coach.' Sid-Ahmed offered a first round of tea. '*Menfadlak*. Have a sip. My wife is the expert, but she's attending to a birth and cannot be here.' Sid-Ahmed talked and talked. Guillermo tried to conceal his irritation, whereas his friend seemed delighted. He was expecting the Saharawi to get the dope out at any moment and sweet talk them into buying it. When they said goodbye at the door with a handshake, Guillermo was disconcerted.

'We'll meet again, Sid-Ahmed,' said Santiago.

'*Ins'Alah*. It'll be a pleasure.'

The street was completely dark by the time they left the shop. They had been talking with Sid-Ahmed for over two hours. At a corner in the distance, they saw the dim light of a streetlamp. It was a dirt road. They walked in the moonlight towards the lamp. Guillermo seemed calmer now. 'And where did you learn all those words in Muslim?'

'It's not Muslim, Guillermo, it's Hassaniya.'

'It sounds like Muslim to me.' Santiago laughed and mocked his friend, but suddenly something hit Guillermo on the head so hard that he held it with both hands. His cap rolled onto the street. Santiago turned around, without understanding what had happened, when his friend knelt down on one knee and supported himself with his hand. There was very little light. It all happened so quickly. Guillermo moved his hand aside, revealing a stream of blood running from his face to his neck.

'Fuck, Guillermo, what happened?' But Guillermo couldn't reply: he just lowered his other knee and collapsed, unconscious. The streetlamp was only a few metres away. Santiago saw the glimmer of a metal bar lying on the ground near his friend. He looked everywhere, but there was no one around. Someone must have thrown the object at them from a window, but there were no lights on. Santiago, still looking around, tried to see how bad the wound was. It was a gash above the temple, and Guillermo was bleeding profusely. Santiago tried to keep his friend's head off the ground, lest the wound get dirty. Guillermo opened his eyes but couldn't speak. Santiago lifted him as if he was a bag of potatoes and threw him over his shoulder. He made it to the corner, but Guillermo was too heavy. More objects started raining down. Now they were stones, and a flowerpot that broke against a boulder. Santiago was terrified. Barely controlling his panic, he carried his friend to the next corner. Guillermo's hands and uniform were stained with blood. When Santiago took a look at him under the next streetlamp his fear increased. He called out for help. No one came out into the street; no one leaned out of a window. For a few seconds he cursed the moment he'd had the stupid idea of coming up to the Zemla quarter. He was trying to lift Guillermo again when someone hissed from a nearby doorstep. Santiago saw the silhouette of a man in a turban but didn't dare to ask him for help. The man went on calling him and beckoning him over. Santiago was unable to move. Eventually the door opened and two young men came out. They carried Guillermo and asked Santiago to follow them into the house. Once inside, a third man closed the door and bolted it. Half a dozen cautious faces stared at the legionnaires as though they were terrifying apparitions. There were two lads and four old men in black turbans, with lined faces and grave countenances. No one said a word; they looked at Santiago San Román, and two of them laid Guillermo down in the centre of the room. It was a rectangular room, with bare white walls and a carpet that took up all the space of the floor. Against the wall was a long bench, barely half a metre high, covered with cushions. The only light came from a fluorescent tube. Santiago was unable to conceal his anxiety. He could only say: 'Help me please, my friend is hurt.' The men looked at Santiago and Guillermo curiously. The oldest one started giving orders, but no one obeyed him. Santiago, not knowing what to do, kneeled down beside his friend. He got even more frightened when he saw his face covered in blood and his vacant eyes. For a moment he thought Guillermo was dead. He looked at the men imploringly. The Saharawis started talking in Hassaniya all at the same time. They were obviously having an argument.

Suddenly there was a loud banging on the door. The six men looked at each other and stopped arguing. A woman appeared in the room. She said something to the young men and one of them went to open the door. It was Sid-Ahmed, the shopkeeper, looking extremely angry. He glanced at Santiago without saying a word and kneeled down beside Guillermo. He pressed his ear to his chest, and when he sat up his cheek was covered in blood. He started shouting orders and got the rest moving without any further discussion. Two other women came in. Sid-Ahmed shouted at them too. Santiago looked on without daring to interfere. He couldn't believe that this was the same shopkeeper who a short while ago had treated them to tea and tobacco with an open smile.

'They cut his head with an iron bar, Sid-Ahmed. Someone threw it at us in the dark. He won't stop bleeding.' Sid-Ahmed gestured at him not to raise his voice and talked to the Saharawis in furious tones. He shouted at them in Hassaniya, and the other replied in a similarly angry vein. For a moment Santiago thought it would come to blows, but nothing of the sort happened.

'He'll recover, don't worry. They'll dress the wound and sew it up.' As he explained this, Sid-Ahmed took Santiago to a small patio surrounded by an adobe wall. It smelled of animals and urine. They jumped over a crumbling bit of wall, proceeded to the neighbouring house, and went through a few more houses.

'Where are we going, Sid-Ahmed? I can't leave Guillermo here.' The shopkeeper gestured to him to calm down.

'Don't worry. Your friend is in good hands. They'll take good care of him.' Santiago didn't dare to ask any further questions or contradict him. He knew he was in a terrible situation. Suddenly he realised he had to be at the barracks in an hour. Without an overnight pass, he could be accused of deserting. He was so nervous he stumbled on one of the walls and fell over. Sid-Ahmed helped him up. Eventually they reached a room where a whole family was watching a TV with lots of static. No one seemed frightened to see them arrive in the dark, like ghosts. Sid-Ahmed, again sounding angry, exchanged a few words with the oldest man in the house, who pointed to the front door. They went out and across the street. Santiago followed the shopkeeper like a frightened child. Sid-Ahmed stopped at a door and knocked. A child opened. The Saharawi pushed the door and dragged Santiago in behind him. Now Santiago's confusion was complete. From among the people drinking tea in front of the TV, a young man got up and approached the legionnaire.

'Santiago, what happened? What are you doing here?' It took Santiago a moment to realise that the Saharawi dressed in an immaculate white *derraha*[10] and blue turban was Lazaar. Santiago couldn't utter a word. Sid-Ahmed took off his shoes and sat down. He spoke so fast that Lazaar's family had trouble following. Santiago kneeled on the carpet, his legs shaking. No one spoke when the shopkeeper finished his story. One of the old men gestured to the women to take the children elsewhere. Only five people remained in the room. Someone handed Santiago a glass of tea; he began to feel better with the first sip.

'I need to go back to Guillermo, but I don't know the way.' Lazaar took a few moments before replying.

'Your friend is fine. Don't worry,' he said, placing his hands on Santiago's shoulders. 'But you shouldn't have come up wearing those uniforms. There are some mean people here.'

[10.] *Derraha*: Traditional Saharawi male dress made, like the *melfa*, of a single cloth but without covering the head. The most frequent colours are white and blue.

'We were only taking a stroll...'

'*Al-la yarja mmum!*' cursed the Saharawi. 'Do you really not know what's happening between your people and mine?' It was the first time that Santiago had seen Lazaar angry. He was taken aback.

'Take your clothes off,' ordered Sid-Ahmed. Santiago didn't understand what for.

'Give me your clothes,' insisted Lazaar. 'The women will wash the blood off.'

'But I have to go back to the barracks.'

'Go back? They would arrest you and ask you a thousand questions.' Santiago started undressing; he trusted Lazaar blindly. 'Tomorrow morning your clothes will be clean and dry. Then we'll take you back.'

'Tomorrow? Who's going to take me over tomorrow? We have to be back in half and hour.' Lazaar raised his voice for the first time.

'Don't be stupid! Do you want to ruin us all? Tonight you'll sleep at my house.'

Santiago finished undressing without asking any more questions. Everyone left the room. In his socks and underwear he felt ridiculous and helpless. He didn't know what to do with his hands. At that moment the curtain opened, and in walked a dark-eyed girl with brown hair. She casually looked the legionnaire up and down. Then she smiled, revealing her lovely white teeth. Without a word, she offered him a blue tunic and took two steps back. Lazaar returned with a turban.

'Andía, what are you doing here?' The girl looked inhibited and confused. She pointed to the *derraha* that Santiago was holding in his hand.

'I brought some clothes for the Spaniard.'

'Well you can go now. He's my guest, not yours.' Andía hung her head and, visibly embarrassed, left the room. Santiago thought Lazaar had been unfair, but he didn't dare to reproach him for it.

'Who was that?' The Saharawi didn't respond to the question immediately, but Santiago kept looking at the door.

'She's my sister. She's a bit nosy, like all the women in my family.'

'You never mentioned you had a sister, only brothers.' Lazaar found the comment strange. He stared at Santiago.

'There are many things you don't know about me.' Santiago slipped on the *derraha* and did up the turban on his head. He'd seen others do it so many times that he knew the movements by heart.

'I've always wanted to wear one of these.'

'Well, you'll be able to wear it whenever you like. All this is for you,' said Lazaar, smiling for the first time. 'And the slippers too. Presents from a friend. Now to bed, it's late.' Santiago glanced at his watch. It was only nine. The Saharawi turned off the fluorescent tube and lay down on the carpet. Santiago did the same.

'What about your family?' Lazaar took a moment before replying.

'The women are cleaning your uniform, and the men are in bed.'

'I hope I haven't disturbed the sleeping arrangements.'

'No, no. You're my guest and need to be comfortable. My grandfather snores a lot. You wouldn't sleep a wink.' Both men started laughing, just like when the Nomad Troops scored a goal.

Santiago couldn't shut his eyes. There had been too many emotions for one day, and things were moving too fast. He was so tired he couldn't think straight. He tried to imagine how Guillermo was doing at that moment. He wasn't sure that leaving him with unknown people had been the right thing to do. And he worried about what would happen if the authorities found out they had not returned to the barracks. It all got mixed up with the image of Sergeant Baquedano and his obscure words. For a moment he wished he had been arrested, so as not to have to report to the regiment; that would give him an excuse not to participate in Baquedano's mission. Time passed very slowly during the empty night. Now and again he was startled by the distant howling of a dog. As soon as he saw light through a crack in the curtains, he got up and went out into the patio. The dawn painted the rooftops red. Only a goat was stirring in a wire pen. The cool of the morning comforted him. His uniform was hanging out to dry under a small asbestos roof; it seemed the only proof that it was all really happening. He badly wanted to smoke. To the right and left of the patio were two low doors, covered by curtains, where, in all likelihood, Lazaar's family were sleeping. Santiago tried to recall how many brothers the Saharawi had, and at that moment Andía peered out from behind the curtains. Her eyes were swollen and her hair was tangled. On seeing him, she smiled. Santiago said good morning in a whisper, so as not to wake anyone up. Andía approached him.

'Are you always up so early?' asked Santiago in a kind voice.

'Always. I'm the eldest sister and I have lots to do.' She said it with pride, and stopped smiling for a moment. Then she picked up Santiago's clothes and folded them carefully. 'They're dry,' she said after touching her lips to the cloth to make sure. 'As soon as everyone's up you'll be able to leave.'

'You want me to leave already?' Andía smiled, revealing her white teeth.

'I didn't say that. You're my brother's guest.'

'How old are you, Andía?' The girl took a moment to reply: 'Seventeen.' She stopped smiling. She handed Santiago the uniform and disappeared behind the curtain. He was lost for words. Perhaps he had offended Andía, who had surely lied about her age so as not to seem like a child. Suddenly she reappeared, smiling again. She took Santiago's hand and put a necklace on his palm. This confused him.

'It's for your girlfriend. A present from Andía.'

'I haven't got a girlfriend.'

'Not even in Spain?'

'Neither in Spain nor anywhere else.'

'I don't believe you. All soldiers have girlfriends.'

'Well, not all.' Santiago smiled at the girl's naiveté. 'Unless you'd like to be a legionnaire's girlfriend.' Andía grew very serious, to the point that Santiago regretted his *faux pas*. He put on the necklace to ingratiate himself, but she no longer smiled. A woman came out from behind the curtain and spoke angrily at Andía, startling them both. Andía went back into the room and Santiago returned to Lazaar's side.

The sun had barely risen when they heard the loud beep of a horn. 'It's Sid-Ahmed,' announced Lazaar after peering out. 'Your friend's with him.' There was an immediate flurry of activity, with women and children coming and going. Santiago ran out into the street. Guillermo, with his head bandaged, was sitting in the back seat of a Renault 12. He didn't look too well, but appeared to be okay. Santiago hugged him leaning in through the window. Sid-Ahmed moved over and Lazaar, dressed in his uniform, got in on the driver's seat. One of Lazaar's brothers got in as well, in the back seat, and told Santiago to do the same. San Román touched his head and felt something missing.

'My cap, Lazaar, I forgot my cap.' He went back into the house and out to the patio. Andía was there, feeding lentils to the goat. She had such a serious expression that Santiago thought she might be angry. 'Have you seen my cap, Andía?' She pointed half-heartedly to the line where the clothes had hung all night. Santiago took it down quickly and put it on. Andía came out of the pen and waylaid Santiago.

'I do want to,' she said, very seriously.

'What is it you want?'

'To be your girlfriend. I want to be your girlfriend.' Hurried and all, Santiago could not contain a smile.

'I'm glad, very glad. I'll be the envy of the Legion. No soldier there has a girlfriend as pretty as mine.' Andía smiled too. Santiago kissed her briefly and said goodbye, but before he left he heard the Saharawi's voice.

'Will you come up and see me?'

'Of course, Andía, I'll be back.'

That morning, Guillermo and Santiago were the first to join ranks. No one could have guessed they had spent the night away from the barracks. As they themselves had done on other occasions, their fellow soldiers had kept their absence secret and covered their backs. No one asked any questions. Santiago and Guillermo entered through a hole in the wall known only to the Saharawis. It was Lazaar who told them what to do. They went round the Nomad Troops' pavilion and reached their building just when reveille was sounded. It all happened so quickly that they didn't have time to reflect about what they were doing. Later, in the soldiers' mess, the two legionnaires were surprised at how easy it was to get in and out of the barracks, and at the fact that the Saharawis knew secrets that no one else did.

Santiago San Román was short of breath when he saw Baquedano's silhouette appear among the shadows. Without his uniform, the sergeant lost the authority and pomposity he had in the barracks. He was wearing a blue jacket with its collar up and synthetic trousers with flared bottoms. Behind him were the two old legionnaires. Although not running, they were walking at some speed. As soon as he recognised them, San Román tensed up. He was lucky to be back in the car, as Baquedano had instructed. When the sergeant got in he had already started the engine.

'Let's get the fuck out of here, San Román! Quick!' the sergeant shouted.

Santiago stepped on the accelerator and released the clutch at the same time. The car lurched forward with a noise of screeching tires. Santiago didn't know which way to go.

'Not that way, you idiot! To the square,' shouted Baquedano. 'I want you to drive twice around it for everyone to see you.

And do one of those spins of yours.'

For the first time Santiago turned to look at the sergeant, and noticed that he had a blue hold-all between his legs.

'And you, cover your faces!' he ordered to the legionnaires riding in the back seat.

In the rear-view mirror San Román saw the two veterans cover themselves with sacks like the one Baquedano held in his hand. The sergeant did the same. As Santiago skidded and did a spin at Plaza de España, he felt naked before they eyes of a group of young people sitting in the gardens. He didn't quite understand what was going on. The sergeant put the hold-all on the floor with a clinking sound.

'To the Smara road,' shouted Baquedano. 'Floor it!'

Santiago obeyed without thinking. As he went past the *Parador Nacional*, he saw a lieutenant get out of his car. Santiago didn't dare to ask the sergeant what was going on. The fear that that man instilled in him ruled out any initiative.

They left the city lights behind. The road looked like a continuation of the desert. The sergeant patted him on the shoulder.

'Well done, lad. You've got balls.'

After about four kilometres Santiago turned into a dirt road. He soon found the Land Rover in which they had left from the Alejandro Farnesio headquarters. He turned off the lights and cut the engine. The sergeant directed every one of his moves. Their eyes took a while to adjust to the moonlight.

'I want you to put on your uniforms and pretend you're just out on leave.'

As they got dressed, San Román looked at the veterans out of the corner of his eye. One seemed euphoric, while the other wore a serious expression and remained silent. Baquedano approached him from behind and forced him to stick his chin out.

'Are you a chicken?'

'No, sir, of course not.'

'Then what are you?'

The legionnaire hesitated but then said, as loud as he could:

'I'm a bridegroom of death, sir!'

'That's right. You should know who your mother is,' said Baquedano, pointing to the flag. 'And who's your bride.'

'Sir...' said the legionnaire, and then went quiet.

'What's the matter? You've never seen anyone get killed?' shouted Baquedano, anticipating the man's thoughts.

'No, sir, never. It's the first time...'

'Be grateful then, as you now know your bride's face.' Baquedano was shouting so much that his neck swelled. Then he took a deep breath and started singing: 'No one in the regiment knew / who that legionnaire was / so fearless and so bold /who enlisted in the Legion.'

Encouraged by the sergeant, the men sang along.

'No one knew his story / but the Legion supposed / that a great pain was biting / his heart like a wolf.'

Santiago, frightened, added his voice to the chorus:

'I'm a man whom fortune / hurt with a beast's claws / I'm a bridegroom of death / who will tightly embrace / his faithful companion.'

As they finished putting on the uniforms and sang at the top of their voices, Baquedano loaded the three hold-alls onto the back of the Land Rover. He took something out of one of them and put it on top of the car. It was a silver chalice. San Román didn't understand a thing. Then the sergeant gave each of them a piece of paper.

'A promise is a promise: here's a week's permit. I don't want to see you near the barracks until the week is out. We're all in this together, and if anyone spills the beans I'll flay them alive.'

Santiago was about to retrieve the keys from under the passenger seat, but Baquedano got there first. He took him aside and said almost in a whisper:

'You stay here. I want you to wait until we're gone. Then

you'll take the Seat and wheel it down that ravine over there. Set it on fire and leave. But don't move until it's completely burnt. You understand? You can be back in El Aaiún in under an hour.'

Santiago didn't reply. He was relieved to part company with the others. Before the sergeant got behind the wheel, he gave Santiago the chalice that he had taken out of the bag.

'Leave this in the back seat. Don't forget it.'

Santiago held it in his hand, touching the relief figures as if they burned. Meanwhile, the Land Rover started and the two legionnaires broke into song, encouraged by Baquedano:

'Just to come and see you/ My faithful lady/ I've become a bridegroom of death/ I held her tight/ And her love became my flag.'

Santiago was tempted to dispose of the chalice and run away, but fear prevented him. He took a deep breath and, in the moonlight, looked around for the ravine that the sergeant had indicated. Like an automaton, he got into the car, threw the chalice onto the back seat and drove down a gentle slope scattered with bushes. In the damp cold night he inhaled the strong smell of earth. A dazzled hare froze in front of the headlights. Santiago thought he saw himself reflected in its terrified eyes. He turned off the lights. He didn't quite know what to do. His uniform burned his skin. After undressing slowly, he put his civilian clothes back on. He opened the petrol tank and threw in a match. He recoiled at the sudden flash.

He walked across the field to the road. From there he could see the car in flames. He headed towards El Aaiún. Not one car came his way. When he arrived, dawn was barely an hour away. It was Sunday and he felt lost. He slumped on a wooden bench, under a palm tree on Plaza de España. And it was at that moment that he realised what had happened. There was a commotion at the entrance to the church. A crowd of people was standing there as though they were at the box office of a cinema. Santiago drew near with a mixture of fear and curiosity. He learned that the church had been robbed. The police were keeping people away. A stretcher was brought out with a dead body covered by a blanket.

'Is that the priest?' asked a woman.

'No, the sacristan. So they say. They've stolen all the objects of value from the sacristy. The poor man must have been sleeping. He never saw it coming.'

Santiago walked away trying hard not to run. He felt cheated, furious, scared. He didn't know where to go or what to do with his seven days' leave. Without much thought he directed his steps to the Zemla quarter. As he started uphill he opened the bag in which he had his uniform and change of clothes; he took out the turban Lazaar had given him and put it on while walking along the empty streets. He wandered about without quite knowing what he was doing. No one took any notice of him. He went into a store and bought some tobacco. He tried to make sense of what had happened. At mid morning he recognised the Renault 12 and the front door of Lazaar's house. He was about to knock when he noticed the door was open. Inside, seated on the carpet, two women were painting their fingers with henna.

'*Salama aleikum*,' said Santiago.

They greeted him back without any sign of surprise, and asked him in. He thought one of them was Lazaar's mother, but they looked so alike under the *melfa* that he couldn't be sure. Suddenly Andía rushed in from the street, nearly out of breath. She had seen Santiago from afar. She smiled, breathing heavily. Then she went out into the patio and started shouting. The men of the family came into the room and, one by one, shook Santiago's hand. Andía lit a small brazier and put the kettle to boil.

'Lazaar is not in,' explained Andía with a smile. 'Now you'll be my guest.'

Chapter Nine

THE CITY'S ARTERIES WERE CLOGGED WITH CARS. TRAFFIC lights no longer served any purpose. The Guardia Urbana was incapable of bringing order to such chaos. Everywhere one looked, children were dragging their parents towards the parade of the Magi. The shops seemed to be in the final seconds of a race against time. Doctor Montserrat Cambra was dazed by the general bustle and the young ones' unbounded enthusiasm. It had taken her nearly an hour to find a free cab and, when she finally did, the driver had to make a detour of several kilometres to reach Barceloneta. Once there she felt her mouth dry up and her stomach shrink. Although she was familiar with the symptoms, she felt as frightened as she did the first time that she had been there.

Years ago the city ended at the Estación de Francia. The steel web of tracks was like a cold, desolate curtain behind which one could only imagine dilapidated grocery stores, huge warehouses and perhaps the sea. Now it looked like a different city. She knew Carrer de Balboa well, but the sadness gathering in her chest prevented her from walking in that direction. Instead, she went into the Palau del Mar building. Her only time in it had been nine years before, at the opening. Her husband and their daughter, Teresa, had come along: the perfect family. Teresa was not yet ten. She could still see her running between the tables of the restaurant. The image hurt – hurt a lot. Montserrat Cambra took the lift to the top floor. As it went up, the pressure in her chest increased. She felt nauseous. A little later she sat at the entrance to the Museo Histórico, fighting back her retching. She tried to take deep breaths to stave off a panic attack. She closed her eyes, but opened them right away because she felt dizzy. Her pulse raced. She feared she might pass out. From her bag she took out a bottle of pills. She put two in her mouth and swallowed them anxiously.

On the other side of the huge window, Barceloneta appeared as if on a cinema screen. Montse opened her eyes and tried to see the landscape as she remembered it. Twenty-six years before, the building she was in was nothing but a store in ruins, about to crumble into the sea. It wasn't unusual to spot large rats which had no fear of humans. The houses in Barceloneta echoed with transistor radios and women's singing. Their terraces were a tangle of rickety aerials and clothes hung out to dry.

Suddenly she pictured her daughter coming out of the museum with her husband. The image was so real she had to close her eyes to blot it out. She needed fresh air. Montse left the building anxiously. The cold January weather brought her back to reality. She headed for Ayach Bachir's house. Although the neighbourhood had changed, everything was familiar. She had no trouble finding the address. When someone came out of the building she slipped in through the door. The smell brought a number of images to mind. The flats were still all very much alike. She sat down on the stairs and waited for the lights to go off. Then she put her head on her knees and effortlessly remembered the first time she had been in the area.

One morning Santiago San Román appeared in front of the shoe shop without a car. 'Today I feel like walking,' he told Montse. She did not raise any objections. She pressed her books against her and walked beside him without replying. The boy had a serious expression for the first time in weeks. She didn't have the courage to ask, but suspected something was troubling him. As they walked by a rubbish bin, she threw in her folder and books. Santiago looked at her as though she had committed a crime. 'What are you doing?'

'No more studying for me.' She took him by the hand and they pressed on along Vía Cayetana. 'I'm going to spend a few days with my parents at Cadaqués,' she lied. 'They really want to see me.' Santiago frowned and stopped walking.

'When?'

'Saturday. My father's coming to pick me up.' San Román was slow to react. He looked bewildered, nearly despondent.

'Saturday! You're leaving on Saturday. For how long?' Montse was deliberately mysterious.

'I don't know: till September, probably.' Santiago opened his eyes as wide as they went. He looked as though he were the brink of a panic attack. 'Unless...' continued Montse.

'Unless...?'

'Unless you tell me the truth.' That was the master stroke. He went red in the face. His pulse raced and his voice trembled.

'What do you mean, the truth?' Montse quickened her step, and he had to struggle to keep up. 'Wait, sweetheart, don't leave like this. I don't know what you're talking about. I never lie to you...' He trailed off when she stopped and glared at him.

They had the last beer of that summer sitting outside a bar. Santiago paid with his last one-hundred-peseta note, offering it to the waiter as if he were entrusting him with his life.

'Are you going to be honest with me?' Santiago checked his fingernails and then sipped at his beer.

'Okay, you're right. I don't work in a bank or anything like that. I made it up.'

'I knew that already,' replied Montse. 'What I want to know is what you really do. Because I'm beginning to think that all those cars are stolen.' Santiago gave a start.

'They're not. I swear on my mother's life. They're from the garage. I pick them up in the morning and return them after I drop you off at home.'

'The white convertible too?'

'Yes.'

'So you work in a garage?' Santiago slouched a bit and lowered his voice.

'I used to.' Montse pressed some more.

'Have you got a new job?'

'More or less. Well, no, they've sacked me.' It was time to cut him some slack. She took his hand and kissed him very tenderly. Santiago went on talking as if his words burnt his mouth. 'Yesterday the boss realised a car was missing. I had it, of course. He waited for me at the entrance to the garage. He says he's going to report me to the police, and he's refusing to pay me all the money he owes me. He's an arsehole. He hasn't paid me since January.'

'And all that money you had?' asked Montse, intrigued.

'I know how to earn a living, what do you think? I fix old parts and leave them as good as new. Stuff you can't find anywhere else. Anyway, that arsehole Pascualín spilled the beans.'

'Pascualín works with you?'

'Naturally.'

'I thought he didn't look like a banker,' said Montse, trying to make him smile.

'Banker! He can barely do a sum. He told the boss about the cars. He said that I'd only been dropping by the garage to borrow cars in the morning and return them in the evening.'

'And all this time the boss had not been to the garage?'

'Like hell he had. He just buys stolen cars, has them dismantled and sells the parts in Morocco. And then lives it up in Tangiers with a stash of dope and a bunch of whores.' Santiago realised he had said too much. Montse grew serious. She wanted to believe him, but the story was too far removed from her world. 'What is it? You asked me to tell you the truth, and that's the truth,' he said. Montse was slow to react.

'I don't care about any of it. I only wanted to be with you. It hurts that you're a liar, though.' San Román stuck his hands in his pockets.

'Are you leaving for Cadaqués on Saturday?' She had the upper hand now.

'It depends on you. If you show me you're sorry, I'll stay here with you.'

'What do I have to do to prove it?'

'Introduce me to your parents.' San Román went quiet. That was the last thing he was expecting. Montse stood up, offended by his silence. 'Just as I thought, all talk and no action.' She stormed off. She was so offended she felt capable of anything. San Román went after her and held her by the shoulders.

'Wait up, darling, I haven't even said no.' Montse crossed her arms and gave him a defiant look.

'Well I haven't heard anything else either. And your face says it all.'

'Fine. I can't introduce you to my father, because I've never met him. I think he's dead, but I'm not sure. I'll take you to see my mother, but she's not well: she suffers from nerves and forgets stuff all the time.'

It was the first time Montse had been beyond Estación de Francia. Had it not been for Santiago, she would never have been curious enough to venture into the area, which felt like a different city. Songs by Antonio Molina spilled from radios out into the street. The smell of stews cooking mixed with that of the diesel heating the shops and the rotting algae gathering in the Dársena de Comercio. Santiago didn't hold her hand once. For the first time she saw that he was embarrassed. With his head lowered, he walked one step ahead of her, and greeted people half-heartedly.

Santiago San Román's mother ran a tobacconist's off Calle de Balboa. It was a run-down little shop, with cracked floor tiles; the counter and shelves were very old, and darkened by layer upon layer of varnish. The glass panels of the door rattled. Santiago gave his mother a kiss and said without much enthusiasm: 'Mum, this is Montse.' The woman looked at the girl as if from the bottom of a deep pit. Then she looked at her son. 'Have you eaten, Santi?'

'No, mum, it's only twelve. I'll eat later.' Santiago grabbed a packet of Chesterfields and slipped it in his pocket. Montse, although she didn't want to appear impolite, couldn't take her eyes off the sickly-looking woman dressed in black from head to toe. Santiago's mother sat at a small table with some knitting patterns and a skein of wool on it. The boy gestured to Montse to wait for him and disappeared in the back room of the shop. She felt tense. She didn't know what to do or say to the woman who was knitting without lifting her gaze from the needles. Standing still, she just looked at the piles of cigarette packs. Time moved very slowly.

Suddenly Montse said: 'It looks like it won't be very hot today.' Santiago's mother looked up, left her knitting on the table and stood up.

'Sorry, I didn't hear you come in,' said the woman, as if it were the first time she'd seen her. 'What would you like?' Montse froze.

'Nothing, thanks. I'm Montse, Santiago's friend.' The woman looked at her, trying to place her.

'Montse, yes, of course. Santi is not here yet. He's at the garage. If you like, I'll tell him you came by at noon.' Montse nodded. The woman sat back down and resumed her knitting. Presently Santiago reappeared, with a hand in his pocket. He kissed his mother.

'I'm going now, mum.' The woman said goodbye without even lifting her head.

Out in the street, Montse tried to smile.

'She's a very handsome woman, your mother.'

'You should have seen her a few years ago, I've got pictures form the time she came to Barcelona and met my...' His face darkened. He took his hand out of his pocket and showed her a silver ring, then slipped it on the finger where it fitted best. Montse smiled at him.

'Is it for me?'

'Of course. It's a family ring. My grandmother gave it to my mother, and now it's yours.' Montse took Santiago by both hands.

'What's wrong with your mother, Santi? Is she ill?'

'I don't know. The doctor says it's nerves. I've always seen her like that, so I'm used to it.' Santiago was anxious, and jumped up and down on the balls of his feet. 'Let's go now; it's very hot in this neighbourhood,' he told Montse.

When Santiago San Román opened his eyes, the sun had already reached the balcony outside Montse's bedroom. It took him a moment to remember where he was. He was surprised to find the girl's body beside him. He had a sweet taste in his mouth. Montse's smell suffused the sheets and the pillows. He inhaled it. Asleep she looked so beautiful he didn't want to wake her. He slipped out of bed and got dressed without taking his eyes off her. The house was in total silence. It was still very early. Santiago knew that, after a day off, the maid would not return until after ten, on the way back from the market. He wandered about the corridors, looking at the paintings and the furniture as though he were in a museum. It was the first time he'd been in a carpeted flat. The living room smelled of leather and the velvet of the curtains. He lingered for a bit in a study with bookshelves covering one wall, and degrees and diplomas on the other. Suddenly he felt out of place. He walked round the corridors again, found the door and ran downstairs. Once in the street he checked his pockets: he only had six pesetas. He followed the road until he reached a rubbish bin. He stuck his hands in it and retrieved Montse's books and folder.

Montse opened the door with her eyes red from crying. She looked at Santiago as if he were a ghost.

'You're an idiot,' she said, leaning against the door frame. Santiago didn't see what the problem was. He showed her the books.

'This is yours. I don't want my wife to be as ignorant as me.' Montse shivered. She took him by the hand and pulled him inside.

'Come on in, we need to have breakfast before Mari Cruz gets here.'

The noise of the key turning in the lock caught them in the kitchen, while they were warming up some milk. Montse pricked up her ears like a hunting dog. Santiago's heart jumped.

'Is it the maid?'

'Yes,' she replied, trying to remain calm. 'But it's too early, it's not even nine.' That was all she had time to say. Then Mari Cruz appeared, covered in sweat and carrying a big basket. She froze on the threshold, her eyes fixed on Santiago. 'This is Santiago, a classmate from the Academy. He's come to pick me up, as we both take the same bus.' Mari Cruz put the groceries on the table without saying a word. Then she left the kitchen.

'She didn't buy it,' he said.

'I don't care. She can't say anything, trust me.' When Montse went to her room to get ready, the maid came back into the kitchen, as though she'd been waiting for her cue behind the door.

'I know you,' said Mari Cruz in a menacing tone.

'Don't think so, it's the first time I've come round.'

'Maybe, but I've seen you in the neighbourhood.' Santiago held his breath and his gaze.

'Aren't you Culiverde's grandson?' He thought of running away without giving any explanations, but something kept him glued to the spot. 'Aren't you the tobacconist's son?'

'I don't know what you're talking about.' Mari Cruz positioned herself in the doorway, with arms akimbo.

'Look, young man, I may not know what you're up to here, but I can imagine. You're looking for a rich kid to cosy up to. But make no mistake. If you try to pull the wool over this girl's eyes, I'll report you. You understand? This is a decent household. You'd do better by helping your mother, she could use a hand.' Mari Cruz fell silent as soon as she heard Montse's steps in the corridor behind her. The girl picked up her books and folder from the kitchen table and gestured to Santiago to follow her. She said goodbye to the maid. ''bye, *señorita*. Shall I expect you for lunch?'

'Not today. I'm eating at Nuria's.'

★★★

The lights of the vestibule startled Doctor Cambra. She raised her head and opened her eyes. An elderly woman cautiously approached her.

'Are you all right?'

Montserrat Cambra stood up and tried to appear normal.

'I'm fine, thanks. I'm waiting for someone.'

The woman started up the stairs with great difficulty, holding onto the handrail. From her breathing Montse could tell she suffered from asthma. Her anxiety had passed. Although she knew Ayach Bachir's address by heart, she checked the piece of paper she had in her handbag one last time.

The Saharawi was a thin man, with clear-cut features and dark skin. He had very short hair and a two-day stubble, and looked about twenty-five. He was casually dressed, in jeans and an unfashionable jumper. He shook Montse's hand feebly, and then invited her in. It was a modest household, with old floorboards and bare walls. In the living room there was very little furniture: an armchair, two chairs, a coffee table, a 1970s unit against the wall, and a lamp that looked even older than the other pieces. The floor was covered by a large, colourful carpet. The room gave onto a balcony, and the window, which was too small, didn't have any curtains. It seemed as though all the furniture had been left behind by previous tenants. The unit was almost empty, as if about to be moved. In the middle of the room were a primus stove and a tray with small glasses and a teapot on it. On entering the room Montse saw a young man looking out of the window. He was younger and more slender than Ayach. She was introduced to him, but was unable to understand his name. Montse sat in the armchair and Ayach Bachir took the chair. The boy sat down on the carpet and, without saying a word, turned on the primus stove and put the kettle on. From the moment she'd come in, Montse had been able to hear a baby crying. It seemed to be coming from a room on the other side of the wall.

After a few polite phrases, Montserrat Cambra took out the photograph and gave it to Ayach. The Saharawi stared at it. He trailed a finger over it, as if he was trying to recover from the paper the touch of his wife. Montse observed a respectful silence. She didn't know where to begin.

'You see, I didn't tell you everything on the phone, because I wanted to discuss the picture with you first. And now I don't know how to say it.'

Ayach looked at her in confusion. The other Saharawi went on preparing the tea, oblivious to Montse's words.

'I don't understand,' said the Ayach.

'Let me explain. I used to know the guy in the *djellaba* – a long time ago, though.'

'The one in the *derraha*?'

'Yes, but that man died many years ago in the Sahara. It happened in Marcha Verde. At least that's what they told me. Now, the other night, after your wife's accident, I found this picture among her personal belongings. I have no doubt it's him, but the date on the back is later than the date of his death. And I know for a fact that the dead don't come back.'

Montse regretted these last words, and Ayach Bachir realised she felt ill-at-ease. They looked at each other without saying anything else, until the Saharawi turned his eyes back to the picture.

'This man is not dead,' he said firmly. 'He came to my

wedding three years ago.'

Montse took a deep breath and asked Ayach to look at the photograph again to make sure. He did so.

Yes, he's my wife's uncle.'

'Mamia Salek's?'

He smiled in appreciation of her remembering the deceased's name. He seemed moved.

'Yes. The last time I saw him was at our wedding. My wife loved him like a father. He used to live at the Bir Gandus *daira*[11], in the *wilaya* of Ausserd.'

Montse could not hide her disappointment on hearing those words. She hung her head and looked at the boy making tea.

'Then there's been a confusion,' she said in a hushed voice. 'The man I was referring to was Spanish, but they look so alike...'

'I didn't say that this man was Saharawi, only that he was my wife's uncle. My wife would have told you lots of stories about him. But one thing I'm sure of is that he was born in Spain.'

'Do you remember his name?'

'Yusuf, they called him Yusuf. I don't know his Christian name. The other man in the picture is Lazaar Baha, his brother in law. He died when Mauritania attacked the capital, like our president. I was born that year.'

'Does the name Santiago San Román ring a bell?'

'No, I've never heard it.' Ayach Bachir fixed his eyes on the photograph once again. 'I didn't see him much. We barely exchanged a few words, I can't remember. My wife had more recent pictures of him. He's changed a lot. He was badly wounded in the war. He didn't strike me as being entirely together. They say the death of his wife upset the balance of his mind.'

The other Saharawi held out a small tray to Montse. She picked up a glass and Ayach Bachir another. Montse's hands trembled as she took it to her lips. Now the child's crying was

---

[11.] *Daira:* A smaller Algerian administrative division, akin to a county.

louder. At that moment she understood it had been a bad idea to come over. The past could not be changed. Not even hers. And yet she could not help asking:

'So he was married?'

'Yes, to my wife's aunt. A daughter of his studies in Libya and his son was killed by a landmine near the Wall.'

What wall? Where was Ausserd? What was a *wilaya*? Montse tried not to think about these things, but questions kept popping into her head. A woman came into the living room and stood still on seeing Montse. She had long black hair, and was wearing jeans. She apologised for interrupting and exchanged a few words with Ayach Bachir in Arabic. The other Saharawi said something as well; he sounded upset. The woman looked worried. All three spoke in low voices, as if they didn't want to disturb their guest. Ayach left the room. The other Saharawi started preparing a second round of tea. He looked up and smiled. Then he went back to what he was doing. Ayach came back and apologised.

'I'm sorry. Fatma's son is ill. And she's worried because she doesn't know what the problem is.'

'Was that him crying?'

The Saharawi nodded. Montse stood up and left her handbag on the armchair. The two men looked at her in confusion. Montse's face, all of a sudden, had grown serious and tense. She looked cross.

'Where is the child?'

'In the women's room.'

Montse went to the corridor and let the crying guide her to the room. Fatma and an elderly woman, both sitting on the floor, were trying to appease the child. The doctor approached and asked their permission to pick him up.

'Don't worry, I'm a doctor.'

Fatma's face lit up. She stood up and gave her the baby. Montse lay him down on a mattress. He must have been four or five months old.

'He's been crying since noon. And he refuses to be fed,' explained Fatma, weeping.

'When did he last suckle?'

'At ten,' said the other woman without hesitation.

The two men looked in from the door, disconcerted, without daring to take part in the conversation.

A sacred silence descended on the room as the doctor examined the baby. She lifted his clothes, undid the nappy and felt his groin, stomach and chest.

'He needs liquid. He's nearly dehydrated.'

'He won't open his mouth,' said Fatma, bursting into tears.

The doctor turned over and examined the faeces in the nappy.

'He's got a strong colic. Don't cry, please, it's nothing serious. We need to give him an infusion of fennel, camomile and aniseed. In babies the gallbladder is not fully developed and it's common for this to happen. For now we'll give him some camomile with a syringe for him to swallow. If it works with cats, it must work with babies,' she said, trying to dissipate the tension and make the mother smile.

Fatma stopped crying. Ayach Bachir looked at Montse awkwardly, without knowing what to say. He still had the picture in his hands. For a moment he tried to imagine the woman's story.

'Tomorrow I'll call Rabuni,' the Saharawi said. 'If this man is the Spaniard you believe he is, then my father must know him. He's got the memory of an elephant: he can still recite from memory the names of all the dead he left behind in our country before he fled.'

Doctor Montserrat Cambra smiled at him with a mixture of gratitude and uncertainty.

Chapter Ten

THE TRUCK IS GLIDING ALONG THE *HAMMADA*. IT ISN'T A long way between the Smara Hospital and the *daira* of Bir Lehru, but to Montse it feels like an eternity. She's travelling in the cab, between the driver and Layla. In the back are three young men and a goat. The Saharawi who is driving has not uttered a single word during the whole journey. Now, as Bir Lehru comes into view in the distance, he exchanges a few phrases with Layla. The nurse seems angry with him. Yet the man remains indifferent to her reproaches. One could even say he enjoys seeing her like that. Montse does not understand a thing, and doesn't dare to ask questions.

The vehicle goes up a gentle slope and stops in front of a humble brick-and-cement building with a whitewashed façade. Layla extricates herself from the truck and helps Montse out. The driver smiles with his pipe in his mouth. By way of goodbye Layla slams the door and utters a phrase that sounds like an insult.

'He's a cretin,' she explains to Montse. 'He won't takes us any nearer my *jaima*. He says it's getting late and has to be home. He's a friend of my father's, but I didn't want to marry him when I returned to the Sahara.'

'Don't worry about it,' replies Montse, amused. 'This is a lovely place.'

In the sunset, the pale colours of the houses in Bir Lehru set off the intense ochre of the desert. The small elevation where Montse and Layla are standing, and on which a special-needs school has been built, commands a superb view of the desert. The roofs of the *jaimas* break up the monotony of the horizon. Against the last slanting rays of sun the water tanks shine brightly. There's a slight breeze blowing, which makes the landscape of the *daira* more pleasant. Now and again, the bleating of a goat shatters the seemingly sacred silence. The bluish green of the *jaimas* contrasts with the much poorer adobe buildings.

Montse takes a deep breath. She feels tired. The beauty of such an arid place sends a shiver down her spine. The desert and the sky meet in an almost imperceptible line.

'Look,' says Layla, stretching her arm. 'Down there is my house.'

Montse looks where she's pointing, but all the *jaimas* look the same.

'Wait a moment, I'd like to enjoy the fresh air,' says Montse. Layla pulls up her *melfa* and sits on the ground. Montse does so as well. In one of the far areas of the camp stands a mud wall, almost completely covered in sand, which surrounds two or three hectares planted with trees and tomato bushes. Montse is surprised to find an oasis like that in the middle of such a hostile desert.

'We built that orchard. It looks like a picture, but it's real. The water is very salty here, but it yields tomatoes and some lettuce.'

'And the school?' asked Montse, pointing to the brick building.

'It's for sick children, mentally handicapped ones, actually.'

'Now, if you've managed to build hospitals and schools, how come you're still living in tents after twenty-five years?'

Layla smiles, as if she had been expecting the question and has a ready-made answer.

'We could lay down foundations for buildings, plan streets, dig drains into the ground. But that would mean we're giving up. We're only here temporarily, because our country is occupied by invaders. Once the war is over, we'll go back. And all this will be swallowed by the desert. Right now the tents can be taken down in two days, and we could be in our country in less than a week.'

Montse doesn't know what to say. She wouldn't have thought that within a fragile-looking woman like her friend lurked such firm courage and resolve. She winks at her and takes her hand. Layla goes back to being her usual gentle self.

'Last night you spoke in your sleep again,' she says, drawing the *melfa* behind her ears. 'There's nothing to be afraid of now. I'm sure that woman is only a mirage. If she had existed, our soldiers would have found her. The dead don't disappear so easily in the desert, although it might seem so. Besides, a scorpion sting causes hallucinations.'

Montse fixes her gaze on the line of *jaima*s below.·

'You're right. I'd also like to think it was a hallucination. But I cannot explain away the nightmare about Tindouf. That really did happen. I feel like such an idiot now…'

Eventually she agreed to cover her head to go out. But when she crossed the door, the lady of the house went after her and didn't leave her side, even though Montse wanted to be alone to try and find a phone. The Algerian wore a serious expression, and was visibly annoyed by the fact that Montse wanted to go out on her own. Montse found the situation so absurd that at times she wanted to laugh. At others, however, she had to struggle not to cry. The children would follow her as well, trailing a few steps behind her. If Montse stopped off, the woman did so too, and if she walked faster, the woman matched her step for step. Both looked thoroughly exasperated. Montse had decided no longer to speak to her. The Algerian barely spoke any French, and Montse knew no more than a dozen poorly pronounced phrases in the language.

After looking for a phone booth at every corner she passed, Montse thought she heard someone curse in Spanish. She turned round and saw an old truck, with a trailer covered by a hole-ridden tarpaulin, parked at a petrol station. Without thinking, she walked straight over. The Algerian woman's shouts did not intimidate her this time. A man of about sixty was talking to the station employee. He was dressed in the remains of various military uniforms, sported a grey beard down to his chest, and had both arms covered in tattoos. Montse recognised the hat of the Legion, and saw a Spanish flag embroidered on each of his sleeves. She approached the man like a castaway who finds a floating plank at sea.

'Excuse me, are you Spanish?' The man turned round as though he could barely believe his ears. He looked her up and down and put his hands on his belt buckle. He was slow to reply, however.

'For the love of God, where did you come from?' Montse was so excited that her explanations barely made any sense. She tried to tell the stranger everything, and seemed incapable of expressing herself coherently. From across the street, the Algerian woman looked at the scene incredulously, without daring to approach.

'I need to make a phone call. They should have collected me from the airport yesterday, but no one showed up. My suitcase is at that woman's house, and they almost didn't let me out.' The Spaniard looked to where Montse was pointing. As soon as the Algerian realised they were discussing her, she covered her face and quickly walked away.

'Don't be afraid, madam, you're safe with me. You've been very lucky to find me. Believe me, very lucky.' In spite of his strong smell, Montse could have hugged him.

'Can you tell me where I can find a phone?'

'I'll do something better. I'll take you to the Spanish consulate and they'll take care of everything.' Montse could not believe it would all be solved so easily after so much trouble. She mentally pinched herself to make sure she was not dreaming.

'My suitcase is still at that woman's house,' insisted Montse.

'I know how to get there, but I would really appreciate it if you came over with me. I don't understand what they want from me.'

'Do you have anything of value in your suitcase?' Montse thought for a moment before replying. Her instinct told her to be cautious.

'Nothing expensive. What little money I have and my passport I carry on me.' The man thought it over. He paid the employee with some dirty, crumpled notes, and said a few words to him in French.

'Get in the truck, madam. We're leaving straight away.' Montse climbed into the cab and soon began to understand that things were not going to be as easy as she had thought.

As soon as the erstwhile legionnaire got behind the wheel, two other men entered the cab. They were Muslims, and were wearing turbans and army boots. From the noise Montse could tell a few other men were climbing onto the trailer. 'They're good people, madam. Real patriots,' the legionnaire said, referring to the Algerians. The truck pulled out, and Montse was caught between the driver and the other two. Their smell was nauseating. Despite the noise of the engine, she could hear the shouting in the back.

'The house is at the end of this street, on the left. Those grey blockish buildings,' explained Montse. The legionnaire put an unlit cigar in his mouth and chewed on it while looking straight ahead. Montse got alarmed when they went past the street. 'It's back there, in those little houses.' The legionnaire smiled.

'Don't worry, madam; going into that neighbourhood is really not worth it. Only riff raff live there, thieves and whores, if you'll excuse the language. Nothing else. If you haven't got anything valuable in your suitcase you'd better forget about it. Trust me.'

As the last houses receded into the distance, Montse's feelings became more and more mixed. On the one hand, she was glad to leave that hellhole behind; on the other, she knew she shouldn't have climbed into the truck without knowing if the man was trustworthy. As her suspicions increased, the legionnaire talked and talked. He seemed to enjoy soldierly bravado. The other two men remained silent, smoking impassively. When the legionnaire paused for breath, Montse saw an opening in which to ask: 'What city is the Spanish consulate in?' The man was slow to answer, and Montse had the feeling he was playing for time. Then he mentioned an Arabic name that she didn't catch. 'And is that far from Tindouf?'

'In the desert, madam, you can never be sure what's near or far. It depends what you compare it with. Did you say you came from Madrid?'

'No, I didn't say that.'

'I beg your pardon, I thought you had.'

'I came from Barcelona.'

The legionnaire went on asking Montse about the details of her journey. She raised her guard, for the questions had turned into a kind of interrogation. Montse tried to disclose only half of the truth; but the man was clever and at times made her contradict herself. Eventually Montse decided to reply with monosyllables or to pretend that she couldn't hear him over the noise of the engine.

It was difficult to say whether they'd been driving for two or three hours. The tarmac gave way to a dry, dusty path which in turn disappeared a few kilometres later. The truck lurched along the tracks left by other vehicles or simply cut across the desert. They seemed to be going increasingly far from anything. When Montse could barely take it any longer, she saw the glimmer of a village in the distance. The dark shapes contrasted with the ochre of the desert. In the dazzling noonday sun, she couldn't make them out clearly, but she was sure that far on the horizon there were signs of civilization. She even thought she could see some rooftops shining in the sunlight. 'Are we nearly there?' she asked, animated.

'Yes, madam. In five minutes you'll be able to rest.'

As they approached the mirage, Montse felt the blood rush to her face. When they were about one kilometre away, she realised that the place was not a town, or a village, or anything of the sort. The dark shapes and shiny surfaces she had seen were in fact thousands of cars heaped up as scrap metal in the middle of the Sahara. There were so many that pathways ran between them, complete with intersections, in what looked like a monstrous cemetery.

She was dumbstruck. Her mind raced ahead of itself. She crossed her arms and tensed up, as though holding on to an imaginary object. When the men got out of the truck, she followed them, terrified but trying to keep her wits about her.

'You told me you would take me to the consulate.'

'All in good time, madam, all in good time. Once we've dealt with a couple of things, I'll take you to the consul.'

'My husband must be in Tindouf already, and he'll surely alert the Algerian police.' Montse's words sounded like the lies of a desperate little girl. With a quick movement, the legionnaire stuck his hand in Montse's pocket and grabbed her papers. She tried to back away, but two men took her by the arms and held her still. She tried to scream, but her voice faltered. A third man checked her other pockets and took out her wallet and passport. He passed them to the legionnaire as a dog would a gunned-down prey. The latter flicked through it and put it away in one of the several inner pockets of his uniform.

'Now, don't do anything stupid. Even if we let you go, you wouldn't get anywhere on foot. You'd die of thirst and hunger first.'

The legionnaire walked off and the two men dragged Montse behind him. Among the wrecked cars was a small hovel, with a window sealed off by two planks. The man unlocked the padlocks on the door, and the mercenaries pushed Montse in. She fell flat on her face. 'You can scream all you want. No one will hear you.' She stifled a cry of pain. Physical resistance, she knew, was futile, but she wasn't even capable of screaming. She let out a moan and lifted her head. Her nose was bleeding.

'Please, please, please,' she whimpered pleadingly. The door closed. Montse sat up and started asking for help in whispers, afraid to raise her voice. She soon realised she wasn't alone. Although there was very little light, she made out three other women sitting on the floor. They looked at her with as much surprise as her own face was no doubt registering at that moment. She felt inexplicably ashamed and tried to regain her composure, but couldn't stop whimpering. There was really no point in screaming and kicking at the door. She looked at the other women. Little by little she made out their features in the shadows. They were dressed the same as the women she'd seen in Tindouf. In spite of their hardened expressions, they looked scared. Montse tried to communicate with them in Spanish, said a few words in French; but there was no reply. One of the women gestured at her to sit down. Montse fell on her knees and buried her face in her hands. Could things get any worse? She cried inconsolably for a long time, until her tears and strength ran out. When she tried to reconcile herself to the idea that this was a hopeless situation, a woman sat next to her and put her hand on her shoulder.

'Here,' the woman said in Spanish. Montse lifted her head as if she'd heard a revelation. The woman held out a ladleful of water. 'You've been losing water for nearly an hour. If you don't drink, you'll get dehydrated.' Montse took the ladle to her lips. She sipped. The water was salty and smelled awful. 'Drink,' said the woman. 'Better to get diarrhoea than to become dehydrated.' Montse drank it up, trying to conceal her disgust.

'Thanks.' The woman went back to her place and crouched down. 'Do you all speak Spanish?'

'Not them.' Montse realised that the woman was dressed differently from the others.

'Are you Algerian?'

'Saharawi.' Montse sat beside her, feeling momentarily relieved.

'From the refugee camps?'

'Have you been there?'

'No, I didn't get that far. I had problems when I got to Tindouf.' Montse started telling the unknown woman everything that had happened to her. The Saharawi listened motionless, clicking her tongue whenever there was a pause. Montse felt much better when she finished the story of her ordeal. The woman didn't take her eyes off her, as if she wanted to make sure that she understood every single word.

'I'm Montse,' she said, breaking the silence.

'I am Aza.'

'And how did you end up here?' Aza made a gesture of despair. She had been shut away in the junk heap with the two Algerians for two days. She'd gone to Tindouf to make a phone call and buy some ballpoint pens. On the way back to the camp, her four-by-four broke down. The two young men who were with her decided to walk the twenty kilometres to their *wilaya* while she remained in the vehicle, waiting for them to come back with help. She had food and water, so there was nothing to worry about. But the Spaniard's truck came by and offered her a lift. The rest Montse could guess. 'And what do you think they'll do to us?' Montse asked naively. Aza's face grew worried, and she buried it in her *melfa*. She didn't say anything.

Time stood still inside the hovel. The first two days seemed interminable. They heard the men talking outside, but couldn't see anything through the cracks in the window. Montse had to be allowed out a few times because of her upset stomach. Seeing the sunlight and breathing in clean air was her only luxury. Aza and the Muslim women endured the imprisonment much better than she did. They could sit still for hours, without moving, drinking or eating. Montse clung to the Saharawi in order not to lose her mind. She did everything Aza told her to: she drank the stagnant water, ate the rotten fruit and tried not to move much when it was very hot. The three women, it seemed to Montse, showed superhuman endurance. When she felt she couldn't take it anymore, she talked to Aza. She learned the Saharawi's strong Caribbean accent stemmed from the many years she'd spent in Cuba as a student. But when Montse asked her about her life in more detail, Aza would shut down and change the subject.

'Who are these men, Aza?'

'Mean people, my friend.'

'But what do they want?'

'I don't know, and I'd rather not think about it until the moment comes.' She would then click her tongue and wave away the flies with extraordinary elegance.

On the third day they heard the engine of the truck roaring again. The four women grew alert, thinking the men would leave them behind on their own. But soon the door opened and they were led into the trailer. In spite of the appalling conditions, the journey felt like a small luxury in comparison with the days shut away in the hut. Montse looked at the immensity of the Sahara through the planks half-covered by the canvas. They drove for more than three hours. The truck finally stopped by the side of a well surrounded by a few trees. It was the only sign of life they'd seen in several kilometres. The rocks were smouldering.

Layla looks serious, engrossed as she is in Montse's tale. After a moment of silence she clicks her tongue and looks towards the *jaima*s, which are barely visible in the declining sunlight.

'Why do you do that?' asks Montse.

'Do what?'

'That clicking with the tongue.'

'It's a habit.'

'Aza used to do just that. She can't be a hallucination.'

'No, it doesn't sound like she was. But let's go now, it's getting dark.'

The *jaima*s are set considerably wide apart, and there are no streets between them. The mud buildings have no identifying feature: they all look the same. Layla moves in the dark as if she were in broad daylight. They walk slowly. When they reach her *jaima*, Layla starts shouting to the people inside. A woman comes out and starts shouting in her turn. She looks angry and startles Montse.

'She's my aunt, don't worry. She's telling me off for being late.'

They walk into the tent, and Montse is amazed by the world that opens before her eyes. Men and women are crouching down on brightly coloured carpets. A fluorescent tube powered by a car battery hangs in the middle of the *jaima*. There are several children about. The women's *melfa*s and the girls' dresses are like bursts of colour in the white light. Montse's heart misses a beat. She takes off her boots and starts to greet everybody. Almost everyone speaks Spanish, with a strong Arabic accent. The children want to touch her and sit beside her. Layla introduces everybody, and Montse cannot remember the names for more than a few seconds. She retains the expression in the eyes, the smiles, the gestures. She feels tired, and finally sits down.

Layla speaks for her. Montse likes to hear her talk in Hassaniya. Someone offers her a glass of tea, which she gladly accepts. Children from other *jaima*s keep pouring in. Layla's aunt tries to frighten them away as if they were chickens, but the children offer resistance. An old man shouts at them and, finally, they reluctantly leave, though they sit outside in the sand, only a few metres away from the entrance. Montse cannot cope with the attention from so many people. For a moment she is overwhelmed. Layla looks at her and understands she is very tired. The nurse stands up and starts making gestures. No doubt she is asking the others to leave. Montse tries to stop her, but Layla is determined. Everyone gets up without a fuss. One by one, the men shake Montse's hand and walk out. Then it's the womens' turn. Layla's aunt lags behind. She keeps giving her niece instructions. By the time they are both alone, Montse is exhausted.

'You shouldn't have sent them away. I'm pleased to meet them.'

'They talk too much. They'll stay here all night if you let them. They are in no hurry. They've been known to spend four days chatting and drinking tea just because there was a visitor from another *daira*.'

Montse smiles but shows signs of fatigue. Layla takes a couple of blankets from the cupboard and spreads them over the carpet.

'Tonight no one will bother you.'

'No one bothers me, Layla. Don't tell me you're sending your aunt away, too.'

'She'll be fine anywhere else. You're my guest.'

Montse has no strength to argue. She looks quietly at Layla, who's looking for something in the cupboard. Eventually she takes out a pair of scissors. She sits down next to Montse and tells her to lower her head.

'What are you doing?'

'I'm cutting your hair. Isn't that what you wanted?'

Montse smiles. She tries to feel as peaceful as Layla seems to be. She draws near and lets her do as she wishes. The Saharawi cuts lock after lock, making a little heap on the floor. The rhythmic sound of the scissors and Layla's hands make Montse sleepy, but she doesn't want to miss a thing. She struggles to stay awake.

'Layla.'

'Yes?'

'I lied to you.' Layla doesn't say anything. 'Well, I didn't exactly lie, though I didn't tell you the whole truth either.'

Montse goes quiet, but the nurse doesn't want to press further lest she give the impression of being too curious.

'I do have a daughter. But she died last year.'

It's the first time Montse has spoken about her daughter since her death. She feels relieved. Layla clicks her tongue and goes quiet.

'She had an accident on her motorcycle. She was nineteen, and her name was Teresa, like my sister.'

After that she only hears the sound of the scissors and the wind beating against the canvas of the *jaima*. The last thing she hears before falling asleep is Layla's voice:

'Thank you.'

Chapter Eleven

SOLDIERS WHO'D NEVER READ A NEWSPAPER IN THEIR LIVES could now be seen queuing up for one, or standing in circles while the better educated read the news from Spain out loud. The Spanish government had sold the largest share of the phosphate mining company Fos Bu Craa to Morocco, but the news arrived quite late in El Aaiún. By the time it spread among the civil servants, the deterioration of public life was apparent. In the barracks the officers barely mentioned the pro-independence revolts taking place in the streets to the troops. The robbery of the church and the murder of the sacristan had upset the precarious stability between Saharawis and Spaniards.

Very few things, apart from sergeant Baquedano's presence, worried Santiago San Román or caused him to lose sleep. Yet the general insecurity in the barracks unsettled him. He often found conversations about politics tedious and difficult to follow. April and May saw the coming and going of troops, new orders from superiors, counter-orders, manoeuvres, and night-time operations. Many blamed the Polisario Front for all the outrages that were being committed, and the desecration of the Church was the straw that broke the camel's back. The press called it a terrorist act. San Román was frightened by the memory of that night, and struggled not to think about his participation in it. He tried to salve his conscience by not adding his voice to the proclamations against the Polisario Front and its supporters.

Guillermo experienced things differently. The building

works at the zoo stopped, and most of his company was assigned to planting landmines on the border with Morocco. When the landmines ran out, they started planting plastic fakes, which looked so real that they caused confusion, which led to some fatal mistakes for the people handling them.

Meanwhile, San Román was required to drive Land Rovers, official vehicles, trucks, diggers, anything with a steering wheel and an engine. Every day he would encounter battalions on the road who were out on a mission or returning in a state of exhaustion to the capital. At least three times a week he had to transport security troops to the Bu Craa phosphate deposits. The fear of sabotage was rife not only among workers but also among the directors of the state company, who lived in the city. Only a year earlier, the conveyor belt used to carry the phosphates to the sea had been set on fire by a group of young Saharawi workers, who were at present serving prison sentences in the Canary Islands. Now soldiers and legionnaires spent endless hours in the blazing Sahara sun, stopping even the foxes from coming near the conveyor belt and its premises. The offices and personal residences of high-ranking civil servants were also guarded by soldiers.

The atmosphere in the streets was charged, which Santiago San Román thought absurd. The Instituto de Enseñanza Media, the *Parador Nacional*, the Gobierno General del Sahara, and the Estado Mayor building, were guarded by soldiers at all times. He had often seen patrols armed with Cetme rifles or machine guns who mingled with the civilian population and were suspicious of anything out of the ordinary. But now everything in El Aaiún was out of the ordinary. Whenever Santiago had to ask a Saharawi for his ID or stop a vehicle, he would look at the papers without paying much attention, exchange greetings in Hassaniya, and send them on their way; people responded with a mixture of annoyance and surprise. Santiago felt awkward during the searches and controls carried out in the main junctions. But he was happy to patrol the street market or the souk. On those occasions he was always on the lookout for Andía, her mother, her cousins or any of the women of her extended family.

Lazaar wouldn't take him seriously. He started laughing whenever San Román spoke to him about his sister. Santiago was annoyed at how frivolously his friend dealt with Andía.

'You're in love with Andía? But she's only a girl.'

'She's seventeen.'

'Is that what she said?' Lazaar asked, laughing. 'You'll soon be discharged, go back to your city and never come back. And you probably have a girlfriend in Barcelona already.'

'No, no. You're crazy, man.'

However, it was different with the family. Santiago was embarrassed to find out that Andía's mother, aunts and younger sisters would do anything to please him. Their house underwent a transformation that he took a while to notice. The walls, initially devoid of decoration, were covered with photographs and posters, the point of which he couldn't quite see. Sometimes it was maps of the Iberian peninsula, or newspaper cuttings about famous people: photographs of Franco, Carmen Sevilla during his Christmas visit of 1957, Fraga Iribarme inaugurating the *Parador Nacional*, calendars showing Julio Romero de Torres, matadors, footballers. He didn't make much of this at first, but later understood they did it to please him. They also started replacing the Saharawi music with pasodobles or boleros sung by Antonio Machín. Santiago tried to repay their kindness in his own way.

The family relations were so extended and complex that he was never sure who was a cousins, brother-in-law, sibling or a distant relative. But he tried to be nice to everyone. He would teach the men how to take apart and clean a carburettor, replacesits hoses, or recognise the faults of an engine from its noise. Andía's little brothers followed him everywhere. However, the real man of the household, since the father's death, was Lazaar. He was revered not only by the family, but by the neighbours as well. Anything Lazaar said was immediately acknowledged as true. And so San Román knew that, until the Saharawi took him seriously, he had little chance with his sister.

Andía, for her part, would sometimes behave like a woman and sometimes like a girl, but Santiago did not dislike the ambiguity. Whenever he found himself with a couple of hours to spare, he would go up to the Zemla quarter and sit down to share some tea with whomever happened to be there. The girl welcomed him in a casual manner, as though she was used to his presence, but she would avoid his charged glances, his attempts to get closer to her, or the covert compliments he paid her. He spent more time talking to the family than to her. Sometimes she would go to another room and not even come to the door to see him off. Santiago found these customs deeply irritating, and would often leave the house promising himself never to return. Yet the presents Andía gave him in secret, her evasive eyes, the small attentions she had for him, or her nervousness when he spoke to her, raised his hopes again and he came back whenever he had a chance.

When he told Guillermo what was happening with Andía, his friend didn't know whether to be glad for him or help him get her off his mind. At least Santiago no longer spoke of Montse, nor asked him to phone or write letters to her. Guillermo was sure that the infatuation with the Saharawi would lead nowhere, but Santiago seemed so taken with her that Guillermo could not be entirely honest. Unlike San Román, Guillermo viewed the situation in Western Sahara with anxiety. Lacking informed opinions, he let himself be influenced by rumours, what he heard in the soldiers' mess and saw in the streets. Planting landmines was a terrible job. Nor did the officers seem to know what was really going on. When he asked a sergeant or a simple corporal, they reprimanded him or told him to shut up. But their faces looked obviously worried.

San Román was only worried by his conscience and by the prospect of meeting Sergeant Baquedano. He was happy when he took part in operations that lasted several days, when he was sent out to patrol the streets, or when he was dispatched with the new recruits to the training grounds, twenty kilometres away from the city, by the sea. Sooner or later, though, he knew that he was bound to bump into Baquedano and would have to stand to attention. This finally happened on a morning when the sergeant entered the regiment riding on the side of a truck. As soon as he saw San Román, he jumped off and quickly walked towards him. The soldier saluted and stood to attention.

'San Román, I've got something for you.'

Santiago started sweating, and tried to conceal the trembling of his legs.

'At your command, sir.'

'I want you to sit the exam for corporal.'

'Corporal, sir?'

'Yes, corporal. You know what that is don't you?'

'Of course, sir. But you need to study and have a head for figures.'

'Don't tell me you can't read and write.'

'No, sir. I mean, I do, sir. Read and write, yes, in my own way. But I'm not really good with numbers.'

'I won't take any nancy-boy excuses. You're a legionnaire, you hear me? You don't need to read or write. All you need is balls. Like these ones. Don't tell me you haven't got any?'

'No, sir. I mean, yes, sir. Of course I have.'

'Then sit the examination, damn it. That's an order! Saturday. Don't get drunk or go whoring on Friday. Saturday at eight I want you at the officers' pavilion. The Legion need patriots like you.'

The following Monday Santiago San Román was already a Corporal of the Legion. His peers, including Guillermo, started to treat him differently. He wanted to impress Lazaar when he turned up at the Nomad Troops' pavilion, but the Saharawi only glanced at his stripes, looked him in the eye and said sarcastically:

'Now you'll get some real girlfriends.'

The phrase hurt him like an act of treachery. So much so, that the following day he refused to be the Saharawis' goalkeeper.

Things were changing apace. A few days later, after returning from a reconnaissance mission, he found Lazaar waiting for him at the football pitch. He looked very serious; Santiago had further reason to worry when he heard Lazaar's first sentence.

'Listen, San Román, I don't know how to tell you this without causing offence.'

The corporal didn't know what to expect. A thousand things went through his mind, but none as bad as what was to come.

'Come on, Lazaar, I'm your friend. Say it. Whatever it is.'

'Are you my friend?'

'Of course I am. You know it. Why do you ask now?'

'Well, then you'll understand that sometimes friends have to do things they don't like, if it's good for the other one.'

'You can ask me whatever you like: it won't frighten me.'

Lazaar looked Santiago straight in the eye. He was holding him by one hand, and had his other on his shoulder.

'I'd rather you didn't come to my house. At least for now.'

Corporal San Román swallowed. It felt as though all his blood had left his brain.

'Of course, of course,' he said, without letting go of Lazaar's hand. 'It's because of your sister, right?'

'No, it's not because of her. I know she's fond of you, although she's only a child of fifteen. It's because of me.'

'Have I offended you?'

'On the contrary. I'm proud to be your friend. But things are not as simple as they look. One day you'll understand, but I can't explain it to you right now.'

These words disconcerted San Román. He couldn't believe there might be any reason other than Andía for him not to be welcome at Lazaar's. He would never have thought that the young Saharawi would cause him such distress. Nor did he believe that he would ever understand what was happening. He felt despondent.

He stayed away from Lazaar's for two weeks. When he patrolled the city he would look up to the stone houses and wonder what Andía might be doing. He stopped eating and sleeping well. Once again a woman had destabilized his life and become an obsession. He still spent his spare time with friends from the Nomad Troops, but his relationship with Lazaar wasn't the same. Santiago felt a mixture of admiration and envy for the Saharawi. He seemed special. He was familiar with the secrets of the desert and the language of the dromedaries; he knew as much about the climate and geography of the desert as an old man. But in the course of two weeks their relationship cooled to the point that they only said hello and exchanged a few polite words.

At the beginning of May, however, something happened which helped San Román get out of the hole he was in. He was driving a truck full of supplies across the Colomina quarter. There was an armed soldier in the passenger's seat, and another one in the back. Santiago was half-listening to the soldiers' talk when he thought he saw Andía in the crowd, walking down the street. He slammed on the brakes and almost called out to her, but was wise enough not to. He knew he could not abandon the truck or go off the set route without a good excuse. The other legionnaire seemed frightened when the vehicle stopped.

'What's going on, Corporal? Did you see anything?'

Santiago was craning his neck out of the window, trying to make sure it was Andía. It was the first time he'd seen her outside her neighbourhood.

'Stay in the truck. I think there's something weird ahead of us. It's a bit strange.'

The soldier went pale. He looked everywhere, holding on to his Cetme rifle, trying to spot the danger. Corporal San Román jumped out.

'I need to make sure,' he shouted with forced authority. 'Don't move away from the truck unless they shoot at you.'

Santiago ran down the street after the girl. When she turned a corner, he approached her. He was greatly relieved not to have been wrong. Andía was with another Saharawi girl who, on seeing him, instinctively covered her face with her *melfa* and blurted out a few words in Hassaniya. Santiago didn't catch their meaning. She was addressing her friend, who couldn't stop laughing as she covered her own face. After a while, the girl went quiet and serious.

'What are you doing here, Andía? Where are you going? Is this a friend of yours?'

'My brother told me you'd gone back Spain, that you'd been discharged.'

'It's not true, Andía. I would never leave without saying goodbye. Actually, I wouldn't leave without you: you're my girlfriend.'

A smile returned to the Saharawi's face, and also to her friend's. Santiago was so nervous he hopped about and couldn't stop putting his hands in his pockets, only to take them out again.

'I won't lie to you. It was Lazaar who asked me not to go back to your house. He says it's not because of you, but he hasn't given me any other explanation.'

Andía found it difficult to understand Lazaar's motives. She wrinkled her brow and took her friend by the hand.

'My brother is a busybody. He treats me like a child; he thinks I'm stupid.'

She dragged Santiago and made him walk with her. The friend stood to one side. They walked across the street and Andía asked him to go with her into a Saharawi bazaar. It was very similar to the stores in Hata-Rambla: same smell, same chaos.

'Do you like dates?' Andía asked. 'No, better take raisins. Do you like raisins? No, no, not those.'

She asked the shopkeeper for a pipe with a case and then put it in Santiago's hands.

'Do you like this?'

'A lot, Andía, I like it a lot. But I...'

'I want to give it to you as a gift.'

The friend asked to see some bracelets and tried them on Santiago. She chose one that fitted his wrist.

'Haibbila wants to give you a present too. She's my best friend.'

Santiago didn't know how to thank them for their attentions. He was confused, and quite surprised that two young girls should be capable of such generosity. He said goodbye promising to come and visit her at home as soon as Lazaar went away on manoeuvres. That evening he slept with the bracelet and the pipe in his hands.

The manoeuvres Santiago referred to were in fact a special mission that the Nomad Troops had to carry out at Amgala. But it wasn't made public until a few days later. Like everything else in those days, the movements of the army aspired to secrecy even if it wasn't achieved. On Monday 5th May, a day before leaving, Lazaar went to see Corporal San Román at the soldiers' mess. It was the first time he'd set foot in that place, which surprised Santiago. The words the Saharawi had prepared surprised him even more.

'You know I'm leaving tomorrow on patrol.' Santiago nodded, trying to anticipate Lazaar's thoughts. 'I don't know when I'll be back, so I'd like to ask you a favour.'

'Anything.'

The Saharawi took his time before saying:

'I'd like you to look after my sister and my family.' He paused and studied Santiago's reaction. 'I know they'll be fine, but keep an eye on them for my piece of mind. My brothers are young and busy with other things. They sometimes don't really understand what's going on in the Sahara.'

'You speak as if you're not coming back.'

'Of course I'm coming back. But the situation is worse than they tell us. Morocco is about to pounce on us like a hyena.'

'That won't happen. We're here to stop it. You're a part of Spain.'

'You must be the only optimist left. Which is fine. But I'll feel better knowing that you'll look after my family, whatever happens.'

'You shouldn't need to ask. I'll be happy to do it. But only until you come back.'

'Of course, only until I come back,' he said, smiling.

They hugged and shook hands looking each other in the eye.

Lazaar's words were bewildering. Santiago didn't fully understand their meaning until the following week, when important news reached El Aaiún. At first the information was confusing, even contradictory. Not even the press relayed the events. But eventually the officers informed the soldiers what had happened. On Saturday the 10th of May, 1975, a Nomad Troop patrol, code named 'Pedro', went over to the Polisario Front. They took two Spanish lieutenants, a sergeant and five soldiers as hostages. This happened in Amgala. The following day, a patrol in Mahlbes did the same, though in this case the Spaniards offered resistance, and a soldier and a sergeant were killed. Seven other soldiers were taken prisoner and whisked off to the Algerian border.

As a consequence of these skirmishes and desertions, the situation in El Aaiún became even more tense. Most civil servants had the impression that their days in Africa were numbered. A few optimists trusted the Spanish politicians and tried to carry on with their lives and habits as usual. However, every day there were more walls painted with slogans in favour of the Polisario, calling for independence, or denouncing the King of Morocco, who strongly supported the Spanish province in international forums. Some riots had to be suppressed by force. Both the Spanish and the Saharawis looked after their own interests.

Santiago would listen to the arguments without fully understanding the issues. Every time Guillermo warned him against the risks of going up to Hata-Rambla, they ended up having an argument. He visited Andía anyway, whenever he had a chance. It took him some time to realise that every member of the family was a supporter of the Polisario Front. When one of Lazaar's uncles asked him, in front of the whole family, what he thought of the current situation, the legionnaire scratched his head and tried to clarify his thoughts out loud:

'We Spaniards are not into politics. I only want what's best for you. I leave the rest to those who know.'

Later San Román proved as good as his word. When certain areas were cordoned off with barbed wire to prevent riots, he used his rank to go in and out of the neighbourhood, bring news from outside, find supplies when they were low, and carry letters for the Saharawi soldiers who were not allowed out of the barracks and remained on alert.

Every once in a while, he would remember Montse: there was nothing he could do about it. Her ghost chose random moments; a song, the face of a girl, to stir up painful memories. He would sometimes calculate how long it would be until she gave birth. The idea troubled him, and he could only get it out of his mind when he was with Andía. The Saharawi still treated him with indifference in front of the family. She knew that, if she looked interested in a man in public, her brothers and her mother would go on treating her like a child. No woman she knew would express her feelings in front of other people. One day she asked Santiago:

'When will you be returning to your country?'

'This is my country, Andía.'

But she meant something else.

'You'll leave eventually, won't you?'

'No, I won't. Do you want me to leave?'

'People say you Spaniards will sell us off to Morocco.'

Santiago did not have an answer for that. The more he heard the officers talk, the more confused he felt.

'I'm not leaving. Unless you come with me. *Jaif*?'

'No, I'm not scared. But I know you have a girlfriend in your country. I can tell from the way you look at me.'

'*Nibguk igbala*. I only love you.'

Andía reacted as though she were offended. And yet, underneath her serious expression, a reluctant smile appeared and her eyes twinkled.

Chapter Twelve

THAT NIGHT THE PILLS HAD NO EFFECT. SHE WAS RESTLESS, worried about something she couldn't name or define. In addition, the tea she'd drunk at Ayach's kept her awake. Yet it was a different kind of anxiety from the one she'd experienced in those last few months. She tossed and turned in bed until two in the morning. Then she got up and switched her computer on. The memories of the past day were a confusing amalgam – they were mixed with flashing images and details that she hadn't noticed at the time.

At eight in the morning on 6th January, the city was asleep or about to go to bed. She walked down the Paralelo towards the harbour, enjoying the silent empty streets. The sky was overcast; it was quite humid. For the first time in her life she walked across Plaça del Portal de la Pau, right down the middle. Eventually she stopped at the pier. She could hear echoes of the music spilling out of the bars across the harbour, and she could see a few exhausted people walking out of them, some actually staggering. Beyond, a cottony mist clung to the sea. The landscape looked beautiful in the sunrise. She'd spent several hours in front of the computer, searching for information on the Saharawi camps in Tindouf. Countless pictures of the desert, of the refugee camps, of El Aaiún and Smara had passed before her eyes. The information was now churning in her brain, in sharp contrast to the calm blue blot of the sea and the leaden light of the first hours of the morning.

Santiago San Román had been dead to Montse for twenty-five years. That had been the reality ever since someone broke the news to her. Now she wondered how she had believed what a stranger had told her. But would things have been any different if she had taken the trouble to confirm it? She wasn't sure they would. She tried to remember how long it had taken her to forget him. Not very long: a few months, perhaps. Back then the tension within the family forced her to look ahead and ignore the bouts of nostalgia that sometimes came over her. Fate had played a dirty trick on her by not letting her read those letters at the time they were delivered. But her brilliant Alberto had filled up the space left by Santiago. Perhaps such a space had never even existed. She wasn't sure their love would have lasted very long if the boy had returned to Barcelona. Suddenly she was troubled by the idea that Santiago might think he had a child in Spain. He brought it up in every one of the letters he'd written from El Aaiún. Perhaps that was the only thing that had kept him interested. Yet Santiago did not strike her as a model father. Not that the magnificent Alberto had been one, either.

The shouts of the people coming out of the bars brought her back to reality. It was too early to pay Ayach a visit. She walked along the pier towards Barceloneta. The sleepless night was taking its toll. Her legs shook slightly and her stomach grumbled. Like an automaton, she walked down the streets of that neighbourhood which had once been a revelation in her own city. Now most windows were closed and no music could be heard in the houses. Yet she still remembered the smell of the stews flooding out into the street at noon. She stopped at the tobacconist's and went in. The place had changed considerably. The old wooden shelves had been replaced by spacious glass cabinets, and the counter was lower and shorter. They also sold newspapers and trinkets for children. She bought a packet of Chesterfields. The last time she'd smoked that brand she'd been eighteen. She shivered just from thinking about it. The owner was a young man. She was about to inquire after the woman who'd run the shop in '76 or '77, but held back. It would have been like digging up a mass grave. She saw a sign on the wall indicating where the nearest pharmacy was: Plaça de la Font. She asked the owner for directions, and he indicated the way.

When she reached the square it felt as though it had been waiting for her all these years. A number of cars were now parked around it, but the place had changed very little. She shivered again. An old lady in a pink robe was walking her dog on the pavement. She'd probably already lived there twenty-six years before. And, if not her, one of the neighbours who would soon be coming down to the square. Quite possibly the woman had been right here back in '74, at a street party at the end of August attended by the whole neighbourhood. Montse remembered where the stage had been, and even the name of the band: Rusadir. She approached the lady with the dog and said good morning. The woman greeted her back.

'Is there a pharmacy near here?' asked Montse, just to hear the woman's voice.

'Yes, right over there.'

Montse thanked her, and the woman walked away, complaining out loud about all the litter young people had left on the square.

'It's always the same. They don't care if we end up covered in shit. Of course, later they go back to their own neighbourhoods, which I'm sure are clean enough.'

Perhaps the woman didn't remember that twenty-six years before she too had been at a party on that square; and that, once the music and the dancing had stopped, the square was a mess in just the same way.

It took place at the end of August. Santiago San Román asked Montse:

'Do you fancy going for a dance?'

'Of course. Are you taking me to a club?' she replied.

'On Saturday there's a street party in my neighbourhood. It's not great, but since you accused me of being so ashamed of it...' It was the first time Montse had worn high heels and lipstick out. She had done so several times at home, when there was no one around, thinking the time would never come when she could put into practice everything she'd learned in front of the mirror. She put on a dress which she had seen her mother wearing in some old pictures. It was a cream-coloured number, with a scoop neck and a close-fitted waistline. The satin skirt reached down to her knees, with folds that revealed a flower print. It looked made to measure. She wore a yellow cardigan over her shoulders, and her accessories were a pearl necklace and matching earrings. She also took her mother's white patent leather handbag and leather pumps. She tied her hair into a ponytail with a hair clip. With a bit of red lipstick the transformation was complete. She stood still in front of the mirror, marvelling at the result. For a moment she hesitated, not daring to powder her face. Although she had dreamed of this moment for some time, she was embarrassed to go out like that.

When Santiago San Román saw her, he was speechless. He suddenly felt like a child. He was wearing his white shirt, beige flares and pointy brown leather shoes, but Montse certainly looked more mature than him. She let him kiss her on the cheek so as not to leave any lipstick on him. At the last minute she had put on some mascara and eye-shadow. 'You look like a bride,' said Santiago. The comment went down very well. 'Shall we walk? I'd like everyone to see how beautiful you look.' Montse knew that Santiago didn't have any money for the bus or the metro, so she accepted the idea as a compliment.

They were the most elegant couple of the night. She couldn't take her eyes off him. He was more tanned than ever, and his hair was combed back with brilliantine. She'd never seen such a handsome boy. She liked the fact that the other girls threw her envious looks. Whenever Santiago looked away, she would take him gently by the hand, and he would smile at her. 'You also look beautiful. The most beautiful boy at the party.' Montse had to insist before Santiago let her buy the beers. She could see he felt awkward, perhaps even embarrassed, as he drank. Whenever someone came over to say hello to Santiago, she felt herself being examined. In other circumstances such looks would have made her uncomfortable, but now she was flattered.

'Tell me something, Santi, do you love me?'

'Of course. If I didn't love you, I wouldn't be with you.' Montse was puzzled by how simply he viewed things. But that was also what she found most attractive about him.

'If you love me, why do you never tell me?'

The band was playing the hits of that summer. Neither Montse nor Santiago were really paying attention to the music. She had always felt slightly sick at the sight of girls who clung to their boyfriends, kissed them constantly, rested their wrists on their shoulders, and wrapped their hands around the guys' necks. But now she was acting exactly like the people she had mocked so many times. 'Shall we dance, Santi?'

'Well, I'm not very gracious, you know.' She actually liked that. Guys who danced well didn't strike her as very masculine. Now and again she would ask for a beer. She had given Santiago her purse, and each time he took out a few coins he felt them burning his hands.

The band started playing a pasodoble called 'Las Corsarias'. San Román felt an itch in his stomach. *Far away on Moorish land / On African land, far away / A Spanish soldier would sing / A tune that went this way.* The younger couples moved to one side, while the older ones started dancing with their arms around each other. *Like the wines from Jerez and from Rioja / Are the colours of the Spanish flag.*

'Now I do want to dance,' said Santiago impulsively.

'You want to dance to this? But it's "La banderita".'

'So? It's a pasodoble. It's the only music I know how to dance to. My mother likes it a lot.' Montse let herself be led to the centre of the square. *And the day I die / If I'm away from my homeland / I want to be covered / With the Spanish flag.* Montse felt everyone was looking at her, but Santiago seemed oblivious to it all, and mumbled the lyrics. *When I'm on foreign land / And see your colours / And think of your exploits / See how much I love you.*

'What did you say?' asked Montse, her eyes fixed on his.

'See how much I love you?' whispered Santiago in her ear, and she touched her lips to his. 'See how much I love you, see how much I love you, see how much I love you. Now you can't complain I never say it.'

'Say it again.'

'See how much I love you.'

'Again.'

'See how much I love you.'

When the song finished, and the younger people regained the dance floor, Santiago and Montse were left kissing in the centre, unaware of the music, the noise and the glances. The floor stopped moving only when they opened their eyes.

Little by little the square emptied. Every corner had been filled by litter. Montse didn't want to part from Santiago.

'I want you to spend the night with me.' The boy grew tense, and Montse noticed straight away. 'What is it? You don't want to come over?'

'No, no, it's not that. Well, in a way.'

'You're not making any sense, Santi, a moment ago you said you loved me and now...'

'It's because of the maid.'

'We won't make any noise on the way in, and she sleeps on the other side of the house. After she leaves for mass in the morning, you can go.'

'She knows me,' he confessed, embarrassed. 'She knows my mother. I wouldn't want you to get into trouble because of me.

If your father finds out... You told me that if your father...'
Montse sealed his lips with a kiss.

'I told you that a century ago. I don't care if my father finds
out. Besides, there's no reason why he should. Mari Cruz
knows she can't say anything. Not with me.' Santiago nodded
in acceptance.

They walked through Barceloneta towards Paseo de Colón.
Montse felt very tired. Her feet were sore. They sat in a doorway.

'These shoes are killing me. I'm not used to them.'

'Have a rest.'

'I'd rather take a taxi.' The street was poorly lit. The dark
warehouses of the harbour, looming large behind the buildings,
lent the area a dismal look.

'We won't find a taxi round here,' said Santiago. 'If we don't
get to the main road there's no chance.'

'I can't take another step, Santi.'

'Then I'll go, but I haven't got any money.'

'I can't stay here on my own.' Santiago San Román had an
idea. There was a bike chained to a lamppost.

'Give me one of your hair clips.' Montse did, without
knowing what for. Santiago unlocked the padlock and took the
bike. Montse started pinching him and telling him to give it
back. 'Didn't you say your feet hurt?'

'You're crazy. You'll get us into trouble.'

'No, no. I'll bring it back tomorrow and leave it right here.
The owner will be so happy to see it.' Montse resigned herself
and mounted behind him. For a moment she tried to imagine
what she might look like sitting there, with her fancy dress and
pearl necklace, and could do nothing but laugh.

Doctor Montserrat Cambra stepped into the building in
Barceloneta more decisively than the day before. She'd been
killing time until eleven in the morning. Only the two women
were in.

'Ayach went out this morning to make a phone call from the Western Sahara office,' explained Fatma as she invited her in.

'It doesn't matter. I've actually come to check on the baby. Did he sleep well?'

Fatma smiled.

'He cried, but then he slept a bit.'

Montse went into the women's room. The baby was whimpering. She took everything she'd bought in the pharmacy out of her handbag, and placed it on a night table.

'Let's warm up some milk to give him with the aniseed. He needs to drink plenty of liquids.' Montse removed his nappy. 'And the cream will soothe the irritation.'

The Saharawis did as they were told, without hesitation. Montse spent nearly an hour with the child, until he went quiet and, finally, fell asleep. When she said she was leaving, the women wouldn't let her. They took her into the living room and made some tea. It gave her a much-needed boost. They wouldn't let her go before Ayach Bachir returned.

'Ayach said he'll try to find out more about the man in the picture. Bachir Baiba knows everyone.'

'Who's Bachir Baiba?'

'Ayach's father. He works with the missionaries in Rabuni. He knows everybody. He used to be a Spanish soldier.'

On coming back, Ayach was glad to see her. He'd made a call to the camps in Algeria, and jotted down some information.

'That man's name is Santiago San Román, although now everybody calls him Yusuf. My father is sure; and he's never wrong.'

'And why did they tell me he died?'

'That, I don't know. It's a distance of four inches.'

Montse didn't understand what he meant. The man smiled.

'That's what we say in my country. Between what comes out of people's mouths and what goes into their ears there's only four inches, but that distance can feel greater than the Sahara.'

Montse listened to the man's explanations expectantly. The two women took in every detail.

'Santiago San Román married my wife's aunt. My father knew her. Her name was Andía, and according to my father she was very beautiful. Been dead three or four years now.'

'Santiago?'

'No, his wife. He's alive. My father saw him about a year ago in Ausserd. His health's not too great, apparently. He's quite a guy. According to my father, he was almost sent to the firing squad in El Aaiún for smuggling explosives out of the barracks. My father is very grateful to him for his help. He was very good to the Saharawis.'

Montse remained silent. She found it difficult to imagine that Santiago was as old as her, that he too had aged. She'd banished him from her thoughts too many years ago. She thought of the woman, Andía, whose name was the only thing she knew about her, and was overcome by a sort of adolescent jealousy. It made her laugh. Fatma stared at her.

'Was that man your boyfriend?'

'That boy. To me he's still a boy. But, yes, he was. Actually, he was a little more than just a boyfriend.'

'One never forgets that,' said Fatma with conviction.

'The thing is, I haven't thought of him for many years. It's bizarre: I almost had a child by him, yet sometimes I can't even remember his face. We did a lot of stupid things, the two of us, but nothing as stupid as what I did on my own later. I wonder what he was doing while I was letting life pass me by as if I could start afresh whenever I wanted.'

Montserrat Cambra took the tea glass to her lips. Fatma looked at her in silence, not daring to disturb her thoughts. Montse looked at her dark eyes. She was very beautiful. Had Andía been as beautiful? Jealousy, inexplicably, made her feel good and smile again.

Chapter Thirteen

LONG BEFORE DAWN SHE CAN HEAR THE NOISE OF THE vehicles driving between the tents. Montse knows it's a special day: The Festival of the Sacrifice. In one corner of the *jaima*, on a wooden sideboard that looks as if it had been salvaged from a shipwreck, are the children's dresses, carefully folded. There are so many kids around that Montse hasn't been able to learn all their names. Nor is she sure who is or isn't Layla's brother or sister. A family resemblance is all she can detect. The women barely speak any Spanish, although they understand it.

The night before, the *jaima* had been crowded until late. Most people were soldiers visiting the family on a week's leave to celebrate the Sacrifice. Some had not seen their wives and children for ten months. Montse had to persuade Layla to let her stay up, as though she were a child. She finds the nurse's motherly ways endearing.

When Montse awakes, Layla is already, busy giving instructions to her nephews and nieces. Although she hasn't slept much, Montse feels quite rested. The light coming in through the curtains touches her feet. Montse stretches as she hasn't done in years.

When she goes out to the pen, Layla tells her off for getting up so early.

'It's such a beautiful day it would be a pity to stay in bed,' explains Montse. 'Besides, I want to come to the celebrations with you.'

'Oh, I'm not going. But Brahmin and my sister will take you. I have to prepare the meal and assist on a circumcision.'

Montse nods and tries to keep some order among the children, who are all trying to take her by the hand.

Brahim has tea-stained teeth and eyes reddened by the wind of the desert. His Spanish is quite basic, but he talks through the whole journey. He drives with his hands close together on the top of the wheel, and keeps a pipe hanging from his lips like most Saharawis. He smiles all the time. Montse can barely understand what he says, but is amused by the young man's verbiage. She doesn't know whether he's Layla's brother or brother-in-law. The sister is sitting between them, and doesn't utter a word. Montse asks Brahim if she's his wife, and the Saharawi responds with a puzzled smile, as if he hadn't understood the question. In the open back of the van are a dozen kids from the house and the neighbourhood. They keep their balance expertly, and wave at every vehicle Brahim overtakes. It only takes ten minutes to get to the place of the festivities, but a kilometre more before they arrive; the desert has become a metallic mass of cars and trucks. Thousands of people congregate in an enormous circle. The black and blue turbans stand out against the ochre of the desert.

Montse has borrowed some clothes from Layla. She also wears a blue *melfa*, so as not to call attention to herself. The men crowd together, praying and speaking in hushed voices. The women stand to one side in silence. Brahim and Layla's sister go their separate ways. Montse joins the women. She imitates everything they do. She sits on the floor and shades her eyes with her hand so she can see everything. Deep in the crowd, someone recites the Koran, aided by a megaphone that launches the lines of the suras into the clear blue sky above the *hammada*. Montse tries not to stand out, but the Saharawi women cast curious glances at her. No one, however, asks her anything. Cars keep arriving, in spite of the fact that the ceremony has already started.

About half an hour later, the megaphone falls silent and the voices pipe up. Montse waits to see what Layla's sister does. As she stands up, she freezes at the sight of a woman's face in the middle of the crowd. It only takes a couple of seconds, because the woman soon turns her back and presses into the throng. But Montse is pretty sure it was Aza. The idea makes her mind race and her heart beat faster. She's about to shout to her, but then holds back. She doesn't want to call attention to herself or look like a hysterical woman.

'I'll be right back,' she tells Layla's sister with a gesture, and quickly walks away.

A moment later she has lost sight of the woman, but remembers the colour of her *melfa* and the exact spot where she first appeared. Several men, standing hand in hand in circles, prevent her from moving any faster. Montse pushes on in a straight line. She is dazzled by the sun. The crowd opens to let her through and swallows her up as the sea would a ship. She stops. Retraces her steps. Takes a good look around. Every woman looks a bit like Aza. Perhaps her mind is playing tricks on her. She searches for an open spot to breathe, and suddenly finds herself among the parked vehicles. She tries to calm down. That woman did look a lot like Aza. She's seen Aza's face in her dreams for too long not to be able to tell. All of a sudden, without rhyme or reason, she realizes that it is Saturday and that she's in the middle of the Sahara. It's a pleasant feeling. She's ready to forget about Aza when she sees a truck parked among the four-by-fours. Her heart jumps once again. She instinctively crouches down between the cars. The hell of Tindouf flares up inside her. The truck resembles the one driven by the Spanish legionnaire, Le Monsieur, as the Algerian women called him. Montse is now so frightened that she even stops breathing normally, in case she makes too much noise. She sees groups of people among the cars, and that reassures her. She fears that Le Monsieur might be nearby.

★★★

When Montse, Aza and the two Algerian women got off the truck, the rocks were ablaze. Montse's idea of the desert did not resemble what lay in front of her. Rather than sand, the place had stone and rocks everywhere. It was the first spot that she had seen some vegetation, though: the odd palm tree, acacias and sparse shrubs. It could be considered an oasis, although it looked more like a dung heap. At the centre was a deep well. The legionnaire's men positioned themselves in what little shade they could find at midday. Three hours on the truck had drained Montse of her remaining strength. She tried to beg them to take her back to Tindouf, but her voice barely left her body. Aza squeezed her hand to silence her. They were taken to a hut built with cement blocks and bare bricks, with an asbestos roof that soaked up the sunshine. Someone opened the door and they were unceremoniously shoved in. There was more space than in the previous cell, but inside there were seventeen other women who shared their bad fortune. The smell was nauseating. There was only one window, blocked with a car bonnet tied to it with wire. The fear in the faces of the trapped women turned to surprise when they saw that a westerner was being treated the same way as them. No one said anything, but they made room for the newcomer to sit on the floor. Aza crouched down, hiding her face in her hands so as not to show her despair.

They spent over a week in that place, only allowed out to use the latrines. By the second day Montse no longer noticed the smell. Their captors gave them dates to eat in the morning and in the evening. Montse tasted them with disgust. They oozed a whitish liquid which made her fear a botulism infection. Aza encouraged her to eat. The basinful of stagnant water was refilled without ever being emptied of its dregs. Outside the men chatted and argued at all hours. Now and again a shot rang out, as if one of them had lost his wits. In the morning the legionnaire would drive off with a group of men, leaving behind two or three mercenaries to keep watch on the women. Most of the women were Algerians and only spoke Arabic and basic French. They showed Montse a kind of respect that at first she mistook for distrust. One of them offered Montse her *burnous* after a few nights, when the temperature dropped sharply in the small hours.

Aza tried to get information from them about the mercenaries, but met with no consensus. Each of the women had her own theory about what was happening. Montse would ask questions insistently, but there were no straight answers.

'The older man is called Le Monsieur,' explained Aza.

'Some of the women say he buys and sells prisoners in Mauritania and Morocco. Others think he's a trafficker for a prostitution ring.'

'We have to get out of here, Aza. No matter how. Better dead than this.' Aza would not say a word. Her mind seemed elsewhere. When the mercenaries fell asleep, Montse would speak to Aza for long stretches. It felt good to tell her whatever popped into her head. Aza would listen as if Montse were reading from a book. Little by little Montse revealed secrets she hadn't shared with her closest friends. When Aza learned the reason for her trip, she stared at Montse as though Montse were a character in a film. Aza was very curious about the details. However, she was too polite to ask questions. Montse mentioned her husband, the days of her youth, her job and Santiago San Román. Sometimes she would fall silent for fear of boring her interlocutor, but Aza would remain attentive, encouraging her with her eyes.

The days went by slowly, and there was plenty of time to think. Little by little Montse started recognising every noise around the oasis. She knew when the men extracted water from the well, rummaged around the engines of the vehicles, took a walk to shoot at rocks, fell asleep or approached the hut. On the tenth day she realised there was absolute silence. Although she could see a vehicle through one of the cracks at the bottom of the door, the men could not be heard. By midday she was sure they had left them on their own. She told Aza:

'I'll try to escape. Look at those boards. A good kick would break them.' Aza looked distressed. She hid her face in her hands as usual.

'You won't make it. Even if you managed to run for three days, they would find you in an hour when they come back.'

'I'll leave in that car. If a group of us go we'll have a better chance of escaping.'

'No, it cannot be done.'

'Tell them.' Aza spoke to the Algerian women. Their faces registered an expression of terror. They all spoke at once, trying to convey to Montse how crazy it was to think one could escape from there. 'Won't you come with me?' Aza replied without hesitation:

'No, not me. If you're sane, you shouldn't even try.'

'I'll definitely go insane if I stay here any longer. I shouldn't have left my home, damn it.'

'You've had bad luck,' said Aza with unaccountable serenity.

★★★

Now these images crowd into Montse's mind. The parked truck brought back bitter memories. When the people started climbing onto the four-by-fours and the vans, she realised she might be in danger. The truck remained there like a beached boat. Suddenly someone taps her on the shoulder, startling her. She's about to scream, but manages to control herself. Brahim's smile disappears. He looks as scared as she is. Layla's sister is behind the Saharawi, and doesn't understand what's going on either. Feeling relieved, Montse hugs her impulsively. She tries to justify her conduct, but the others don't understand a thing. Then she casts a defiant glance at the truck, and is no longer sure that it belongs to Le Monsieur.

For Muslims the day of the sacrifice is also the day of forgiveness. During the festivities, the Saharawis visit their relatives, especially the elderly. It is a time to ask to be pardoned for acts that may have offended others. Montse listens attentively as Layla explains this. Later, while the nurse prepares the feast with the help of the women of the household, and the men collect the carcass of the sacrificed animal, Montse takes a walk with Layla's nieces. Brahim keeps an eye on them from afar, as if that were his job. The girls have put on their best dresses, and some are wearing shoes for the first time in many months. Shod in patent leather, they walk with difficulty. The boys cast envious glances at them, because the Spanish woman lets them lead the way. The girls take her to the corrals to see the goats. They sit down at the top of a hillock on stones laid in a circle. A few metres from there, a one-eyed boy looks at them. He's rooted to the ground, like a tree. Montse asks him to come closer, but he doesn't reply. She doesn't even know if he's one of Layla's relatives.

After eating couscous and desert, Montse is full. She cannot remember a feast like this one. She's eaten all she can. Yet she still tastes everything she is offered. At times she smiles with her mouth full, incapable of eating anything else. Everyone showers her with attention, especially Brahim, who fills her glass with water or juice, passes her dishes, offers her bread, a napkin, more meat. Layla smiles away. At one point Montse asks her quietly:

'Tell me, Layla, is Brahim your brother or your brother in law?'

The nurse opens her eyes wide and holds her breath, as if the question disconcerted her. But she also tries hard not to look surprised, and her eyes fix on the food. Montse is bemused. She asks again, thinking that perhaps Layla did not understand.

'No, no, he's nothing of the sort.'

'Who is he then?'

'My fiancé. We're getting married after the summer.'

Montse swallows with difficulty. She is about to laugh, but Layla's seriousness dissuades her.

After the banquet, the men go out and sit on mats around a primus stove. It seems to Montse that the women are nervous. They do everything in a hurry and whisper to one another, as if annoyed by the fact that the men have taken so long to leave the *jaima*. Soon she understands what's going on. Layla's aunt opens the dresser and takes out a small TV. She places it at the back of the room and connects it to a piece of wire that leads to an aerial. She plugs the TV into a car battery. Montse cannot help smiling when the mystery is revealed. A few neighbours come in, and eventually more than twenty women are settled in front of the screen.

'It's a soap,' explains Layla. 'From Mexico, but we get it from Algerian television. We can go out if you like.'

Montse doesn't want to miss the sight.

'Wait, I'd like to watch for a bit.'

The spectacle around the Mexican soap dubbed into Arabic astonishes Montse. The women are completely silent. When the heartthrob appears on scene, they cheer him on as if he were a hero, calling him by his name. Montse can barely believe her eyes. Every time she tries to say something to Layla, the women glare at her angrily. Eventually she and the nurse go outside. A few girls take them by the hand, fighting amongst themselves to get closer. By now Montse knows some of them by name. It is very pleasant to stroll between the *jaima*s, feeling a warm breeze blow. In every household there's a flurry of activity, as visiting relatives come and go. The men's *derraha*s look clean and starched. The women have donned their best *melfa*s. Layla and Montse stroll away from the *jaima*s.

'It's hard to believe that so much beauty can survive alongside the pain of exile,' says Montse. Layla smiles. She knows the desert can captivate foreigners. 'I feel like I've been shut away for the last few years.'

'My family here feels the same. I'm lucky to have spent a long time abroad. But some people have been here for twenty-six years, trapped in a place without walls or doors.'

They stop, Montse a few steps behind her friend.

'What is it?' asks Layla.

'Do you know who that boy is?'

The nurse looks where her friend is pointing. A few metres off, the one-eyed boy walks in a parallel line to theirs. His head is shaven and covered in small cuts. Layla looks at him, shading her eyes with her hand.

'No, I don't. A stone must have hit him in the eye. It's quite common here.'

'No, that's not why I ask. This morning I saw him near the corrals. He follows me everywhere but he never comes close.'

Layla smiles:

'There's no reason to be surprised. You're an attractive woman. Brahim likes you a lot, you know.'

Montse feels embarrassed. She cannot quite understand the way Saharawi men behave in front of women. Yet she doesn't want to ask any questions. Everything seems strange to her.

'Tonight we're invited to a party,' says Layla. 'A colleague from the hospital wants to have us all round.'

'Me too?'

'Of course. She insisted you come.'

The afternoon drags on. Brahim drives Layla's family to the dunes in his vehicle. The sunset is an unparalleled spectacle. From the top of the highest dune Montse can see the sun almost level with the desert. The other side of the dune is almost dark. Montse rolls down the hill of sand like a child, and the little ones imitate her. Meanwhile, the men prepare tea and snacks.

Back at the *jaima*, Montse feels both tired and euphoric. She'd like to lie down and listen to the wind beat against the canvas, but she doesn't want to miss a thing. Alone in a small adobe room, Montse and Layla wash themselves and change their clothes. They put on some perfume and darker *melfa*s. At nightfall, they say goodbye to the family and make off along the streets of the camp.

Layla's colleague's house is in another sector of the *daira*. Montse finds it difficult to believe that people can tell the neighbourhoods apart, the streets, the *jaima*s. They all look the same. She stumbles along in the dark as Layla leads the way. The Saharawi has put on a pair of black boots and is carrying a bag. She strides as elegantly as on a catwalk.

Near the house, Montse is surprised to see a man crouching down, relieving himself in the street. When he spots the two women he runs away, his genitals in plain view and his *derraha* rolled up to his waist.

'Don't worry,' says Layla. 'He's an old man, and he's not right in the head. He goes whenever nature calls, like a child.'

Montse carefully sidesteps his excrement.

The nurse's house is not a *jaima*, but a construction made of adobe. As soon as they peer through the door, Layla's friend stands up to welcome them in. Montse recognises her from the hospital, although she cannot remember her name.

'Do you remember Fastrana?'

'Yes, of course I do.'

Most of the women are nurses. There are barely any men. Montse casts a quick look around at the people and discovers Brahim sitting in a corner; he smiles at them. She finds the situation both amusing and disconcerting.

'You didn't tell me your fiancé was going to be here,' says Montse with a touch of sarcasm.

'With men you never know,' retorts Layla.

Bob Marley is playing on the tape recorder. Montse sits down among the nurses, and recognises most of them. The women are speaking in Cuban Spanish, and the men in Hassaniya. Suddenly a man bursts into the room, shouting. It's the same man who startled her in the dark a moment ago. He stands in front of Montse and speaks to her as though she were able to understand him.

'*Musso mussano? Musso mussano?*'

Fastrana's smile reassures Montse.

'Don't worry. The poor old man is crazy.'

'And what is it he's shouting?'

'He asks if everything's all right,' translates Layla.

'Tell him it is,' says Montse. 'Ask him his name.'

'We call him The Demon,' replies Fastrana. 'The kids started calling him that. My mother takes him home in the evening and lets him sleep in the kitchen when it's empty.'

The Demon picks up the banana that Fastrana offers him. Then the nurse gestures to him to leave the room. He does so by leaping about like some kind of court jester.

People come in and out of the house all the time. Montse cannot tell who's who. She lets someone paint her hands with henna. It takes hours.

It is very late by the time they finally say their goodbyes. Brahim stays behind, drinking tea and chatting with the nurses. Layla and Montse are tired. A starry sky casts its light over the camp. It's a very cold night.

'How long have you known Brahim?'

'Five months. But he loves me. He likes to make me jealous. He thinks I'll love him more that way.'

'And do you love him?' asks Montse, instantly regretting her words.

Layla smiles. Her white teeth stand out against her dark skin. She really is a beautiful woman.

'Look,' says Montse, stopping. 'Isn't that the one-eyed boy again?'

'Yes, it's him. He seems to have taken a shine to you.'

'What is he doing up so late? Doesn't he have school tomorrow?'

'He's on holiday for ten days.'

'Call him. Ask him his name.'

Layla gestures to him, and calls out without shouting.

'Esmak? Esmak?'

The boy looks at them from afar, but doesn't say his name.

'Eskifak?'

When Layla tries to approach him, he runs away and disappears among the *jaima*s. Montse is very tired now, but her heart is beating fast on account of all the tea she's drunk.

'That boy is not from this *daira*. Otherwise I would've seen him before,' says Layla with great certainty.

Chapter Fourteen

CORPORAL SAN ROMÁN LAY AWAKE THE WHOLE NIGHT, looking at the shadows on the ceiling and the lights coming in from the aerodrome. Over the last week he'd barely managed to sleep one or two hours a day. He was wracked with anxiety in the guardroom, and his perception of reality had been growing erratic. It was barely six paces from one wall to another. The latrine gave off a nauseating smell. When he was about succumb to tiredness, the dripping of the tap in the silence of the night would attract his attention; the more he focused on it the less able he was to sleep. For more than a week he heard the drops hit the cement, an unceasing, unnerving dripping.

Following Guillermo's unexpected visit, he felt even more edgy. He knew he would never see his friend again, and regretted the way he had treated him in the last few months. Guillermo did not deserve that. But it was now too late to make amends.

He tried to forget the memory of Andía, which was a worse kind of torture than the dripping. He felt betrayed, a bitterly familiar sensation. Even with his eyes closed he could see the girl's face; hear her child-like voice, her adolescent laughter. It was only possible to cast her image aside when he thought of Montse. Her memory made him anxious too. He had tried to write her a letter, but was incapable of stringing two sentences together. Words did not flow. He would never have thought it was so difficult to express one's feelings. At times he tried to picture Montse with her newborn child, his son, and was overcome with anxiety and confusion. The memories he had been able to keep under control would then resurface, flickering on his mind like a flame he had never entirely managed to extinguish.

Suddenly he thought of his mother. Something he rarely did. Now, however, he was troubled by the idea that Montse might have learned of her death. It seemed unlikely. But sometimes he wanted to believe that the girl, out of remorse, had taken the baby to meet its grandmother. If that had been the case, no doubt Montse knew the old woman had died. For a moment he imagined his mother in her black dress, lying on the bed, her arms crossed over chest, her face pale and waxen. He felt guilty: guilty of being far away, of not having attended the funeral, of assuming she would live forever, in spite of her illness.

It had been Guillermo who'd given him the news of her death. This was in late May. Guillermo had been looking for him all morning, and eventually found him at the Nomad Troops' pavilion. He went straight to the point, as if it were the most natural thing in the world. Santiago looked at him without fully grasping his words. His whole past, his mother included, lay dormant in his memory. He had only called her twice in all his time in El Aaiún. Now it was too late to do anything about it.

In the face of the situation unfolding in the Western Sahara, any news that reached them from Spain seemed unreal. When Major Panta called Corporal San Román to his office, Santiago already knew why: his mother was dead. He listened without blinking, with a grave expression. The major thought it was the shock of the news that prevented him from reacting, but in fact Santiago's mind was elsewhere.

'Events at the moment are very serious, Corporal. You know it as well as I,' the major explained. 'But the army appreciates that the sorrow caused by the death of your mother goes beyond any other problems we might have here.' Santiago nodded, almost without moving. The major took out some papers and passed them to San Román. 'And so, even though in the present circumstances all permits for leave are suspended, we are prepared to make an exception. You have fifteen days to go to Barcelona and be with your father, your brothers and sisters – in short, your family. The loss of one's mother is irreparable, but no doubt sorrow is more bearable when shared.' It didn't occur to Santiago to tell the major that he had no father, brothers, sisters or, indeed, any family. He puffed out his chest and stood tall to convey his gratitude. 'There's a plane leaving tomorrow for Gran Canaria,' explained the major, summing up the documents he'd just given him. 'There you'll catch a connection to the peninsula. You have fifteen days to be with your family. We expect you back on the 15th of June. You may leave now.'

'At your command, major, sir.' Santiago San Román walked out into the blinding sunlight in a daze. Every soldier he knew would have given everything they had to get a permit like his. And yet, the idea of getting on a plane and returning to Barcelona barely six months after leaving filled him with anxiety.

On the 24th of March, the governor of the colony, General Gómez Salazar, had set in motion Operación Golondrina (Operation Swallow), in order to evacuate the Spanish population from the Sahara. Classes in both the primary and secondary schools were suspended a month before the end of term. Although some civil servants left the city that they considered home in tears, many others did not even look back, knowing full well what was coming.

The Saharawi demonstrations in favour of independence were increasingly frequent. Any excuse served to put out flags and sing chants supporting the Polisario Front. The Territorial Police and the legionnaires would cordon off the most riotous areas as soon as conflicts erupted. News from other cities was hardly encouraging for the Spaniards. The civil prison in El Aaiún was filling up with detainees.

Santiago packed up the following day and walked to the car park from where he'd been told a vehicle was leaving for the airport. He was lost in thought, going over his plans, and didn't spot Guillermo, who was coming to meet him, until he practically bumped into him.

'Leaving without saying goodbye?' Santiago looked at him as he would a stranger.

'I thought you were out on patrol,' he lied.

'I asked after you and they said…' Guillermo gave him a hug, cutting him short. 'Let go, now, or they'll think we're queer.' Guillermo smiled. In view of the news, his friend's behaviour did not seem particularly strange. He wished Santiago good luck and stayed behind as he walked away. Corporal San Román felt in his pocket, where he'd put his money and the permit. The idea of abandoning the Sahara at that moment made him anxious; but he had other plans. He changed course little by little and, instead of walking to the car park, directed his steps towards the gates. He showed his permit and left the barracks behind, walking decisively. An hour later he walked into Sid-Ahmed's store, dressed as a Saharawi, trying to hide the bag where he'd put his uniform.

Santiago spent his fifteen days' leave at Andía's. The girl could barely hide her excitement. For two weeks he didn't leave the boundaries of the neighbourhood. He would sometimes stroll along the streets of Hata-Rambla, or spend the evenings with Sid-Ahmed at the store, smoking and drinking tea. No one found his presence strange; the neighbours treated him as if he were a relative of Lazaar. Yet when the men gathered together in the house, Santiago felt marginalised. Their shared familiarity did not extend to him. He remained silent, offering tea and listening to them argue. Not that he understood much. They spoke in Hassaniya, and whenever they addressed him in Spanish it was only to utter trivial remarks out of politeness. Santiago was sure they were discussing politics. He knew they supported the Polisario, but no matter how much he had done for some of them, he was far from gaining their trust in that respect. Sid-Ahmed, when they were alone, would reveal certain things, but Santiago still had the feeling that a lot was kept under wraps.

Two days before his permit expired, Santiago confessed to Andía that he had no intention of going back to the barracks. The girl looked at him with enthusiasm and ran off to tell her mother. The mother told the girl's aunts and, before an hour had gone by, Sid-Ahmed appeared in the house, visibly shaken. For the first time his characteristic kindness had disappeared.

'What's all this about deserting?'

'I'm not deserting, I'm just not coming back.'

'That's desertion, my friend.'

'So?'

'Do you have any idea what they will do to you when they find you?'

'They won't. No one knows I'm here.' Sid-Ahmed laughed with humbling sarcasm.

'Everyone knows you're here. Everyone, except your friends.' His words were so categorical that Santiago didn't doubt them for a second. 'Our people know everything that happens inside and outside the barracks. Do you think we are stupid?' San Román felt helpless. At that moment he regretted not having taken the opportunity to travel to Barcelona. 'If you really love that girl,' said Sid-Ahmed, referring to Andía, 'tomorrow you'll turn up at the barracks. Otherwise she and her family will be accused of housing a deserter. Can you imagine what would happen to them?' It was impossible to counter this argument. Sid-Ahmed's words crushed Santiago. He hung his head in shame. The man was teaching him a lesson without even meaning to. Santiago nodded in agreement. The Saharawi changed his menacing tone and once again became his usual self. 'Andía is very attached to you. You have behaved like one of us. Don't spoil it now.' The phrase touched the bottom of his heart. No one else had taken his feelings for Andía seriously. They shook hands and drank some tea in silence, without further discussing the matter. That evening the house filled with men. They talked and drank tea until dawn. Once they left, San Roman told Sid-Ahmed:

'At the end of the day, you Saharawis always look happy.'

'Not always, my friend, but tonight we had good reason to be so. Our brothers have triumphed in Guelta.'

Santiago didn't understand these words until the following day, when he went back to the barracks. The situation was one of near chaos, and amid the confusion no one noticed that he hadn't used his permit to travel to Spain. News about the Polisario travelled from mouth to mouth, inflated by rumours and surrounded by official silence. The army's retreat from Guelta was seen as a step towards the definitive withdrawal of the Spaniards from the Sahara. In the first two weeks of June, the prison filled with Saharawis arrested in demonstrations and street riots. Santiago's job, on his first day back, was to act as a guard at the civil prison. The building, barely in use a few months previously, was now full of men who had barely any space to sleep in the crowded cells. It was situated at the end of a long street off Edchera. From afar one could see the huge security operation run by the Spanish Army. Most of the detainees were forced to spend their days and nights in the courtyard. Orders and counter-orders were given by sergeants who did not quite know how to deal with such a critical situation. The phones rang off their hooks. Soldiers ran up and down, carrying out commands that were reversed a minute later. Amid the chaos, Santiago recognised the faces of a few Saharawis. He spoke to some of them, trying not to attract the soldiers' attention. In just one morning he promised at least twenty people he would give their families news of their whereabouts. Although all permits had been cancelled until further notice, it wasn't difficult for Santiago to reach Hata-Rambla. And, as soon as the locals got wind that many of their relatives were still detained in El

Aaiún, they started entrusting him with messages. His role as a messenger became an everyday occupation.

That summer was the saddest one in recent memory. Civil servants continued to be repatriated. In July a number of bars closed for the holidays. The population surmised, and it was later confirmed, that these holidays would last many years. The Oasis shut its doors. The summer cinema never opened. Fewer and fewer children were seen in the streets. By August only half of the population remained in the city. It was most noticeable in the suburbs: many houses were empty and locked up. More shops closed down. People would walk hurriedly along main roads with very little traffic. The street market reflected the suspicion and desolation which was taking hold of the city. Although the evacuation became better organised than it had been in spring time, everyone was in a hurry to sort out their affairs: selling off cars and television sets, calling in loans, settling the rent.

News of the Caudillo's illness did nothing but increase the uncertainty. Although many refused to believe that Franco would die, even high-ranking officers were waiting for first-hand news in the telegrams and calls that came from Spain. Yet the result of all this information was a perpetual confusion that swelled the numbers of sceptics.

In mid-October a rumour that had circulated among the best informed became fact. An hour before dinner, the TV in the canteen showed the king of Morocco addressing his people. His voice sounded resolute. Almost no one paid attention, but Santiago was hypnotised by the seriousness in Hasan II's face. He didn't understand much beside a word here and there which didn't make a lot of sense. But, before his speech ended, Santiago told Guillermo:

'Something's not right.' Guillermo looked at the screen without much interest. He didn't understand the troubles in Morocco and the Sahara. 'I don't know what it is,' said Corporal San Román, 'but something strange is going on.' He stood up and walked briskly to the Nomad Troops' pavilion. Security had been tightened inside and outside the barracks. As soon as he stepped in, he knew his intuition had not failed him. The Saharawis had the TV on, but no one was paying any attention to the Moroccan propaganda. Instead they were all sitting around an old radio. No one noticed the legionnaire until he asked them what was happening.

'Nothing, Corporal, nothing.'

'Don't treat me like an idiot. I know something's going on.' The soldiers knew him well. Many of them had sent messages to their families through him. He'd been playing football with them for several months. He knew many of their fiancées, and had been invited to a number of the soldiers' houses. And so he stood his ground, and, annoyed, asked: 'What did Hasan say on TV?'

'He says he wants to invade Sahara and annex it to Morocco.' San Román did not see how that would be possible.

'But he can't: we have the superior army,' he said naively.

'He's asking civilian volunteers to enter the Sahara. He says it'll be a peaceful occupation. He's mad.'

San Román stayed with the Saharawis until the call to quarters was sounded. When he lay down on his bunk, those words were all he could think about . He stayed awake but motionless until they sounded reveille. That day the barracks were in great confusion, with orders and counter-orders being given all over the place. Rumours spread faster than ever. At times it seemed that they were all getting ready to march towards the North. At others, it looked as though they would evacuate Africa that same day. Amid the chaos, Santiago San Román managed to leave the barracks the last Friday of October. His plan was to walk up to Zemla. But it proved quite difficult to get there.

The situation in the area was as confusing as in the rest of the city. People were stocking up on food. Most shops had no supplies left. The first thing Santiago did was visit Sid-Ahmed. The Saharawi tried to sound reassuring, but he looked unusually nervous. They went over to Andía's house together. The girl did not seem to be aware of what was happening. She was aloof and annoyed at the legionnaire for not having visited her in almost three weeks. They drank tea for over an hour. When the moment came to say goodbye, Santiago noticed that the family made an effort to leave him alone with Andía. It was the first time they tried so hard to please him, and so he didn't at first realise what was happening. The girl sat in front of him and let him take her hands.

'When the time comes to leave, I'll take you with me to Barcelona. You'll like it. You'll like it a lot.' Andía smiled. It wasn't the first time Santiago had made promises to her.

'And what about your girlfriend there?' Santiago pretended to get angry. He knew it was a game.

'There's no one waiting for me, I swear.' Eventually, as usual, she smiled, pleased.

'I want to ask you something, Santi. It's a favour for me, just for me.'

'Of course, anything.' She put her hand in her *melfa* and took out an envelope.

'This is for Bachir Baiba. Tell him it's from her sister Haibbila. You can read it if you like.' San Román smiled. He knew Bachir well. He'd been to his house, and knew his family. His sister Haibbila was a close friend of Andía's; it was she who had offered Santiago a bracelet as a gift. He had no intention of taking the letter out of the envelope, even if it was open. It seemed rude. Besides, he was sure it would be written in Hassaniya.

The letter reached Bachir Baiba. It was the first thing Corporal San Román did on arriving at the barracks. The Saharawi read it in front of him, and his serious expression did not make Santiago suspicious. He started to say goodbye, but Bachir asked him not to go yet. They drank tea and smoked for a while. Bachir Baiba was kind but distant. When it was finally time for Santiago to leave, the Saharawi asked him:

'When are you going back home?' San Román understood immediately.

'I'd like to go up tomorrow, but it's become very hard to get a permit.'

'I see,' Bachir said, trying to find a solution. 'We have no way of getting out of here. They've taken away our arms and there are no permits at all.'

'I know.'

'Will you do a friend a favour?'

'Tell me.'

'When you get a permit, come and see me. I've got stuff for my mother: dirty clothes and stuff like that.' Santiago knew what the other meant, but he raised no objections.

On Friday 31st October, Santiago walked to the exit gate carrying a bag that weighed over fifteen kilos. He naively thought that no one would take any notice of a corporal leaving the barracks on foot, like so many other times, and so he didn't realise that, near the sentry box, a lieutenant and two sergeants were exchanging nervous looks and shaking their heads.

'What have you got there, corporal?' The question caught him unawares. He blushed and his voice trembled.

'Here's my permit,' he replied. The lieutenant didn't even look at the piece of paper.

'I'm not asking you for that. I'm asking you what you have in your bag.'

'Dirty clothes and stuff like that.' As soon as he said it, he understood he was in serious trouble. The bag was too heavy. When he put it down it made a suspect noise. Before he even opened it, the two sergeants were pointing their guns at him. When the contents came out, the lieutenant went pale and nearly dived for cover. Among the clothes were hand grenades, detonators and explosives. In less than an hour, the news had spread throughout the barracks like the darkest of omens.

Insomnia and fleas were turning the guardroom into a dungeon. But it was the absence of news that most distressed San Román. He felt terribly alone, more alone than ever. He could picture the commotion that would erupt in the barracks as soon as the death of the Caudillo became known. Yet all he cared about was his own situation. That day he finally slept normally, at the usual hour. But no one deigned to explain to him what was happening. He kept his eyes and ears open to every noise, every movement outside. Any moment now they would come for him and take him to the Canary Islands or Spain. Worse than the wait was the fatigue. His eyes stung, and his whole body ached as if he were running a temperature.

In mid afternoon the door opened and Guillermo turned up in uniform, armed with a Cetme rifle. He only said:

'Time for your walk, Corporal.' And stepped aside. Santiago went out, deeply moved. He walked towards the end of the runway, as he'd done in previous afternoons. Guillermo followed a few metres behind, holding the Cetme with both his hands.

'I'm really sorry, Guillermo. I'd like to have your forgiveness for everything,' said Santiago without turning back.

'I don't want to hear a word from you, Corporal.'

Tears welled up in San Román's eyes and rolled down his cheeks. It felt good. 'I'm so sorry I wasn't a good friend, I'm sorry I…'

'One more word and I'll shoot you.'

Santiago knew he didn't mean it, but did not say anything else. When they reached the end of the runway, Guillermo walked away a few metres. He stood with his back turned to Santiago, looking at the dunes, seemingly oblivious to everything. Santiago made a run for the Land Rovers. With each step he felt closer to freedom. He jumped into one of the vehicles, retrieved the key from under the seat, and drove off as fast as he could. Guillermo started shooting into the air. No one reacted, no one noticed what was going on. In a few minutes, the vehicle disappeared down the road, leaving a trail of black smoke behind.

Santiago had never thought he would see the city so desolate. The streets were almost deserted. None of the shops were open. Some areas had been completely evacuated. Others, however, were now cordoned off with barbed wire, and no one could leave. His uniform and the military vehicle did not attract anyone's attention, given all the units deployed by the army. It wasn't hard to reach the Zemla area. He drove to Andía's house and got out of the car without even cutting the engine. Inside he only found the women. He asked where Andía was, and someone went to fetch her. The girl ran to see him, short of breath. On seeing him she burst into tears. She knelt down on the floor, and started to tear her hair out. The women tried to calm her. San Román was frightened. This was not the reaction he had been expecting.

'I thought you were dead, Santi,' Andía was saying through her sobs. 'They told me you'd been executed.'

Santiago had never seen anyone cry like that. He forgot all the reproaches he wanted to make to her. The neighbours turned up, and started shouting. Disconcerted, unsure of what to do, Santiago went out into the street. Someone had gone out to inform Sid-Ahmed he was there, and the shop-keeper came running to meet him. He tried to give Santiago a hug, but he pulled away.

'It's my fault, not the girl's,' said Sid-Ahmed. 'She's only a child, you can't blame her.'

'I thought you were my friend.'

'And I am. That's why I trusted you. You have *baraka*, my friend, you have *baraka*. Now you're one of us.'

Santiago thought at first that he was being tricked, but the Saharawi's words got through to him. Eventually he let Sid-Ahmed hug him.

'They are invading us, my friend. Didn't you know? There's

no time for arguments between ourselves.'

'You only needed to ask. Just that. I would have done anything for you. Anything. There was no need to deceive me.'

Sid-Ahmed took him by the arm and led him into the house. Andía was laughing and crying at the same time. She clung to Santiago like a little girl and spoke to him in Hassaniya. Santiago could no longer pretend he was angry. He drank a glass of tea, accepted a cigarette and settled himself on the floor against a wall. Andía would not leave his side. The legionnaire's eyes slowly closed. Suddenly all the tiredness accumulated in the days previous took hold of his body. His eyelids, his arms felt heavy. He had no strength left to talk. A moment later he was completely asleep.

Chapter Fifteen

Doctor Belén Carnero went into the canteen of the hospital and saw Montse sitting at the back by the window. She'd been looking for her. After negotiating a few obstacles, Belén approached the table and sat down beside her.

'What took you long? I was about to leave, Belén.'

'It was a long operation. And the worst thing is, that poor man nearly died in there because of you.'

Doctor Cambra raised her eyebrows.

'How do you mean, because of me?'

'Well, you know, Montse, that story of yours intrigued me so much I nearly overdid it with the anaesthetics.'

Montse was about to protest when she saw the cheeky smile on Belén's face. 'What? Where's your sense of humour?' Montse covered her face with her hands.

'I'm not sure I ever had one.'

'Of course you do. Remember how much we used to laugh together?'

'You're right. But it's been so long I can barely remember.'

They looked each other in the eye for a moment, as if they were trying to read each other's thoughts.

'Listen,' said Belén eventually. 'Why don't you come home and pick up your story where you left off.'

'I haven't got time. I have to go home, take a shower and…'

Belén knitted her brow. 'Is this what I think it is?' she asked.

'Well, yes, there's no point hiding it. I'm going out to dinner with Pere.'

'The most eligible bachelor. Well, none of my business really, but why don't you finish telling me about Santiago San Romo.'

'San Román.'

'That's it. You were telling me about your pregnancy. You were... nineteen?'

'Eighteen. Eighteen years old. That's all there is to it. But times were different then, and you know what my family has always been like.'

'I do. That's why I'm so intrigued. I can't imagine you telling your mother you've become pregnant by a boy you barely know.'

'Actually, I knew all I needed to know.'

'You were saying you saw him with a blonde.'

Doctor Cambra searched through her handbag and took out a pack of Chesterfields. She lit up a cigarette. Belén looked at her without saying a word.

'Why the look?'

'I didn't know you smoked. Is it a new thing?'

'A stupid thing, I'd say. I haven't smoked since I was eighteen.'

'You're full of surprises, girl. No wonder Pere is crazy about you.'

Monte blew the smoke in her face. Belén started coughing and laughing at the same time.

That October was among the saddest ones in Montse's life. Her father was proud of her when she started university, but that feeling was in sharp contrast to her apathy. She remembered the recent summer like a princess's dream. To be again living in a household with fixed hours and a controlling mother was almost unbearable. As were the prolonged periods away from Santiago. Meanwhile, her sister Teresa lived in a world of her own. Montse often looked up to her. The little sister had a life of her own. She seemed the older of the two. Teresa was better at putting up with their father's demands, their mother's reproaches, and the stifling control they both exerted on their daughters. Yet Montse found it impossible to get on with her sister. At times she saw her as a child; at others she thought Teresa too advanced for her years. In reality she was afraid to find out what her sister would think of her if she knew what she was secretly experiencing.

The longer she spent away from Santiago, the harder it was to get him off her mind. Now they only saw each other on Saturday afternoons and Sundays. Montse had to be back home by ten, and Santiago had nothing to do except be with her. When he told her that by the end of the year he had to be in Zaragoza to start his military service, she tried to look indifferent, as though it were the most natural thing in the world. But at home she counted down the days with anxiety. Things couldn't get any worse, surely. There, Montse was wrong.

The worst happened on an already unpleasant Autumn afternoon. As she had done so often, she was accompanying her mother on a visit to her aunt's house. This was an unavoidable obligation. Nothing bored Montse so much as spending two hours sitting at a small round table while her mother and aunts discussed trivial matters and told colourless anecdotes about people who were already dead or whom she didn't even know. But on that afternoon something broke the routine. Whilst walking past a café, Montse, with a coquettish gesture, looked at herself in the window to tidy her hair. She froze. Santiago was sitting at a table near the door, smoking casually, with a blonde beside him who was laughing as if he'd told her something truly hilarious. Montse only saw them for two or three seconds, but she was sure it was Santiago. Her heart jumped. She held her mother's arm tightly and matched her step. She blushed, and her cheeks burned. She feared her mother might notice something was amiss. Although she didn't want to look back, the image had lodged itself in her head. A number of ideas rushed through her mind. Without further thought, she excused herself and told her mother to carry on to her aunt's without her. She'd forgotten something at home. Her mother went on her way grumbling to herself.

Montse was not in control of her actions. She made sure it really was Santiago and then positioned herself across the street, her eyes fixed on the door of the café. She was shaking. A couple of times she pictured herself as if from the outside and found what she was doing ridiculous. She started to cross the street, but held back at the last moment. For the first time in her life she didn't mind not having an excuse to justify her behaviour in front of her mother. Time moved incredibly slowly.

Santiago San Román exited the café with the blonde. She couldn't have been over nineteen or twenty, but her clothes made her look older. Even from afar, Montse could tell she wasn't a natural blonde. Santiago spoke to her as if they were old friends. He made her laugh all the time, which further annoyed Montse. She followed them from a distance, across the road. Perhaps what Montse really wanted was for Santiago to see her there, but he only had eyes for the blonde. Montse had hers fixed on them to see if they held hands or if he passed his arm round her shoulder. But they did nothing suspicious. They simply strolled to the nearest bus stop and stood there for ten minutes, the girl laughing all that time. How come Santiago was suddenly so funny? More than once, Montse felt the impulse to walk away, or even approach them, but something stopped her. Eventually the bus appeared, and the girl let everyone else on first. At that moment Montse saw them hold hands. Or, rather, it was a tentative, nervous holding of hands, until the girl threw her arms round his neck and pulled him close to her. They kissed. Santiago wasn't simply kissing her good-bye, and he certainly didn't pull back. They untangled when the bus was about to pull out. Santiago remained fixed to the spot, looking at the girl, who was trying to find a seat on the bus. And there he stayed, looking into the distance, even after the vehicle had disappeared from view.

The following Saturday Montse did not turn up for their usual rendezvous. When Santiago rang her, pretending to be a friend from university, she didn't answer the call. She took three days to come to the phone and, when she did, it was only to say:

'Look, Santi, I don't want to hear from you ever again. You understand? Ever. Pretend I'm dead.' Then she hung up. Santiago didn't get an explanation for another three days, when he approached Montse in the street. She was carrying some books, and had just enough time to catch the bus. But he stopped her. He was angry, but on seeing Montse's face he went pale.

'Will you tell me what's wrong with you?' His voice wobbled. Montse changed course and walked on. He followed, trying to get a word out of her, but she gave him no chance. Eventually, fed up with his insistence, she stopped.

'Listen, I don't know what your game is, but you're not going to mess me around like this.'

'First I'd have to know what you're talking about. If you don't explain yourself…'

'Explain myself? You're the one that owes me an explanation. For a start, who's that peroxide blonde you were kissing at the bus stop the other day?' Montse stared at him until he grew very serious and red in the face. Yet Santiago did not retreat.

'If you're jealous, there's no reason for it. She's no one important.' She turned red with anger.

'And me, am I someone important?'

'Of course, the most important person in my life.'

'Well, you've just lost that person. Go and cry on that fake blonde's shoulder.' Whereupon she strode off, with him trying to catch up.

'Listen, sweetheart, that blonde, she's no one. There's no reason to be jealous. Didn't you have any boyfriends before me?'

'Yes, lots,' she lied. 'So what?'

'Then you'll understand: that's all she is, an ex from way back.'

'Well, and do you go around kissing your old girlfriends?'

'I don't. But we met by chance, we had a coffee…'

'Did she pay for it?' Santiago was struck dumb. Montse had hit where it hurt. He stayed behind. Montse eventually stopped walking, turned, and blurted out: 'I'm pregnant. That's right, pregnant. Don't ask me if I'm certain or I'll tell you to f… Now you know. I don't ever want to hear from you, see you or have news of you again. I've got enough on my plate as it is.' Santiago's face crumbled, and he remained glued to the pavement, without taking his eyes off Montse as she walked away. At that moment he realised that people had stopped to watch them as if they were a street act.

★ ★ ★

Doctor Cambra was no longer impressed with fancy restaurants and male gallantry. Sophistication bored her, although she felt at ease with it. She let Pere Fenoll choose the restaurant, the wine and the table. There was something touching about him, though other things grated with her. In fact, she was not sure how the balance stood between what she liked and what she didn't. She knew that in her forties she was still beautiful, perfectly able to seduce a man, but felt terribly lazy when it came to using her charms. Besides, Pere was not very good at the game. He talked about work, his specialism, problems in the health service. And whenever Montse got him off the subject, he would grow pensive, as if taking a spoon to his mouth were a difficult procedure he couldn't quite grasp. Still, he was an attractive man, with good taste and impeccable manners. Montse liked him as much as she found him exasperating. She began teasing him, being seductive in small doses, at moments when Pere seemed at his most receptive.

She guessed the evening would end in his bed; his image was tinged by the wine in her glass. The drink made her pleasantly dizzy. She was wearing her best dress. When Pere went silent he gained a lot of points. He wasn't a good lover, but nor did she need that right now. She remembered him in his underpants and couldn't help smiling.

'Do you find this funny?'

In fact, Montse had not been listening. She was good at switching off without showing her lack of interest.

'Not really. It's the way you tell it, rather,' she justified herself.

Pere blushed. Montse stared at him until he looked down at his glass.

'Sorry,' he said, 'I've been talking all evening, and you've barely managed to say a word.'

'No, what you were saying – it was very interesting. I don't want to interrupt. Besides…'

Pere Fenoll raised his head and expectantly searched for the end of the phrase in Montse's eyes.

'Besides?'

'Besides, I think I'm a bit tipsy, and I wouldn't want to sound too silly.'

'Well, you don't look it. You look as fresh as if you'd just got out of bed.'

Montse smiled and was momentarily lost in thought. They'd finished their dinner, so sooner or later he would invite her back to his for a drink. She felt like talking. The idea of going home on her own, to memories and silent walls, did not appeal at all.

'Have you ever thought of taking time off work?' asked Montse. 'I don't know, three months, six months, a year, even.'

'An extended leave of absence?'

'Something like that, yes.'

'No, I've never thought of it. Maybe later, when I'm…'

'Older? Is that what you were going to say?'

'When I feel more tired, that's what I meant.'

Montse tucked her hair behind her ear. The wine had lifted her spirits in a way she thought she had forgotten.

'Well I'd like to. Three months, half a year. Who knows, I

might ask for it at work.'

'And what would you do in all that time?'

'A million things. Read, enjoy the city, travel. Traveling in the off-season is wonderful.'

'On your own?'

'If I did it, would you come with me?' she replied at once, as if she'd been waiting for her cue.

Pere smiled, and blushed once again.

'It depends. If you asked seriously... Are you about to ask me?'

'No, not now. Don't worry. It's only an idea that keeps popping up in my head.'

Pere Fenoll took the opportunity offered by her frankness to ask his ready-made question.

'Shall we go to mine for a drink?'

Montse smiled, making an effort to look spontaneous when she nodded. Still, she could not manage to feign surprise.

After settling the bill, they barely exchanged a word. They walked out a bit tense and got into Pere's car. It was cold. Montse pulled up the collar of her jacket and curled up in her leather seat. She wanted the drive to be long, so she could warm up while listening to Wagner.

'Are you tired?'

'No. It's just the wine. I'm fine.'

The traffic was heavy at that time. Montse was absent-mindedly looking at the people on the pavement as Pere talked once again about work. Suddenly she thought she saw Fatma, who was walking alone, with her hair covered by a red *melfa*.

'Stop for a second, please, Pere. I've just spotted a friend.'

'You want me to stop here?'

'It'll only take a moment; no need to park.'

Pere stopped at the side of the road. He was annoyed, and saw Montse's sudden reaction as a pointless whim. Montse got out of the car and caught up with Fatma. The Saharawi was glad to see her, even though they had last met only three days before. They greeted each other with a kiss and held hands, asking after this and that, as if they hadn't seen each other for a long time.

'Is the baby okay?'

'Yes, he's fine. He's a good boy.'

The two women were not in a hurry. But Pere Fenoll beeped the horn impatiently. This startled Fatma, who only then realised that someone was waiting for Montse. Not wanting to take any more of Montse's time, she said goodbye. They promised to meet soon.

Pere had a serious expression on his face when Montse got back into the car. She was annoyed, and had to make an effort not to have a go at him for his impatience.

'Well, Montse,' he said sarcastically. 'I wouldn't have thought you had such exotic friends.'

'Exotic? Do you not approve of my "exotic" friends?'

'No, no, on the contrary. I think one should get to know all kinds of people.'

Montse didn't like his tone. Before the car started moving, she opened the door again, got out and said:

'You know what, Pere, I never thought I would say this to someone, but then I never thought I'd go to bed with someone like you either. Fuck off!'

Pere Fenoll was speechless. He knew he had blown it, but it was now too late to make amends. He stayed in the car with Wagner playing in the background, while Montse quickly walked away, cursing him.

Chapter Sixteen

WHEN MONTSE AWAKES, THERE'S NO ONE IN THE *jaima*.
Once again she feels embarrassed to be the last one to get up.
Layla's aunt is cooking in the kitchen. They say good morning
in Arabic. Montse is a fast learner. For breakfast she has coffee
and goats milk, bread with marmalade and an orange. The food
revives her. The Saharawi starts explaining to Montse that Layla
is at the corrals on the outskirts of Bir Lehlu. She understands
without difficulty. The children are running everywhere,
making the most of the holidays. As soon as they see Montse,
they come to say hello. The morning sun is beginning to make
its presence felt.

Montse decides to go for a walk. She covers her head with
a scarf to protect it from the sun. A few little boys are playing
football. Others are fighting over the only bicycle. Suddenly
a kid who is sitting on his own, far from the group, attracts
her attention. She recognises the one-eyed boy from the day
before. He's looking at her without moving from his place.
Montse approaches him slowly, as though she were just strolling
by. Once near him she says hello. The boy doesn't reply. His
head has often been hit by stones and bears the marks. Montse
doesn't want him to run away, and so keeps her distance. It's
Layla's nieces who run away, as though they were frightened
of getting close to the boy. Montse asks him his name, again
without getting an answer. She decides to leave him alone. And
then, after taking a few steps she hears him say something.

'Spanish? Spanish?'

She turns and stares at him.

'Spanish, yes. And you, Saharawi?'

The boy stands up and comes close to her. Seeing him up-close, with his hollow eye-socket, Montse understands why the girls have scampered away. The boy put his hand in his pocket and takes out a piece of paper. The moment she takes it, he starts running away and soon disappears from view. Montse is so intrigued that she nearly tears the paper as she unfolds it. It is a squared sheet from a notebook, a school notebook no doubt. The handwriting is both careful and elaborate.

> *Dear friend,*
>
> *I thank Allah for having saved your life. The news fills me with joy. I have travelled this far only to see you. I have got news that might be of great interest to you. I think your Spanish friend is still among us. Mohamed will tell you where to find me. He's my sister's son. Don't speak of me to anyone, I beg you.*
>
> *Aza*

Montse's hands start shaking. She can barely finish reading the note. When she takes her eyes off it, she cannot see the boy. She calls out his name. She walks in the direction where she saw him disappear. There are children everywhere, but none is Mohamed. She wanders around the *jaima*s and eventually gives up. She puts the note away after rereading it several times, and holds on to it in her pocket. Then, without hesitating, she makes for the corrals to get Layla.

The nurse notices how nervous Montse is as soon as she sees her. She carefully reads the note, then looks at Montse, looks back at the note and rereads it. Layla put her hand on her forehead and a moment later clicks her tongue in her characteristic way.

'It wasn't a dream, Layla. I told you Aza existed.'

The nurse does not speak. She looks around to make sure no one's watching. They are alone. Montse looks calmer now. 'But her nephew has disappeared. I don't think I'll find him again, Layla.'

The nurse smiles. Her calm face contrasts with Montse's gestures.

'I wouldn't be so sure. If I'm not wrong, he's hiding behind those rocks there.'

Montse looks in the direction that she's pointing but sees nothing. Layla calls out Mohamed's name, uttering phrases in Hassaniya. Presently the boy appears. He was right where she said he had been. Mohamed approaches them with a look of embarrassment. Layla shows him the note and exchanges a few words with him. She sounds cross. Montse quickly asks her to translate.

'It's true, his aunt is Aza. She's in Edchedeirîa.'

'Where's that?'

'Not far. It's a *daira* in Smara,' she says, pointing to the horizon, where all that can be seen are rocks and sand. 'It takes a while at a brisk pace.'

'Come with me, please.'

'On foot? No way. You'd get dehydrated.'

Brahim drives with both hands on top of the wheel. His pipe hangs from his lips. Montse's sitting in the middle and Layla by the door. Mohamed is riding in the back, as he's refused to sit between the women. Brahim exchanges phrases with Layla. He sounds angry. Montse asks the nurse if he's annoyed at having to drive them, but she says he isn't.

'Not at all. He's happy to take us, but he likes to grumble. If men don't grumble, they're not real men.'

Montse laughs. Brahim smiles at her; he doesn't understand a word.

There's no difference between Edchedeiría and Bir Lehlu. The landscape of *jaima*s and adobe constructions is identical.

Mohamed jumps out of the truck and runs away. Brahim goes straight after him. He has to drive carefully as there are a lot of children running around, chasing a plastic ball. Eventually he stops at the door of an adobe house. The two women enter and take off their shoes. Aza stands up, covers her face with her hands, slaps her forehead, takes her hands to her heart and finally hugs Montse. She seems to be praying. Her words sound like a pitiful litany, like prayers said after someone's death.

'My friend, my friend,' she says, in Spanish. 'You have *baraka*, my friend. I assure you of that.'

The presentations take nearly an hour. Aza introduces her to all her family in Edchedeiria. Montse introduces Layla. The two women talk for quite a while in Hassaniya. Brahim, who has stayed outside, is soon chatting to the neighbours. He seems to know everyone. The women of the household offer Montse some tea, and bring her perfume for her hands and face. The girls present her with necklaces, bracelets, and wooden rings with pretty decorations. She lets them *fête* her. Layla speaks with everyone as if they'd known each other for years.

'You didn't tell me you had a boyfriend who was a legionnaire,' says Layla after listening attentively to the others.

'You didn't ask,' jokes Montse, laughing. 'But it doesn't matter, really.'

Aza and Layla smile. Montse feels it's the right moment to talk about Santiago San Román. But, at the same time, she's embarrassed about making her story so public. After all that's happened, everything to do with Santiago feels very remote.

'I think I've found the man you spoke of,' explains Aza, waiting for Montse's reaction. 'Other Spaniards like him settled here, but most have died, or gone to Mauritania.'

'It seems my story made an impression on you. After all we've been through, you haven't forgotten what I told you.'

'Not a thing. My mother helped me. She's very old, but has a good memory. She put me on the right track.'

'I'm not so sure I want to see him now.'

Layla and Aza look at each other, disappointed at the Spanish woman's reaction .

'Are you out of your mind?' says Layla reproachfully. 'Now you have to find out whether he's been thinking of you all this time.'

Montse smiles. She has the impression the two Saharawis regard all this as a soap opera.

'Fine,' says Montse, 'tell me what you know.'

'In Ausserd there's a Spanish man who fled with the refugees. He used to be a soldier, and now lives in La Güera, like me.'

'Do you know his name?'

'Not his real name, no. But I think they call him Yusuf or Abderahman, I'm not sure.'

'Have you seen him?'

'I've met him, but I didn't know he was Spanish. He looks like one of us. I haven't seen him for a long time, though. His children attended my school.'

'Are you a teacher?'

'Yes.'

'What other surprises have you got in store for me?'

Aza goes quiet and smiles. Layla clicks her tongue.

As they travel through a *hammada* without paths or roads, Montse wonders what might move a man who wasn't born in the desert to be anchored for so many years in this part of the world. The beauty of the landscape and the generosity and hospitality of the Saharawis do not seem reason enough. Neither does love.

Brahim drives in silence, with his hands on the top of the wheel. The three women have squeezed together in the cab of the pick-up. It feels like a lengthy journey, with the difficulty of the terrain. La Güera is no different from the rest of the camps. Amid the *daira*s one can see the two white buildings where the school is. They look like ships stranded at the bottom of a dry sea. Aza gives directions to her house. They welcome them pretty much as they had in Edchedeiría. Aza's mother is an old, nearly blind woman. She speaks Spanish as if she were salvaging it from the depths of her memory. At once she sets everything up to look after her guests. Presently Brahim strikes up a conversation with the men. Montse knows she'll have to wait for the rite of hospitality to be over before asking after the Spaniard who lives in La Güera, so she doesn't say anything yet.

They eat with the whole family. Brahim has been invited to the neighbours' *jaima*. In the course of the meal, Montse learns more about Aza and her family. Her father was once the mayor of the old Villa Cisneros, and a member of parliament at the Cortes Españolas. When Morocco and Mauritania invaded, he was taken prisoner by the Mauritanians. Aza was a child back then. They spent more than ten years in the country. Eventually they were allowed to go, along with the rest of the Saharawis, to the Algerian *hammada*. Aza's mother recalls her dead husband with contained emotion. Then she explains to her daughter once more where to find the man they're looking for.

Montse is very nervous. Her food feels stuck in her throat. At times it all feels like a dream. She has imagined a possible encounter with Santiago San Román many times, but not at all in the way it is happening now. Suddenly, a Saharawi steps aside from the group of men talking to Aza, offers Montse his hand, and greets her in Spanish, with a strong Arabic accent. He's wearing a black turban and a blue *derraha*. His skin is as dark as any Saharawi's. His eyes are red like theirs, and his teeth are tea stained. His gaze is as piercing as that of the men from the desert. It's hard to judge his age, like most Saharawis after thirty. Montse feels that the hand which squeezes hers is actually burning. Aza speaks to him in Spanish, and he replies in that language and sometimes in Hassaniya.

'Yes, I've been a legionnaire,' he tells Montse. 'But that was many years ago.'

Montse is almost certain that the man cannot be Santiago San

Román, but when she looks him in the eye she wavers.

'My name is Montse. They told me about you, and I didn't want to leave without saying hello.'

The man is obviously very flattered. He smiles. He finds the foreigner's attitude a bit strange. He invites all three women to drink tea at his house. Layla excuses herself, explaining they should be getting back to Smara. The man insists. Now Montse is sure it's not him. But she cannot help asking:

'Did you know a young man called Santiago San Román? He was a soldier like yourself.'

The man thinks for a moment, tipping his turban slightly backwards. Under the cloth appear a few grey hairs.

'I'm not sure. There were thousands of soldiers like myself. He must have gone back home when he was discharged. I stayed.'

'He stayed too.'

'Some died or were taken prisoner,' the man explains, smiling all the while.

Montse knows this is leading nowhere. But deep down she's relieved not to be in front of Santiago San Román. It's a paradoxical feeling.

On the way back, Brahim drives more slowly. Aza has stayed back in La Güera. Montse has promised to visit her at the school in a few days' time. She and Layla are both silent. The sun is setting at their back. Little by little the sky turns a deep red that takes Montse's breath away. When they are near Smara, she asks Brahim to slow down. She wants to preserve the beauty of that sunset in her memory. Layla seems indifferent to it. Suddenly she points something out to Montse. A few metres from the tracks, a dromedary lies on the ground, dead. It is a vision that makes a deep impression on the foreigner. Montse asks Brahim to pull over. He does so without replying. Intuitively, he can guess the kind of feeling a sight like that might give rise to in a European woman. In the distance, one can see the *jaima*s of Bir Lehlu.

There in the desert, the body of the dead dromedary is like a red brushstroke on a white canvas. Montse cannot look away. There are no flies, no carrion-eating birds. Brahim smokes leaning on the pick-up and the women stand a few metres away from the carcass. There isn't even a bit of wind that might profane the silence of the evening. Layla tries to understand what it is that so captures her friend's attention. Montse looks into the horizon. In the middle distance, on a slight elevation, some rocks stand out in profile.

'What's that, Layla?'

'The cemetery. That's where we bury our people.'

Montse feels that death is as much a part of the desert as nature, as the wind, as the sun. They stroll over to the boundary of the cemetery. The tombs are nothing but stones placed at the head and foot of the dead. There are no signs to differentiate between them. It's beginning to get dark, and the light is poor. Montse shudders. They are about to go back to the pick-up when, suddenly, they spot a shape a few metres away. Montse is startled. At first she thinks it's a dog, but Layla's face looks terrified, and she huddles against Montse, screaming. A Saharawi, who until now was half-buried, rises up from the earth. Even in the semi-darkness Montse can tell he's almost naked. The man holds his clothes and runs away with his turban on. Brahim runs towards them, alarmed by Layla's scream. When he realises what's going on, he starts throwing stones at the crazy man.

'What was he doing?' Montse shouts to Layla.

'I don't know. I didn't seen him either.'

Brahim says something to his fiancée. Layla translates.

'He says it's the old man we saw last night. The Demon. He's not right in the head, you know.'

'Let's go,' says Montse, nervous. 'It's getting dark.'

Chapter Seventeen

From the rooftops in the Saharawi area of Hata-Rambla, the city looked like a ship sinking into a sea of sand. One could hear the echoes of the commotion taking place in the modern part of El Aaiún. Few people really knew what was happening, so everyone moved with suspicion, trying to deal as best they could with the chaos of the evacuation.

In Hata-rambla there was a general feeling of consternation. No one had any idea what might happen to those who chose to remain in the city. The population assumed, without entirely accepting it, that sooner or later a great catastrophe would occur. Those Saharawis who lived on the outskirts were looking for vehicles in which to leave the city immediately. The most pessimistic, fearing the danger of invasion, would set off into the desert on a cart drawn by a donkey, loaded with barely enough supplies to survive for a few days. Ownership of a vehicle became a great privilege. The Territorial Police, meanwhile, patrolled the exits of the city, and forced anyone trying to escape to turn back. Nevertheless, the desert was difficult to patrol, and in the middle of the night people would flee in all directions.

Santiago San Roman spent his mornings on the rooftop of Lazaar's house. He felt like a bird perching on top of its own cage. The neighbourhood was like a prison, and it was very difficult to go in and out. Although every man found a way to evade the controls and move around the city, those who lived in Zemla were not prepared to leave behind their women and children. The Moroccan television broadcast disquieting news. Morocco had announced it would organize a peaceful invasion, but the reports coming from the north indicated otherwise. Over ten thousand soldiers had already crossed the border, and were now marching towards the capital.

Sid-Ahmed found Santiago sitting on top of the house, his legs dangling over the façade, smoking a cigarette. Ever since he'd come back, the legionnaire had been acting strangely. He showed little interest in current affairs and did not seem to understand what was going on. He just sat on the rooftop, listening to the noise in the street. The shopkeeper sat down beside him and lit up his pipe.

'I need you, my friend,' aid Sid-Ahmed. 'You're the only one who can help me.'

San Román could only smile when he thought of the last time Sid-Ahmed had asked for his help. However, he didn't say what was on his mind; he remained silent, staring at the desert.

'I'd like you to drive me and my father away in your car.'

'You can have it whenever you like. You know where the keys are.'

The Saharawi searched for the right words.

'I know, my friend, but I don't want your car. I need you to drive us. Later you may return.'

'You're not coming back?'

'No, no, of course not. I'm leaving forever.'

'Then you can keep the Land Rover forever,' replied Santiago tersely. 'I don't think the Army will mind.'

'No, still you don't understand me. I want you to come back to the city in the car. My children and my wife are staying here. I need you to look after them. That's all I can say for now.'

Santiago came back to reality, suddenly abandoning his self-absorption. Sid-Ahmed's words sounded sincere. The Saharawi's face was serious, very serious. Santiago had almost never seen him like this. For the first time he felt they were on an equal footing.

'Where do you want to go?'

'I don't know yet. I only want you to take us out of El Aaiún. I'll tell you later where to drop us off. You'll be back here in the morning. I've discussed it with my family and Andía's. They all agree. I can't do anything here, and my people need me.'

'Your people?'

'Yes, my friend, my people. They won't let me out on my own, but if I go with a legionnaire there won't be any problems. Do you follow?'

He did. That same night he filled up the radiator with water, checked there was enough fuel in the tank, and got ready to take Sid-Ahmed and his father out of the city. They waited until it was completely dark and said goodbye to the whole family. The Saharawi's wife wept in silence. Andía hugged Santiago, and he had to make an effort to disentangle himself. Although her expression was serious, Santiago's spirits rose when he saw how moved the girl was. It was a brief, self-controlled farewell.

Corporal San Román didn't find it difficult to leave Hata-Rambla. The soldiers guarding the gates had their minds on other things. In spite of their orders, the guards were not too zealous, and when they saw the Corporal's stripes, they didn't stand in the way of the vehicle. Later, Santiago, instead of heading for the road to Smara, followed Sid-Ahmed's directions. Despite what the Saharawi had said earlier, he seemed to know exactly where he was going. They drove to the Saguía river and followed it upstream. There was barely any water, and, in the moonlight, one could make out the reddish tinge of its shallow pools. The Saharawi knew every path, ford and track.

'If we've got far to go, we'll run out of petrol,' warned Santiago.

Sid-Ahmed didn't heed the warning. Santiago drove on for two hours with no idea where he was going. There was neither road nor path. The Land Rover lurched across the desert, at times following an old track, at others ploughing across the stony ground. Santiago, who had always admired the Saharawis' sense of direction in the night, let himself be guided through the desert, himself unable to tell north from south. He trusted Sid-Ahmed.

About thirty kilometres away from El Aaiún, the vehicle ran out of fuel.

'I warned you, damn it, I did warn you. The journey's over.'

Sid-Ahmed remained impassive beside him, without taking his eyes off an imprecise point in the horizon.

'Calm down, my friend. Nothing's going to happen to you. Allah will help us.'

San Román had heard that phrase many times, but it had never before sounded so hollow. He tried not to look disconcerted. The silence was terrifying. The Saharawi helped his father out of the car. He sat him down against an acacia and went back to the vehicle. He returned with a teapot, glasses, sugar and water. On seeing this, the legionnaire had to resign himself to the calm temperament of the men of the desert. And when he saw Sid-Ahmed make tea, he knew somehow that nothing would happen to them in that inhospitable place. However, it was beginning to get very cold. The Saharawi walked away a few metres and pulled off some dry branches of an argan tree. Then he cut the white spikes of the acacia. He dug a hole in the ground and made a fire. While they waited for the water to boil and the old man warmed himself, Sid-Ahmed began talking about football. Santiago didn't know whether to laugh or scream.

They drank three glasses of tea, and they would have continued drinking if a light had not appeared at the top of a hillock. The legionnaire stood up, a bit shaken, and alerted the two Saharawis.

'It's all right, my friend. Stay here.'

San Román obeyed. He couldn't do otherwise. The number of lights doubled. Presently he could clearly make out the headlights of two vehicles. They must have seen the fire. They approached slowly, dazzling them with the full beam of the headlights. Sid-Ahmed neither moved nor said anything. The vehicles stopped by the Land Rover of the Nomad Troops. Three or four men came out and walked very slowly toward the acacia. As they proceeded they recited the customary series of greetings, and Sid-Ahmed replied to them casually.

'*Yak-labess.*'

'*Yak-labess.*'

'*Yak-biher. Baracala.*'

'*Baracala.*'

'*Al jamdu lih-llah.*'

Suddenly, when they were near the fire, Santiago's heart jumped. The man leading the group was Lazaar. He was dressed as a soldier, but not in the Nomad Troop uniform. He was smiling broadly. Corporal San Román couldn't muster the strength to stand up. Lazaar greeted the old man respectfully, placed his hand on the man's head, and then helped Santiago up. He gave him a heart-felt hug.

'My friend. I knew I would see you again. Thank you.'

'Why "thank you"?'

'For looking after my family. They've told me everything.'

'Told you? What have they told you?'

'I know you were taken prisoner for collaborating with us. Andía is very proud of you.'

'Andía? How do you know what Andía thinks?'

'She writes to me and tells me everything. Besides, Sid-Ahmed is a good source of information.'

Santiago did not inquire further for fear of sounding stupid. Sid-Ahmed remained calm, as if the encounter were perfectly normal. He set about making more tea. No one seemed to be in a hurry that night except Santiago, who grew frantic in the face of the men's laidback attitude. For hours they discussed the cold, the wind, foxes, potholes, sheep, goats and camels. And for the first time he felt acknowledged, since they did so not in Hassaniya but in Spanish. Sid-Ahmed's father slept through the conversation. The cold became very intense, yet no one complained. When all topics of conversation seemed to have been exhausted, Lazaar addressed Santiago San Román.

'You're here for a reason, it was not only to drive Sid-Ahmed and his father. I asked him to bring you along.'

Santiago knew that asking questions only meant delaying the answer, so he didn't interrupt him in spite of his curiosity.

'I need to ask you a favour, San Román: I'd like you to get my family out of El Aaiún and take them to Tifariti. We're gathering everyone we can there.' The legionnaire still refrained from asking any questions. 'They're invading us from the north, and, if certain reports are true, the Mauritanians want to enter the territory as well.'

'And you want to take them to Tifariti? All of them?'

'Yes, my friend, all of them. My mother, my aunt and my brothers. Sid-Ahmed's wife too. His children are already with us.'

Santiago thought this would be quite a mission. For the first time he realised how serious the war was. An array of possibilities crowded into his mind, and he felt a considerable weight on his shoulders.

'I'm not even sure how I'll get back. The tank is empty,' he said naively.

Lazaar did not stop smiling.

'We'll take care of that.'

'And will I know how to get to Tifariti?'

'Allah will help you.'

'Are you sure?'

'Of course. If I weren't, I wouldn't be asking you.'

The legionnaire did not sleep a wink that night. He felt the cold in his bones, and his stomach was tied into a knot. The Saharawis cleared everything up with utmost calm, and then filled the tank of the Land Rover, using a hose to transfer diesel from their vehicles. When it was time to say goodbye, Santiago felt the need to be frank, even if it meant looking pathetic.

'I don't think I'll be able to find the way back. All the bushes look the same to me. Besides, I couldn't see a thing last night.'

'Forget about last night,' Said Sid-Ahmed. 'We took a short cut, but you can go back following the river.'

'What river? There's no river here.'

'Look, do you see that hillock over there? Go over it and carry on facing the sun. You'll come to a dry riverbed. You can recognise a dry riverbed, can't you?'

'Of course.'

'Follow it towards the north. Do not veer off. After some ten kilometres you'll see water, which will take you to the Saguía. Follow the current and you won't get lost.'

'What about Tifariti? Won't I get lost on the way there?'

Lazaar cut an acacia branch and placed two stones on the ground. He traced a line and gave him directions.

'Don't take any roads. Always drive across the desert. If you bear east you won't get lost. Carry on towards Smara, and as soon as you come across tracks going south east, follow them. Always keep to those tracks. All the people who are escaping to Tifariti leave their marks in the desert. Everyone's going that way. We'll see you in three days. Also, don't enter into any villages, however small they may look: they might be already occupied, which would be very dangerous.'

Santiago drove away in the Land Rover, keeping an eye on the rear-view mirror. Once the vehicles were out of sight he focussed on the hillock. Not even when he'd been caught carrying the explosives had he been as frightened as he was now. He carefully followed Sid-Ahmed's directions, trying to drive as confidently as the Saharawis. He thought that the men had placed too much trust in him, but after two hours driving, when he made out the white houses of el Aaiún, with their eggshell-like roofs in the distance, he knew that nothing would prevent him from reaching Tifariti with Lazaar's family.

They welcomed him as if he'd been gone for months. Santiago

recounted the encounter with the eldest brother in detail. Lazaar's mother and aunt listened without even blinking. As soon as they were told they had to leave, they started preparing themselves. In the main room, boxes containing clothes, food and all manner of utensils started piling up. Sid-Ahmed's wife came into the house too. The legionnaire tried to organise the escape as if it were a military operation. He first reviewed the troops. Three adult women, four girls, and six young men. The youngest girl was about three, and the oldest boy over eighteen. Fourteen people, in any case, was a lot for one vehicle. He told Andía, trying to remain calm, but the girl did not think a detail like that mattered.

Santiago decided to go down to the city and steal a car. The eldest of Lazaar's brothers went with him. This time, however, it wasn't so easy to move freely in the streets. There were legionnaires posted on the pavements, as if they were about to start a parade. The Territorial Police stopped any vehicles which contained more than two people or looked excessively loaded. Few cars circulated along the main roads, and there were even fewer parked by them. Some had broken windshields or busted locks. Others had been robbed of spare parts and their dead engines were clearly to be seen under their open bonnets. At a junction Santiago stopped dead and made the Saharawi take cover round the corner. A few metres from there, at a street control, they were searching a group of Saharawis, whom they had ordered out of their car. The Spanish soldiers, with their Cetme rifles slung over their shoulders, had them against the wall with legs and arms apart. Santiago froze on hearing a painfully familiar voice. It was Baquedano. Santiago experienced both fear and a *crise de conscience*. The sergeant was furious. He shouted at the Saharawis as if they were dangerous animals. Suddenly he slapped the youngest one of them and threw him onto the floor. The lad tried to escape, but Baquedano placed his boot on his face and then started kicking him. Santiago San Román wished he had a loaded gun. Anger replaced fear.

'I'm going to kill him,' he told Andía's brother, but the Saharawi stopped him.

'You have to drive us to Tifariti. We can't leave on our own.'

They went back to Hata-Rambla, ready to leave the following day as soon as it got dark. The family's luggage seemed of greater volume than the vehicle.

'We can't take all that. It won't fit. And where will you go?'

'On the roof,' said Andía calmly. 'We'll squeeze up.'

Santiago knew it was impossible, but was reluctant to disappoint her. Although he didn't say anything, he had a night-long nightmare in which people, luggage and animals came in and out of the car's window in a sort of never-ending game of tag. The following morning he went to look for diesel. It wasn't easy, but he managed to obtain three cans in exchange for a goat. Yet their problems had only just started. Some rumours were confirmed by the locals: El Aaiún had been sealed off by the military. On the 1st of December explosives were found at the *Parador Nacional*. It was initially thought that the Polisario was behind the attempted attack, but it was later discovered it was the work of a Spanish mayor and a sergeant who was an expert in explosives. The explosives, in fact, turned up next to some cans of butane on the courtyard of the Parador. After that the news spread that a few dignitaries from Morocco and Mauritania were staying there, ready to take over the administration of the territory. Security was tightened. Stop-and-search became indiscriminate. On that December day it was impossible to go around El Aaiún without being stopped and frisked by troops. Santiago had to inform the family that it was impossible to leave the city.

The legionnaire's new plan was to escape on foot, crossing the river in the middle of the night. With a little luck they'd all manage it, even the small children. He would then come back and try to leave the city in the Land Rover, dressed in his corporal's uniform. He tried to make them understand that, if they saw him loaded with all those boxes and people on the roof of the vehicle, they would not let him through. Lazaar's mother seemed to think he would manage it anyway. Yet, after the thwarted attack, it became completely impossible to flee. All San Román could do was wait for a more propitious moment. In any case, they would not make it to Tifariti within the stipulated period of time.

Days passed in anxious uncertainty. They all asked the legionnaire what he was waiting for, and although his precautions were justified they would not understand why he did not honour his word. On the 10th of December, one of the rumours circulating in the city was confirmed. The news was broadcast loud and clear on Mauritanian radio: the Army of Mauritania was invading the Spanish province from the south. El Aaiún, from that moment, was like a mouse-hole. As soon as Santiago learned this, he opened the bonnet of the Land Rover and started talking to the engine as he would to a person. He checked and double-checked the hoses. He cleaned the terminals of the battery. He made sure the oil and the water in the radiator were at the right levels. He let some air out of the tyres. Then he took a walk around the city. Before midnight he was back. He went into the house, nervous, and told everyone now was the moment to leave. No one had gone to sleep. It seemed that the Saharawis had guessed what was about to happen.

'Quick. Everyone in the car. We're leaving.'

'And the guards?'

'There aren't any. It's an open city. Something serious is going on.'

When Santiago saw how they all squeezed into the vehicle, he could hardly believe it. The three women and the two little girls climbed in the front. In the back were Andía and her three sisters. Every bit of free space was filled with bags and supplies, so that the girls were squashed against the windows. The six lads clambered onto the roof with the rest of the luggage and held on to the baggage rack. The eldest one positioned himself at the front to stop the little ones from flying off if the breaks were slammed, and the second eldest did the same at the back. The legionnaire didn't say anything, although he knew it was madness to travel in those conditions. He climbed in and, just before turning the ignition, felt something at his feet. He almost screamed. It was two chickens. At the women's feet he saw a shape that looked like a dog. He recognised the goat. Lazaar's mother smiled to him with a calm that seemed wholly inappropriate in the circumstances.

'We cannot leave the city without any food,' she said.

Santiago did not raise any objections. The vehicle moved with difficulty. The legionnaire thought it would grind to a halt before they reached the end of the street, but it didn't. Then they took an earthen road strewn with rocks and drove across the neighbourhood. There was not a trace of the Spanish troops. The Land Rover struggled on, spewing out black smoke. Santiago took the Smara road out of the city, with the headlights off. They advanced almost as slowly as a man on foot.

San Román remembered Lazaar's warning never to follow the road. As soon as the terrain levelled off he started driving across the desert. The rocks under the tyres were like sharpened knives, but the vehicle kept on going. Santiago knew the way, at least up to the crossroads where the road to the phosphate mines of Bu Craa started. Although the path was lost from view, Santiago oriented himself by the hillocks. He'd done the journey several times, and was familiar with the sparse bushes and the line of the horizon. It took over three hours to reach the crossroads where the Smara road forked in two. In normal circumstances he would cover the same distance in half an hour, but the vehicle barely crawled forward. Judging by the tracks in the desert it was obvious that many Saharawis had decided to stay off the road. Even though they were driving at a snail's pace, Santiago could not afford to take his eyes off the terrain. A patch of soft ground might turn into a soft pit, and when he drove onto sand to avoid the sharp rocks the vehicle started to sink and skid. The boys would then jump off and push, or clear the sand with their hands from under the wheels. No one said a word. Everyone looked into the horizon as if they could speed up the journey with their gaze. At the Edchera junction, on the way to Gaada, Santiago decided to leave behind the stony ground and take the road, otherwise it would have been easy to get lost. He had the impression that, across the desert, they moved in a tortuous zigzag. And if they continued that way they wouldn't have enough diesel to cover the four hundred kilometres to Tifariti. Miraculously, the Land Rover lurched on in spite of its heavy load.

The road looked like a car cemetery. Every few kilometres they came across an abandoned car or truck, all going towards Smara. Santiago, well aware of the need for spare parts, stopped every time. Yet the vehicles had been taken apart by their owners or by other drivers who'd had the same idea. If there was a tyre left it was because it had burst. The tanks had no fuel. Batteries, carburettors, headlights, even steering wheels, had been plundered. When a vehicle broke down, its owners took it apart and continued on foot. Small groups of people camped by the road to recover their strength before journeying on. One could see entire families with their belongings loaded onto a donkey and a goat in tow. Every now and again a truck or a van overtook the Land Rover, but none kept to the road. San Román, however, did not dare leave it. Every hour he stopped and opened the bonnet to let the engine cool off.

In ten hours they did barely fifty kilometres. By midday Santiago knew they couldn't go on like that.

'We have to leave some stuff behind. The Land Rover is about to burst.'

Sid-Ahmed's wife shook her head. Santiago found the family's stubbornness exasperating. He tried to fill the radiator of the vehicle with water, but one of the boys dissuaded him.

'If you pour water into the car, we'll die of thirst. Better for the car to die.'

'But if the car dies, we'll die too.'

After arguing with each and everyone of them, he was allowed to pour in half a litre. Eventually he decided that for that morning they could not go any further. It was too hot. The bodywork was on fire and the tyres were going soft, even though it was only December. The cars abandoned by the side of the road were a compelling argument for stopping. They drove a kilometre off the road and settled at the bottom of a hillock. While Santiago checked the tyres, the family improvised a tent. Everyone appeared to know what to do. Santiago sweated more than anyone else. When he realised how quickly the water left his body, he decided that he would not fill up the radiator without making sure that there was a well nearby.

He soon understood that the goat was a lifeline. Its milk and some dates provided a meal for the whole group. Afterwards everyone lay in the shade, trying not to move or waste energy. Not even the sound of the wind disturbed their peaceful rest. Santiago fell sound asleep.

A light breeze started blowing which relieved them of the heat but also carried a disconcerting noise. The Saharawis alerted Santiago to it. He listened intently.

'Trucks,' said San Román.

He climbed to the top of the hillock and lay flat on the ground, trying to find out what it was.

A column of military vehicles was coming down from Gaada. As soon as he saw them he guessed the reason.

'They're headed for El Aaiún. Coming from the north. They can only be Moroccan.'

'What are we going to do now?' asked Andía, who had come to lie down beside him.

'We can't move. If they see us they'll make us turn around.

Either that or they'll take us prisoner.'

They waited without moving until well into the night. Then they broke camp and resumed their journey. From then on they could only travel across the desert. The road was too dangerous.

It took them six days to cover the two hundred kilometres to the sacred city of Smara. Miraculously, the vehicle only once got a puncture. When the city came into view, Santiago breathed out in relief. But his worries were not over. He had to press on further south-east, to the border with Mauritania. And he feared coming across the invading Mauritanian vehicles. Every now and again, a vehicle would overtake them, or they would see whole families fleeing on foot. Some had left El Aaiún more than a month previously. At every encounter they would stop, pitch camp, prepare tea and catch up on the rumours that travelled from one corner of the Sahara to the other. Meanwhile, Santiago would pace up and down, nervous, hesitant, worried. He felt very guilty of the fact he had not honoured his word. He'd promised Lazaar to take his family to Tifariti within three days, but at the pace they were going there wouldn't be anyone left at the military camp by the time they got there.

But the worst was still to come. In the middle of the night, battling against a sandstorm, Santiago lost sight of the tracks. Suddenly he found himself in front of an impassable hill. He went back the way he'd come from and again got lost. Now he couldn't even find his own tracks, and the terrain became steeper. When he realised he should stop it was too late. His heart sunk on hearing a peculiar noise coming from the engine. He heard it over the wind. The radiator was running out of water. He got out, but the sand blinded him. At first he couldn't lift the bonnet, and when he finally managed it the sand covered everything. He fell on his knees and started repeating a prayer in Arabic that he'd picked up having heard it said so often.

The storm didn't blow over until mid-morning. At least it wasn't too hot. The Land Rover was by then almost buried in the sand. The women once more set about pitching camp, while the young men gathered dry branches to make a fire for tea. They'd been living on dates and goat's milk for over two weeks. Lazaar's eldest brother stayed with the legionnaire to help him with the vehicle.

'We can't fill up the radiator,' said Santiago.

'Why not?'

'It's got a crack somewhere. Even if we poured in all the water we've got left, it would leak out again.'

'No car, no water. We can't go on my friend.'

Santiago slumped onto the floor, defeated. Andía, who never left his side, wiped his brow. She was sure the legionnaire would get them out of there. Judging by her smile, she didn't doubt it for a moment.

The first thing Santiago did, after getting his strength back, was try to find his bearings. The boys started walking, and he followed them with some difficulty. Although it took time, they eventually came across the tracks left by other vehicles. They had strayed four or five kilometres off course. San Román tried to remain calm. It would still take a few days to get to Tifariti. He thought they should all rest for a while and then set off, leaving the baggage behind. By now he knew the goat was their only means of survival. On foot they might reach Tifariti in a week. As he was wondering how to broach the subject with the family, he had a brainwave. On getting back to the camp he took one of the empty fuel cans and urinated into it. Lazaar's mother grew very serious, but the children burst out laughing, as if the legionnaire had gone crazy. He then asked everyone to urinate into the can. It seemed like a stupid idea, but soon everyone accepted that the Spaniard must know what he was doing. In an hour, Santiago collected the urine of fourteen people and, with a funnel, filled up the radiator. Fortunately it hadn't emptied completely, and so Santiago was able to calculate where the crack was. The children, as in a game, looked under the chassis until they found the exact point. It was easy. A puddle formed on the floor right under the leak. Santiago took out a bar of soap and crawled under the vehicle. He'd never thought he would use this crazy trick he'd learned among the Nomad Troops, but he rubbed the soap on the radiator until it formed a paste.

For nearly two hours he rubbed the soap over and over, the caustic soda chafing his fingers. Then he squashed it onto the metal with the palm of his hand. He came out from under the car and lay down, exhausted. The Saharawis watched him uncomprehending, as if he was putting on a bizarre show.

'Now we'll wait a few hours for it to dry. And after that, everyone will need to pee again.'

It took them two days to fill up the radiator: as they didn't drink much water, they didn't urinate much. Eventually Santiago turned the ignition and the engine rumbled into life. He waited to make sure the leak had stopped. Andía kept laughing and shouting things to him in Hassaniya. In under an hour they took down the tent and loaded the vehicle once again.

Five days later the landscape began to change. The number of vehicles and people on foot indicated that Tifariti wasn't far. They arrived on the 24th of December, thirteen days later. It had been the hardest journey that Santiago had ever undertaken, and they were almost a month behind schedule. Several kilometres before Tifariti, the Polisario Front tried to impose some order in the reigning chaos. Their trucks picked up those who arrived on foot, they removed broken-down vehicles from the road, handed water to those who didn't have any left, and indicated where they should go from there. Santiago San Román let Andía's mother deal with the soldiers. He was convinced that his cropped hair, and the fact that he was a legionnaire, would not go down well with the people from the Polisario.

The Spanish Army had abandoned the Tifariti square. The soldiers' barracks and the souk had been captured by the Saharawis. Around these, in an area of several square kilometres, the new arrivals were settling down. The nomads who already lived in the area offered their *jaima*s to others. Each family tried to organise themselves as best they could. Corrals for the animals were cobbled together. They even built a precarious hospital for small children. Trucks and vehicles of all kinds kept arriving. Although the newcomers spread encouraging news, some Saharawis had been there for two months. Little by little they were beginning to move east, in search of security on the other side of the border, in the not very hospitable Algerian *hammada*.

On the evening Santiago reached Tifariti a sandstorm broke out such as he had never seen in the whole year he'd been in the Sahara. The whirlwinds pulled out the *jaima*s and whipped up clouds of dust. Their camp came apart in barely a few minutes. The women dug holes in the sand, put the children in and lay on top, trying to protect themselves with their *melfa*s. One couldn't see further away than two metres. Santiago and Andía stayed inside the Land Rover. Wind and sand came in through every tiny aperture. The lack of water vapour was so pronounced that he felt his eyeballs were drying out − a very unpleasant sensation. He told Andía, worriedly, and the girl licked his eyelids, but a moment later they were dry again. For a while he thought he was going blind. The dryness was unbearable. Andía tried to calm him down. At daybreak, when the wind had finally abated, Santiago couldn't open his eyes. He lay still, and very afraid, under the tent the boys had promptly put up, while Andía stayed, caressing his arm.

The girl's brothers looked for Lazaar everywhere, but he was nowhere to be found. They asked around for him for three days. It was almost impossible to find a single person in the camp. The number of Saharawis living there increased daily. Although no official estimates existed, there must have been about fifty thousand refugees. In the daytime the sun blazed on the sand, and in the hours before dawn the dry cold would creep into the bones of those forced to sleep more or less in the open air. The army got water from those oases which had not been poisoned, but food was scarce. Under the circumstances, everything they had managed to transport on the Land Rover was considered a treasure. The few eggs laid by the chickens and the goat's milk continued to feed the family. The tea was also much appreciated – until it ran out, as did the sugar.

Santiago's eyes got better, but he was very weak. The water from the wells gave him terrible diarrhoea. Andía did not leave his side. His body did not adjust to the rigours of the desert until mid-January. By then he was pretty sure he would never see Lazaar again. But one cold morning the Saharawi turned up accompanied by one of his brothers, with an old Kalashnikov slung over his shoulder. He kissed his mother and a moment later hugged his close fried Santiago.

'They tell me you've been ill.'

'No, no. It's the water from the wells and the wind, I'm not used to them.'

Lazaar looked at his sister, who was, as always, smiling.

'Does Andía look after you properly?'

Santiago was overcome with emotion. His eyes filled with scalding tears.

'Better than anyone…' he trailed off. 'I didn't keep my promise. The roads in your country are not as good as you think.'

Lazaar hugged him again.

'Look who's here.'

Only with difficulty did Santiago recognise Sid-Ahmed. His eyes were not as good as they used to be. The former shopkeeper now had a camera hanging from his neck.

'Are you going to take a picture of me, Sid-Ahmed?'

'Right now if you like.'

'Sid-Ahmed works for the Polisario now. He's in charge of documenting what's happening, for the world to see.'

'Stand over there, in front of the car.'

The friends did as they were told. Behind them the Bedouins' tents flapped in the wind. Santiago adjusted his blue *derraha* and undid his turban, letting it down over his shoulders. He smoothed down the moustache he'd grown in the last month. Then he took Lazaar's Kalashnikov and held it up in his left hand. The Saharawi, in turn, lifted his hand and made the 'V' sign. They both threw an arm around the other's shoulder and, beaming at the camera, held their heads together, as though they feared they wouldn't fit into the picture.

That evening, sheltered under the awning that served as a *jaima*, they related their difficult exodus to Lazaar and Sid-Ahmed. Lazaar filled them in on the current situation. The Saharawi population was fleeing towards the Algerian desert, many of them on foot. News of those who'd stayed in the cities was in short supply, but no one envied them, in spite of the suffering experienced on the journey.

Once the wind died down, a deadening silence seized the camp. Neither the goats nor the dogs made a noise. Someone said, a long time later, that that silence seemed like an omen of what was to come. But on that night no one could imagine what the new day had in store.

At nine in the morning, on Monday 19th of January, nothing indicated that that day in Tifariti would be any different for those who had already lost everything. Except for the absence of wind, the morning was identical to so many others in the last few months. It had been a very cold, restless night before the wind abated. Lazaar's brothers had already gone to fetch water and were tidying the *jaima*. Santiago was still asleep, cuddled around Andía to keep her warm. The girl was awake but liked to stay like that, lying still until the legionnaire woke up. Yet a sudden noise shook her out of her stillness under the blanket. Santiago awoke.

'What is it, Andía? Do you want to get up already?'

'It's not that. Listen, Santi.'

Santiago didn't know what she meant. All he heard was the clinking of the teapot and the glasses. Or a goat braying in the silence. But Andía knew what she'd heard. She knew what planes sounded like.

'I can hear a plane.'

Once again Santiago failed to hear it. He only realised how serious it was when one of Andía's brothers came running into the *jaima*, shouting.

The attack came from the north. The planes flew in low from behind the rocks, where no one would be able to see them until they were almost above the camp. They didn't even do a reconnaissance flight. It seemed as though they knew exactly where they were heading. San Román went out and shaded his eyes with his hand so he could see them. Three French F1 Mirages. He knew them well: the best aircraft in the Moroccan army. They approached in a 'V' formation, accurately dropping their deadly load. The first bombs threw the whole camp into a panic. Napalm and white phosphorous razed the *jaima*s to the ground as if they were made of paper. The noise of the explosions was followed by the flash of flames and gusts of hot air that swept everything in its wake. As the planes flew over they left a scar of fire and destruction in the village. But they were certainly coming back, and everyone ran for cover. The craters made by the bombs were so big that they could comfortably hold a person standing upright. For some the fire blocked the escape. Santiago looked for Andía, but she wasn't there. A hundred metres off he saw some tent canvases on fire. Suddenly it was very hot. There was a nauseating smell of burnt things. Santiago ran the other way and saw what was happening. The planes were once again discharging napalm over Tifariti. Whoever was caught near the explosion died instantly, but even several metres away the women's *melfa*s would light up on contact with the hot air. Some people, burnt from head to toe, managed to run for a bit before dropping dead, charred by the phosphorous. No one knew where to run. They all bumped into one another. Amid the confusion Santiago stopped and looked at the sky. He felt the ground shake beneath his feet. Then a blast threw him into the air. He landed on his back, but couldn't sit up. His body felt heavy. He knew his face was scorched. The voices died down in his head until he was completely deaf. His left arm, he realised, was badly burnt. He looked at it and saw a mass of flesh and blood. His hand and half his forearm were missing, but it barely hurt. He understood how useless it would be to stand up and run. The sky became red with fire. A moment later he felt someone grab him by the neck, trying to make him sit up. It was Andía. Her face was filled with horror. She was crying and shouting, although he couldn't hear her. He told her that he loved her, that it was going to be all right, and his words echoed in his chest as in an empty box. Andía pressed her face to his chest and hugged him as if she were trying to keep him from going over the edge of an abyss. Then Santiago San Román no longer felt anything.

Chapter Eighteen

ALBERTO WAS THE LAST PERSON SHE WANTED TO MEET IN
the corridors of the administrative department of the hospital.
Montse left the director's office convinced that she had made
an important decision. She knew her conscience would throw
up objections, but she was used to such internal debates. She
felt good, as if she had just got rid of some ballast and her mind
felt lighter. For the first time in several months she viewed the
future with optimism. Perhaps this was the light at the end of
the tunnel people often talked about. She made plans: go to a
churrería, have a breakfast fit for a queen, call up her sister, check
train timetables, make a list of everything she needed for the
trip and, finally, choose a destination. It was like walking into a
building you have only seen from the outside, but which exerts
a powerful attraction on you. Then her thoughts darkened. She
was used to ghosts coming and going. But this ghost was real.

At that moment Alberto, who was still her husband, walked
out of the lift, a briefcase in his hand and a mobile glued to his
ear. He smiled at her, still talking on the phone. Montse felt
her optimism slip away. Her heartbeat accelerated. She'd always
been slow to react. By the time she felt the impulse to turn
around and go back the way she'd come it was too late. She
should have foreseen the possibility of an encounter. Alberto
was now walking towards her and saying goodbye to the person
on the phone. He had a heartbreaking smile and was impeccably
dressed, as usual. He casually kissed Montse on the cheek. She

let him do it, trying not to show her discomfort. She only wanted the moment to be over soon so she could go back to her previous mood: the buoyancy, the light at the end of the tunnel. But Alberto didn't realise, or didn't want to realise, that he was making Montse upset. They exchanged polite phrases. Montse tried to hold his gaze but found it difficult. She had to admit that he could be very charming, even if one knew all his tricks. When Alberto asked her what she was doing there, Montse decided to test his reaction.

'I've just asked Human Resources for an extended leave of absence.'

Alberto didn't bat an eyelid. He smiled his best smile.

'Well, Montse, that is some news. Are you stressed out?'

'On the contrary, I'm too relaxed. I need an experience which might be a bit more… fulfilling.'

'I see, I see. It might be a good idea. Mind you, I've thought of it myself. I might follow your example. Are you going to travel?'

'Yes, that's what I had in mind.'

'It's wonderful to travel in the off season.'

The phrase felt like a blow in the neck. She was annoyed at thinking like Alberto – having her thoughts, even her words, stolen by him. He'd done that ever since they met. For a long time she'd thought Alberto had such a strong influence on her that she wasn't the mistress of her own words. Montse said goodbye in a rush, feeling she was about to cave in, to collapse. Alberto was like a screen between her and what was real.

The ride on the lift seemed never-ending. She needed air, and almost ran to the street for a breath of fresh air. She was carrying her pills in her handbag, but did not want to take them only because of the encounter. Feeling nauseous, she leaned against a car. In spite of the cold, she was sweating. She was sure she didn't love that man. Sometimes she doubted she had ever loved him. But she had come to depend on her husband in a way that went beyond love. Alberto had a puzzling influence on the people around him. He'd had it on Montse's parents, on her sister Teresa, and on their daughter. He'd had it, no doubt, on the lovers that shared his bed while Montse searched for unlikely explanations after discovering small signs of betrayal. No one had left an imprint on Montse's life as deep as that of her husband. No one had manipulated her so much, nor done her as much harm.

Alberto had always looked more mature than he actually was. Montse had met him during her last year at university. He was studying on a scholarship in his final year at the department chaired by Doctor Cambra. Her father had never invited students home, but Alberto was different. At the age of twenty-four he already spoke like an experienced professor, sure of his opinions. He was handsome, elegant, polite and cultivated. He warmed the hearts of Doctor Cambra and his wife. Even Teresa had a twinkle in her eye when the scholar turned up in the house. Alberto was attentive to everyone, but especially to Montse. He was so different from Santiago San Román that everything she saw in him helped to bury the memory of the dead boy.

The news of Santiago's death had been more painful than her confinement in Cadaqués and her parents' silence after the miscarriage. Montse had started university without applying herself. She had decided to hide her pregnancy from her parents until it no longer became possible. Nor was it very difficult to refuse to extend to Santiago the forgiveness he so desperately asked of her. She was so angry she barely knew what she was doing. In December, when the phone calls stopped, she felt relieved. She thought she would forget Santiago in the year it would take him to complete his military service. But things went from bad to worse when she could no longer hide the growth of her hips, belly and breasts. After her parents found out that she was indeed pregnant, the household descended into a kind of mourning. Yet Montse didn't cry as much as she thought she would. She had run out of tears. Under pressure from her father, she confessed that she'd met someone in the summer and had fallen in love. Doctor Cambra wanted to know more, but she didn't say another word. Just picturing her father talking to Santiago San Román made her feel sick. An enforced marriage was the last thing she wanted, and she knew her parents would never accept the boy. A few days before Christmas, Montse moved to Cadaqués to spend the winter and spring away from Barcelona. Mari Cruz, the maid, went with her. It was the saddest Christmas of her life. Everyone made her feel guilty, even the maid. Her studies were put on hold. The Doctor invented a trip to Germany in order to justify her absence, and the lies told by the family acquired epic dimensions.

Meanwhile, the winter by the sea passed slowly, monotonously, governed by boredom. The family visited Montse in Cadaqués every weekend, but she always wished it was Monday so she could be alone. She thought of Santiago, of his silence. Now she felt guilty for not having given him one last chance to explain himself. Her hope that he might have called her at home remained, but no one ever brought her any news or letters. Whenever she asked if anyone had called her in Barcelona, Teresa refused to discuss it. Even her sister seemed to be against her.

In February Montse started bleeding and having contractions. Her father came from Barcelona with a doctor he trusted. Two days later Montse had to be operated on and the child didn't survive. It was a painful experience, but she felt relieved. Thereafter the family kept a resentful silence. Montse stayed in Cadaqués until Easter. On her return, although she had recovered, she remained in very low spirits – everyone was led to believe she'd been in Germany, attending university. She resumed her studies, but barely passed a subject in June. That summer the family didn't holiday in Cadaqués. While Montse revised for her September exams, the rest of them moved about the house in silence, as if they were standing guard. Every time the phone rang she was startled. Montse only studied out of fear: her heart was not in it. Books and wall charts felt like flagstones under which she might end up crushed. But she was so afraid of her parents that she would have done anything to please them. Little by little Santiago's image lost its contours. She would swing from nostalgia to hatred, from hatred to melancholy, from melancholy to despair. She was sure the boy had forgotten her already. Yet she sometimes would dream of him and wake in a sweat, nervous, fearful. She constantly tried to imagine what he might be doing at that precise moment, an exercise that increased her anxiety. This went on until October.

Alberto appeared in the autumn. His presence proved healthy for the sad atmosphere in the household. Doctor Cambra's mood changed when the young man paid them a visit. Alberto had a winning way with people. Even Mari Cruz, the maid, succumbed to his charms. Whenever he came round for dinner, she made something special and laid the table with the best china. Montse did not appear particularly impressed. And perhaps that was why he showed an interest in her. She was rather aloof, did not listen to the stories he told, and seemed to be thinking of other things when he was present. She would ask to be excused and go to her room as soon as she could. Such indifference hurt Alberto's pride. He came to be captivated by Montse. Doctor Cambra realised this and secretly approved, but his major concern was that Montse should start her university career without distractions.

At the end of the year, Santiago San Román was still very much on Montse's mind and in her heart. She knew that sooner or later he'd be discharged and come back to Barcelona. More than once she was tempted to go to his mother's tobacconist in Barceloneta, but the thought of Santiago's finding out filled her with embarrassment. Nor did Santiago make the slightest contact with her during the first few months of 1976. Montse's feelings started to cool. She often compared Santiago with

Alberto and realised that she'd been blind for over a year.

It took her some time, but eventually she went to the tobacconist. It was a difficult decision. She didn't know what she would say. At the last moment she came up with an excuse: to give back the silver ring the boy had given her. If it really had belonged to her grandmother, it might have some sentimental value.

Something had changed, though. The door was new. She walked in a bit hesitantly. Santiago's mother was no longer behind the counter. In her place were a couple who must be around fifty years old, both plump and kind-looking. Montse froze, again not knowing what to say.

'I'm looking for the owner of the shop,' said Montse eventually.

The woman tensed up, thinking she was trying to sell her something.

'I'm the owner, how can I help you?'

'Oh, well, I was looking for a lady who used to own this… some time ago.'

'Yes, Culiverde's daughter. She was very ill. She died.'

Montse wasn't counting on that, but tried not to appear surprised.

'And her son? She had a son called Santiago. He must have finished his military service one or two months ago. He was in Zaragoza. You see, I have to give him back something which belonged to the family.'

Montse showed them the ring on her palm. The man came out from behind the counter to talk to her more easily. He'd become serious. A customer walked in.

'You say he was called Santiago?' said the shop keeper. 'Yes, I think that was his name.'

'A tragedy,' the woman put in. 'He was killed in an accident in the Sahara.'

'In the Sahara?'

'Yes, during Marcha Verde. Isn't that right, Agustín?'

Agustín was the customer who'd just walked in.

'Who are you talking about? Culiverde's grandson?'

'Yes, this young lady here is asking about him.'

'The poor lad. He was caught in that mess in Hasan last year. They say he was blown up by a grenade.'

'It wasn't a grenade,' corrected the tobacconist. 'It was one of those tanks; you know, ran him over.'

'It was a grenade. They say it was in the papers.'

'Anyway, a grenade, a tank, what's the difference?' concluded the woman. 'The thing is, this girl here was looking for him.'

Montse heard the conversation as if from a great distance. She didn't feel anything. She simply stood there with her hand still stretched out, the ring on her palm.

'Let me see that, love.'

The woman picked the ring and examined it from up close. She was disappointed when she saw that it wasn't valuable, and presently gave it back. When Montse left, the other three carried on their discussion about the exact cause of Santiago San Román's death.

From then on Montse started being more receptive to Alberto's attentions. Yet it still took him two years to persuade her to go out for dinner. His career, meanwhile, took off. He was offered a position in a hospital at an age when most doctors are still revising for entry examinations. Doctor Cambra didn't quite approve of his leaving his academic career, where he had a brilliant future. But he tried to hide his annoyance in public. The young man would shine in any field he chose.

★★★

Ayach Bachir pressed the bell, and Montserrat Cambra buzzed him in. The Saharawi arrived with a smile. He offered his hand as he always did, limp and slightly tilted. Following a rite that she enjoyed, Montse asked him about work, his family, Fatma, the baby, the car, and his broken-down fridge. Ayach asked questions too, smiling at every reply. In fact, they had seen each other only two days before. Montse offered to make him a cup of tea with a teabag, but Ayach preferred coffee.

'I've been looking for you in the hospital,' said the Saharawi. 'I thought you'd be on duty, but they told me you wouldn't be coming into work for the next few days.'

'For the next few months, Ayach. I've taken some time off.'

As Doctor Cambra made the coffee, Ayach went on talking about this and that. She was sure the man had come to speak to her about something important. But she knew he was in no hurry: first he had to receive his host's attentions, drink some coffee, smoke a cigarette, and only later would he say what he had to say. She found the behaviour at once amusing and irritating, but was getting used to it.

'There's something urgent I need to tell you,' explained Ayach at last.

Montse could only laugh. Now she understood why, as she had read somewhere, the rate of cardiac arrest and angina pectoris was abnormally low among Saharawis.

'I'm listening. What's so urgent?'

'You see, in five days there will be a flight to Tindouf. I can book you a seat if you want. There are three left.'

Montse fidgeted in her armchair. Destiny was putting her to the test.

'Tindouf? Me?'

'Yes, it's a safe city. It's quite far from Algiers, so it's not affected by terrorism. You can reach the Saharawi camps in an hour.'

Montse froze. Her eyes glazed over for the first time in a long while. She wasn't sure of anything. Ayach Bachir appreciated her silence. He looked her straight in the eye. At last Montse smiled.

'Do you really mean that?'

'Of course. I wouldn't be coming to your house to play a joke like that on you. What do you say?'

'I don't know.'

'Have you got a valid passport?'

'Yes.'

'Then you decide. That's all I need for the visa.'

Montse felt the floor move under her seat. She stood up, left the room, and came back with the passport in her hand. She was visibly shaken. It had not expired. First she put it on the table, then in her pocket. Ayach Bachir smiled, trying not to look disrespectful.

'If you make up your mind, I'll speak to my father tomorrow. He's travelling to Libya in three days. Politics. But he'll send someone to pick you up. You can stay at my sister's *jaima*. It's a humble place, but she'll be very happy to have a guest like yourself.'

'I'm not sure, Ayach. I don't know what to say.'

'Yusuf will be glad to see you. I'm sure he hasn't forgotten a woman like you. Or should I say Santiago?'

'You're a sweetie, Ayach. But just the thought of it terrifies me.'

'Are you afraid he won't remember you?'

'No, of course not. He wouldn't remember me, I'm sure. Or would he? I don't know. I need to think about it.'

The Saharawi poured himself some more coffee. He tried not to force a decision out of her; but he was honest when Montse asked:

'What would you do in my place, Ayach?'

'I'd go. If Allah wants you to find him, you'll find him even if you stay here or hide in the last corner of the earth. And if He doesn't...'

Montse took out her passport and got a pen and some paper.

'So what do you need for the visa?'

Chapter Nineteen

A STRONG WIND IS BLOWING AT NOON WHICH TESTS THE strength of the *jaima*s. Sand comes in thorough the tiniest gaps. Montse is surprised at the transformation of the landscape. The dogs bark furiously, maddened by the wind. She has spent all morning in the kitchen, helping Layla's aunt. When she goes out, she has to cover her face with a scarf and close her eyes. The sand gets into her clothes, her nose and ears. Although she keeps her mouth shut, Montse can feel sand on her palate and between her teeth.

After lunch, the *jaima* fills with the neighbours who come in to watch the soap. Montse doesn't want to miss this. She sits behind the women and takes in every last one of their reactions. Layla sleeps amid all the noise, lying in a foetal position, with her face covered by the *melfa*. It's an image of great beauty. Suddenly the wind stops and the silence outside captures Montse's attention. Once again she can hear the bleating of the animals. She begins to feel a kind of numbness. Her legs go limp and her eyes are heavy. She seems to be hearing the voice of her daughter Teresa in the distance, as if she were in another room. Yet she knows it's only her imagination. The memory, now, is not as painful as it used to be. Teresa would have liked to see this place. Hazily, Montse thinks of all the things her daughter didn't get to see. The sound of the TV washes over her thoughts. Far away she hears someone whistling. It is a popular song. She cannot quite place it, but she's heard it several times. The jingle is part of her adolescence. Without quite realising it she comes round from her reverie. The whistling is not in her head. It startles her. She really is hearing it. There's someone whistling the tune in the street. She tries to place the music. It's a pasodoble: she's sure of that. When she recognises the chorus, her heart misses a beat. The women have not noticed the whistling. They are engrossed in the Algerian programme. Layla sleeps, oblivious to it all.

Montse stands up and goes out. No one takes notice of her. There are no people outside. There is no wind. And the whistling too has stopped. Specks of sandy dust are still floating in the air, like clouds or a dry fog. The sky is overcast, but the heat is dry and stifling. Montse cannot understand why she's suddenly so nervous, so restless. She decides to take a walk. In the distance, on top of the low hill, she can see the school for handicapped children. Her steps take her in that direction. The first time she saw Bir Lehru it was from up there, and the view struck her as beautiful.

She walks with her eyes fixed on the ground and her feet. And so she doesn't realise that nearby there is a man crouching down, with his back turned to her. When she finally sees him she stops. Should she approach him or continue on her way? Perhaps the man is praying. Suddenly he stands up and Montse is startled. He holds his *derraha*, lifted up to his waist, in one hand. The Saharawi has not seen her. The white skin of his buttocks contrasts with the dark skin of others of his race. Montse is embarrassed at the idea of his finding her there, looking at him. But by the time she decides to turn around it is too late: the man has seen her and is walking towards her. He stops about five metres from her.

'*Musso mussano? Musso mussano?*'

She recognises him and calms down. It's The Demon. He doesn't look so old now. His skin is sunburnt and his lips are covered in blisters.

'*Les bes, Le bes,*' replies Montse. 'I'm fine.'

On hearing her, the Saharawi opens his eyes wide. His *derraha* is all twisted, like a nightgown.

'You Spanish?' he asks in a strong Saharawi accent.

'Yes, I am.'

'I got many friends. Many Spanish.'

Now that she sees him from up-close, he looks harmless. Were it not for the expression in his eyes, she wouldn't have doubted the man's sanity. He says something in Hassaniya. He seems to be reciting verse. Montse interrupts him to ask him his name.

'Can't remember. I forget things. Spanish, beautiful ladies.'

Montse smiles. She doesn't want to offend the man by turning her back on him. The Saharawi clumsily lifts his *derraha*. Montse thinks he wants to flash at her. But she's wrong. He's looking for something in his pocket, and on finding it approaches her. He offers Montse a stone. At that moment she realises the man's missing an arm. His stump peeks out of a *derraha*, cut off almost at the elbow. She tries not to stare, and looks at the stone instead. It's very beautiful. A rose of the desert.

'For Spanish woman,' the man says.

'*Shu-cran*,' thanks Montse. 'It's quite pretty.'

'Spanish women pretty.'

The Saharawi's eyes fix on something. Montse realises he's not looking at her. His mind is elsewhere. For a moment she feels awkward. She holds the rose of the desert in both her hands.

'It's very beautiful,' she says. Her voice sounds forced.

The Saharawi turns around and walks off without saying a word. She looks at him, finding it impossible to calculate his age. It must be very difficult for a mentally ill person to survive in such a hostile environment. She cannot get the image of the stump off her mind. Montse looks at the present the stranger has left her. She walks on towards the school.

And then, as if she were still dreaming, she hears the whistling again, though now loud and clear. She looks around but does not see anyone. In spite of the heat, her whole body shivers. The old singsong, clumsily whistled, takes her back to an August night many years ago: a square full of people, a band playing on a metal stage, and a pair of dark, beautiful eyes that won't stop looking at her. The most beautiful eyes of all.

Brief background to the Conflict in Western Sahara and information about Sandblast

WESTERN SAHARA IS AFRICA'S LAST REMAINING COLONY. Since 1975, it has been the site of a little known conflict for territorial control between Morocco and the Polisario Front, the Saharawi independence movement. The disputed territory is wedged between Morocco to the north, Mauritania to the south and Algeria to the east. Roughly the size of Britain, it enjoys a coastline over 1000 km long and is legendary for its rich fishing waters. For many centuries, this coastal desert patch was home to the Saharawis, a nomadic and tribal people.

The closest Canary Island lies only 80 km away from Western Saharan shores. This strategically important archipelago provided the pretext for Spain's colonial interests in the region, at the end of the 19th century. The colony later became incorporated into Spain as its 53rd province, in 1958, after abundant phosphate deposits were discovered near the capital of Al-Aauin. But by then, anti-colonial winds had begun to blow strongly across the continent. With the rise of the armed Polisario movement, in 1973, Spain felt the pressure to decolonize. However, when it finally withdrew two years later, the Saharawis faced a double invasion rather than the freedom they had expected to achieve through a promised referendum vote.

Politically weakened by Franco's imminent death, the metropolis had opted for a rapid withdrawal from its colony. It signed a secret but illegal accord to hand administrative control over to Morocco and Mauritania, who also claimed Western Sahara as theirs. In return for thirty-five per cent rights to the phosphate deposits, Spain had gone against the Saharawi will and the Advisory Opinion of the International Court of Justice, which on October 16th 1975 had firmly rejected the above sovereignty claims. Determined to be a free people, the Polisario forces resisted. This sparked a war that carried on with Morocco for sixteen years, but led to Mauritania's defeat and withdrawal in 1979.

The conflict divided and dispersed the Saharawi population. Over half fled the invasion and the Moroccan aerial bombardments of napalm and cluster bombs to become refugees in the Hammada, a notoriously inhospitable part of the Algerian desert. Tens of thousands more remained stuck under the rule of their neighbours. Then in the mid-80s, at the height of the war, Morocco built a 2,500km long Berm in Western Sahara to defend its occupation against Polisario attacks. This reinforced sand and stone wall, protected by over 5 million landmines and 100,000 Moroccan soldiers divided the territory as well as every Saharawi family. West of the Berm, under Morocco's occupation, the Saharawis endured systematic human rights violations and were largely outnumbered by Moroccan settlers, the army and security forces. East of the Berm, in the area known as the 'liberated zones', the Polisario military forces controlled the remaining 1/5th of Western Sahara.

In 1991, both sides put down their arms in favour of a Settlement Plan which sanctioned the UN to organize a referendum in Western Sahara for the Saharawis to vote for either independence or integration with Morocco. Scheduled for early 1992, it has yet to take place, although the cease-fire still holds.

Saharawi Art and Culture and the Historical Struggle

In their nomadic past, rich oral traditions were the primary means by which the Saharawis transmitted their culture and history. Expressing a cultural fusion of Berber, African and Arab-Islamic influences, this transmission was largely done in Hassaniya – an unwritten Arabic dialect which became dominant after invading Yemenite tribes successively conquered the Western Saharan region in the 11th and 13th centuries.

Poetry was by far the most highly respected of the oral traditions and poets were held in great esteem for their prodigious language skills and memories. With the rise of the Saharawi anti-colonial movement in the early 70s, this medium was harnessed to mobilize the still largely illiterate masses. Many Saharawis today will recount how they were moved by the power of a poem or a song, to join and fight with the Polisario Front.

When the Polisario emerged, its founding members (a group of university students studying in Morocco, influenced by radical ideas of the times), aspired to eradicate tribalism and all forms of inequality in their quest for independence. They regarded the realm of art and culture as prime terrain for expressing these aspirations and forged a new Saharawi identity that bridged the past with the future. But sadly, the tragic turn of events which unfolded at the end of Spain's rule, meant this vision would only be implemented in the context of a refugee existence and not in an independent country.

Ironically, the intensely isolated state of exile brought on by the war years bred new cultural and artistic developments. In this period, the arts played a primary role in rallying the spirits and emotions, with the struggle and its political aims as central themes. Saharawi music groups, for the first time, formed to sing to the world about the injustices they faced. Drawing on their musical tradition of *el howl*, they innovated through the use of new instruments, such as the electric guitar and keyboard-synthesizer and modernized their rhythms. The stigma of being associated with the caste of professional artists, known as *iggawen* in Mauritania, was overcome by the fact that they were singing for the struggle, not for money. Money, in fact, played no part in the first twenty years of camp life and relations between the refugees and the Polisario leadership operated on the basis of an exchange: the movement secured their basic needs and provided free access to health and education; the refugees gave their labour and skills.

The impact of the Moroccan occupation on Saharawi identity had another unforeseen dimension. Speaking Spanish transformed into an expression of resistance rather than a symbol of colonialism and so very soon after the Saharawis became refugees, Spanish began to be taught in primary schools as a second language. In exile, the Spanish language has become one of the most important legacies Spain left the Saharawis and has been integrated comfortably into the Saharawi identity – a trend reinforced further by the large number of young Saharawi refugees who studied in Cuba. The education of thousands of young Saharawis abroad also meant new influences were being introduced into the lives of the refugees – new forms of creative expression such as painting, photography, theatre and film. But these new interests also meant facing prevailing social and religious taboos, especially when it came to figurative painting.

Since the cease-fire in 1991, the Saharawis have entered a new phase. No longer rallied around the call of war they have been waiting in frustration for a long overdue referendum. The arts, in this context, have had to search for a new direction and meaning. The camps have not been immune from the forces of globalization either and growing consumerism has placed pressures on the arts to meet economic ends. The once collective nature of artistic expression is also seeing erosion by individualistic trends. But on the positive side, waning of political interest and support for the arts has freed them from existing only to serve the cause. Introspective, personal and sometimes critical tones have begun to emerge. However, it is always shaped by the reality of the harsh conditions the refugees live in and by their longings and anxieties of what the future holds. In the absence of war, art and culture are vital in affirming their existence and the evolving complexity of their identity.

The Refugee Camps

The Saharawi refugees are based in South West Algeria near Tindouf in four large camps. Each camp – Al-Auin, Smara, Ausserd and Dakhla – is named after a hometown in Western Sahara. Locally referred to as *wilayas* they are run like provinces of a state. Each *wilaya* is further divided into six or seven districts called *dairas*, also named after places in their homeland. The four *wilayas* together are home to almost 200,000 refugees who are living in an extremely hostile and barren landscape.

The Polisario-run refugee camps provide a temporary base for the Saharawi government in exile – the Saharawi Arab Democratic Republic (SADR), self-proclaimed on February 27th, in 1976, as the last Spanish soldier withdrew from its former colony. Although no Western government recognizes it, the SADR enjoys full diplomatic ties with over seventy countries. In exile, the government has sought to develop a democratic system and involve a high percentage of female participation. Of its nineteen ministries, three are headed by women. A third of the elected members of parliament are women, reflecting their prominence in public life and the central role they have in running the camps.

This role began from the first days of exile. With the men away fighting at the war front, it was the women who were primarily left with the huge responsibility and task of setting up the camps. But promoting the women's position in the society also fitted with the movement's progressive ideals and the National Saharawi Women's Union was formed to ensure women's rights were advanced. By 1978, the first women's vocational school was set up, a residential school known as February 27 and now a woman's vocational school exists in each camp.

The educational achievements of the refugees are by far the most remarkable aspect of their experience. Again here, the Saharawi women have made impressive strides. When the exodus began less than five per cent were literate. Today more than ninety per cent can read and write. This fact is largely due to the goal of the nationalist Polisario Front's to equip the Saharawi population with the knowledge and skills to run an independent Western Sahara in the future.

While education is compulsory and free in the camps, it cannot be provided beyond primary school. Further education is possible through scholarships offered in the main by Algeria, Libya, Cuba and Syria. For the thousands of Saharawis who received their education in Cuba, many left as children and did not reunite with their families until adulthood, sometimes being apart for periods of twenty years or more. A proportionally high number of the young Saharawi adults hold university degrees, including PhDs. But widespread unemployment in the camps and the lack of opportunities, means few are able to apply their hard won university training and knowledge.

Healthcare in the camps is also universally accessible. Over more than three decades of exile, the refugees have built four regional hospitals and a national one. These are run mostly by Saharawi doctors and nurses. Not surprisingly, prevailing diseases are related to the extreme climate and poor nutrition.

The harsh and extreme desert climate of the Algerian Hammada, has made it impossible for the refugees to survive without critical dependency on food aid. But the persistence of this long-term humanitarian situation has exposed the Saharawis to aid-fatigue and assistance in recent years has often being irregular and insufficient, at times covering but a mere 1/3 of the nutritional requirements.

Human rights

The darkest phase of the Moroccan occupation in Western Sahara was unquestionably between 1975 and 1991, when the practice of 'disappearances' was widespread. Men, women (including pregnant women), children and the elderly were targeted if they had either any known Polisario relatives or were suspected of harbouring pro-independence or pro-Polisario views. Major human rights organizations, such as Amnesty International (AI) and Human Rights Watch believe that at least a thousand Saharawis 'disappeared' in that period. The last major wave of disappearances took place in 1987, when mostly Saharawi youth staged the first demonstration since Morocco annexed the territory in 1975.

In 1991, the 350 officially recognized 'disappeared' Saharawis were released by Hassan II in a royal pardon. Until then, the Moroccan kingdom had vigorously denied holding any Saharawi prisoners of conscience, much in the same way it had denied the existence of notorious secret detention centres such as Agdz, Kalaat Magouna and one in Al-Auin, where hundreds of prisoners are known to have died under terrible conditions. Since then, the Moroccan authorities considered the question of disappearances a closed chapter, but according to AFRAPREDESA, a Saharawi human rights organization formed by family members of the disappeared, more than 500 still remain unaccounted for.

After 1991, the pattern of human rights abuses in occupied Western Sahara shifted from long-term imprisonment and disappearances to one of repeated arrests and shorter-term prison sentences. Nevertheless, the practice of torture during detention is still known to take place on a regular basis, and according to AI, the number of reported incidents appears to have risen sharply since 1999. Many human rights abuses are believed to take place during the period of *garde-a-vue* (pre-arraignment detention). Human rights activists, both in Morocco and the occupied Western Sahara, assert the Moroccan state practices the policy of criminalizing all political activity.

Hundreds upon hundreds of Saharawis have been arrested since 1991 as a result of staging protests against high-level Moroccan visits to the territory or demanding improved economic conditions, which then became political in nature. The most prominent instances were in 1992, 1995, 1999 and 2001. Long lists of Saharawis were tortured in order to extract false confessions and given excessively long prison terms, many of which were reduced thanks to effective pressure from international campaigning groups such as AI. In 2001, the longest-serving Saharawi prisoner of conscience (of twenty-three years), Sidi Mohammed Daddach, was released and awarded the Norwegian Rafto prize in recognition of his sacrifice to the Saharawi cause.

More recently, in the large scale peaceful uprisings of 2005, Moroccan repression was brutal in the extreme. Women, children and the elderly were equally affected, but this time the Moroccan authorities particularly targeted human rights activists. Prominent figures such as Aminatou Haidar, who was beaten within an inch of her life, were caught on camera with a defiant expression covered in a veil of blood. For her tremendous courage and continued advocacy for peaceful resistance she won the Human Rights Kennedy Award in 2008.

More subtle forms of human rights abuses, such as the lack of freedom of expression, association, movement and systematic discrimination in the workplace, are a constant feature of the Saharawi experience under occupation. These ongoing restrictions are coupled with the more sinister Moroccanization

policy, which deprives Saharawis from learning their own history and language.

When the UN High Commission for Human Rights finally visited Western Sahara for the first time, in 2006, it expressed its alarming findings in a subsequent report:

> 'The situation of human rights is a source of real concern, especially in the territory of Western Sahara administered by Morocco. Currently, not only is the Saharawi population denied their right to self-determination, but they are also being harshly deprived of exercising other kinds of rights...'

Many of these human rights abuses are eloquently expressed in the resistance poetry of the Generation of Saharawi Friendship, largely based in Spain. Writing in Spanish, this group of Saharawi poets have been inspired by figures such as Neruda and Lorca, and they have published numerous books as individuals and anthologies. Aauin, *Shouting What We Feel*, was published in 2006 to express their outrage at the 2005 Moroccan repressions.

---

by **Danielle Smith**, founding director of **Sandblast**,
a London-based arts charity promoting Saharawi rights.

www.sandblast-arts.org

About Sandblast

Sandblast works to empower the Saharawis to tell their own story, promote their own culture and earn a living through the arts. Through its Saharawi Artist Fund (SAF), Sandblast addresses

the lack of opportunities for Saharawis to develop artistically and helps them showcase their talents and gain recognition for their culture and aspirations. Through SAF we:

- **run workshops** in the refugee camps to teach art and enhance income generation.

- **help outstanding talent** access residencies, master classes and international platforms.

- **provide** small bursaries for aspiring artists to pursue their creative ideas.

- **promote** and showcase Saharawi arts.

Founding director, Danielle Smith has been involved with the Saharawi refugee community for over twenty years. She taught English in the camps for extended periods in 1993/94 and made two documentaries, including the award-winning *Beat of Distant Hearts*, on the role of the arts in the Saharawi independence struggle. She was associate producer for *Western Sahara: A Forgotten War*, broadcast by BBC2 for their *Correspondent* series in 1998. Danielle Smith has spoken widely on the Western Sahara at universities, for the media, the British Parliament and the United Nations.